IT BEGAN WITH THE SUDDEN THUNDER OF HOOVES THAT COULD BE FELT IN THE GROUND.

"Load!" Riker commanded in a loud voice.

Robertson found a good firing place near the company commander. "We're gonna have to hit 'em before they close in on us."

Riker only nodded. "Aim! Fire!"

A scattering of attacking Sioux went down with their horses.

"Goddamn your eyes!" Robertson shouted in a fury. "Fight like infantry!"

This time the volley struck hard, hitting so many attackers that several of the Indians farther back rode into their fallen comrades. In moments the momentum of the attack was broken by the deliberate, disciplined fire of the army riflemen.

"They're pulling back," Riker said. "I don't think we'll see them again today."

Robertson shook his head. "No, sir, but they'll try again tomorrow. And there ain't no way we're gonna keep this up. When they attack again, we're gonna be dead meat."

GUNSMOKE AT POWDER RIVER

PATRICK E. ANDREWS

ZEBRA BOOKS
KENSINGTON PUBLISHING CORP.

This book is dedicated to
THE UNITED STATES INFANTRY

ZEBRA BOOKS

are published by

Kensington Publishing Corp.
475 Park Avenue South
New York, NY 10016

Copyright © 1991 by Patrick E. Andrews

First printing: January, 1991

Printed in the United States of America

ROSTER OF COMPANY "L"

Captain Charles Riker
First Lieutenant Frederick Worthington
First Sergeant Gordon Robertson
Sergeant Aloysius Donahue
Sergeant Thomas McCarey
Corporal Josef Bakker
Corporal Raymond Marteau
Corporal James O'Rourke
Corporal Karl Schreiner
Trumpeter Uziel Melech
Private Theodore Albertson
Private Samuel Anderson
Private Czaba Asztalos
Private Mack Baker
Private Daniel Black
Private Gustav Braun
Private Harry Brown
Private George Callan
Private Roger Carpenter
Private Zbigniew Czarny
Private Harold Devlin
Private Paddy Donegan
Private Ion Dulgher
Private Albert Franklin
Private Hiram Gold
Private George Hammer
Private Christopher Harrigan
Private John Holihan
Private Nathaniel Jones
Private Lars Larson
Private George MacReynolds
Private Ian MacTavish
Private Michael Mulligan
Private Pietro Nero
Private Timothy O'Brien
Private Charles O'Malley
Private Thomas O'Reilly
Private Isaac Patterson
Private George Raleigh
Private Thomas Saxon
Private Ludwig Schwartz
Private David Silver
Private Lars Snekker
Private Timothy Sweeney
Private Edward Tomlinson
Private Bohumir Zlato

In war, three-quarters turns on personal character and relations; the balance of manpower and materials counts only for the remaining quarter.

— Napoleon Bonaparte

Chapter One
The Roman Camp

The early morning dew lay over the bivouac like a chilly, damp blanket. The moisture covered the waterproofed canvas of the tents, beading up into little bubbles that sometimes dribbled down the sides and dripped into the thick prairie grass. In the large Sibley tents that housed the officers, all was dry and cozy. But inside the dog tents, each shared by two enlisted men, some of the droplets seeped through the shoddy material and dripped down on the soldiers inside.

Out on the cavalry picket lines, the horses, already awake as the dawn glowed pinkly on the horizon, snorted and shuddered as they stomped their heavy hooves in anticipation of a feed of oats.

The dew also covered a soldier who sat on the ground away from the warmth of the small fire that comforted the sergeant of the guard and the off-duty sentries who slept there. The man, enduring what the army called being "bucked-and-gagged," was trussed up with his wrists bound to his ankles. A stick had been forced into his mouth and was held in place by a bandanna tied cruelly tight. All feeling and sensation in his arms and legs had gone hours before. The trooper, though in pain, felt no animosity toward those who had done this to him. He had gotten drunk on duty and, being a professional soldier, regarded the punishment philosophically, accepting it as his just deserts. He expected nothing less.

The notes of Reveille, sounded by the cavalry duty bugler, gave the prisoner a sense of relief. The release from the torture was now close at hand.

Sergeant Thomas McCarey poured himself a cup of coffee from the kettle set on the hot coals of the fire. He took a sip and stood up. "Are ye awake, Baker?"

The soldier who was bucked-and-gagged spoke as best he could. "Uh huh."

"Now ye're a sorry sight then. But take heart. Ye've not much longer to go now," McCarey said almost apologetically. "I'd loosen ye up, but I won't have the likes o' the first sergeant getting me for it."

Mack Baker, who understood, tried for the hundredth time to flex his legs a bit. But there was absolutely no feeling in the limbs from his hips all the way down to the tips of his toes.

"Ye've a terrible weakness for whiskey, boy," McCarey said. "And I swear to sweet Jesus above it's gonna kill ye some day. In an army of drinkers, ye're the champion." He laughed. "I've never seen any man wit' a thirst like yours. And that includes Ireland too. If they gave stripes for the amount o' likker drunk, ye'd be a regimental sergeant major, Mack Baker." He took another sip of coffee. "But that's not the way o' the game. Instead ye're a poor old soljer all tied up like a pig for the slaughterhouse." He looked over at the camp proper. "Ever'body is formed up for the reveille now. As soon as it's over, the first sergeant will be coming here to turn you loose."

Baker nodded, the effort making him roll over on his side. He struggled to get up, but the numbness in his body prevented any efficient physical action on his part.

McCarey set his coffee down and walked over. He grabbed Baker by the hair and pulled him upright.

"Oow!" came the muffled yell through the gag.

"Sure and it's better'n grabbing you by the ears," McCarey said. "So don't ye be complaining to me, Baker." He went back to the fire in time to see First Sergeant Gordon

Robertson approaching. He waited for the company's most senior noncommissioned officer to appear. When the man arrived, McCarey raised his coffee cup in a quasi-salute. "Top o' the morning, Sergeant Robertson."

"How are you, Sergeant McCarey?" Robertson inquired. He wore the three stripes and lozenge of his rank. He was a tall man deeply browned by the sun. A heavy black moustache flowed out from under his nose and curled up as if by command. Robertson was all soldier and he demonstrated a near-zealous observance of proper military courtesy. "You set that cup down and button your blouse, Sergeant," he said softly but firmly. "I'm here to receive the official report of the company guard."

McCarey immediately obeyed. "All quiet through the night, Sergeant. The last relief is on post and the pris'ner is still in custody."

Robertson smiled. "Ah, yes! Our drunkard, hey?" He walked over to Baker. "Good morning."

Baker looked up at him in a sort of dumb-animal patience.

Robertson nudged him hard with his boot. "Want a drink, Baker?"

Baker shook his head in a negative manner.

"Want that gag taken out of your mouth, Baker?"

Knowing how to respond, the soldier nodded in an enthusiastic manner.

"I'll bet you do, you son of a bitch," Robertson said. He stood looking down at him for a full minute. Finally he bent over and undid the knot on the bandanna.

Under normal circumstances a man might immediately spit out the offending stick in his mouth. But Baker knew better where Robertson was concerned. Keeping it clenched in his teeth, he waited.

Robertson's voice was calm. "You can spit the stick out now, Baker."

Baker did so. "Thank you, Sergeant Robertson."

"You're welcome," Robertson said. He squatted down and methodically untied the ropes holding Baker wrist-to-

9

ankle. "Get up now."

Baker tried, but his limbs could not respond.

Robertson nudged him again. "I said get up!"

Baker made another attempt, but all he could do was roll around on the ground a bit.

"Want some help, Baker?" Robertson bent down and grabbed the soldier under the arms and pulled him up to his feet.

Baker groaned as the blood rushed rapidly back into his limbs, making them tingle in pulsating pain. "Thank you, Sergeant Robertson."

Further conversation between the two was interrupted when McCarey abruptly shouted, "Atten-hut!"

They snapped to the position of attention—Baker a bit sloppy on his wobbly feet—as Captain Charles Riker, their commanding officer, walked up to the fire. Even that early in the morning, his tall, erect figure was sharp and soldierly. He was a slim man with dark, handsome features; the uniform he wore seemed as natural to him as did warpaint to a Sioux warrior. The officer scarcely gave Baker a glance. "I've been called to a staff meeting with General Leighton," Riker said to Robertson. "Lieutenant Worthington has a meeting with the quartermaster, so you'll be in charge until one of us returns."

"Yes, sir!" Robertson said.

"It shouldn't be long," Riker said. Now he looked at Baker. "What's happened here? Has Baker gotten drunk again?"

"Yes, sir," Robertson said.

Riker, following military custom, spoke of the soldier as if he weren't there. He shook his head. "I swear that if we were out in the sand dunes of the Sahara, that man could find liquor."

"Yes, sir," Robertson said. "He's been bucked-and-gagged all night, sir."

"Where did he get it?" Riker asked.

"One of the quartermaster teamsters, sir," Robertson answered.

"And he probably took a month's pay for a bottle of rot-gut the post sutler couldn't sell," Riker said.

"You know about Baker and his weakness for liquor, sir," Robertson said.

Riker studied the sheepish veteran soldier who was not able to assume the proper position of attention. He sighed and once more shook his head. "Carry on, Sergeant," the captain said, walking away.

"Yes, sir!"

Riker commanded L Company of his infantry regiment. He and his men had been detached from their parent unit and assigned to a small expeditionary force commanded by Brigadier General James Leighton. A squadron of four troops of cavalry and quartermaster supply wagons made up the rest of the group. Working out of Fort Keogh on the Tongue River in Montana, Leighton's mission was to seek out and engage Sioux Indians along the Powder River. The job encompassed moving down south into Wyoming and mounting a pursuit with the cavalry if necessary. The foot soldiers were there to man any strongpoints that might be constructed.

Riker, on his way to the meeting at headquarters, strode through the camp. It had been laid out precisely, with company streets, horse pickets, wagon parks, and even the latrines placed in strict geometric patterns. Contrary to appearances, this was not going to be a site occupied for any great length of time. The elaborate detail, despite location in a temporary place for a brief stay, was the idea of General Leighton. A serious student of military history, the officer followed the example set by the Roman legions.

"In those days," Leighton had lectured the officers at the start of the mission, "at the end of every day's march, the legion's surveyors moved forward to lay out the site of the night's camp. They marked the four corners and the places where the gates would be located. When the remaining troops arrived, they dumped their gear to the ground and immediately began digging a ditch around the entire area. This task was tended to before resting or eating. Once this was done, stakes were driven into the top of the banks of dirt produced by the digging, and the great leather tents were pitched in a formation which created proper streets. As every camp was exactly like previous ones, each legionary could find his own unit's place even in the dark. Not only was it convenient and orderly, but the legion was prepared against any attack, no matter how strong. And that, gentlemen, is exactly what I intend to do on this expedition's march into Sioux country."

Thinking of the trouble caused by the obsession with intricately organized bivouacs, Riker continued his walk across the camp. As he passed the cavalry camp, he caught sight of the horse soldiers' senior officers ahead of him. They were on their way to the same staff meeting. The five—a major and four captains—were old acquaintances of Riker's. He'd worked with them before in the fourteen years he'd spent out on the frontier.

"Yo the cavalry!" he called after them.

They stopped and looked back at him. "Riker, old son," the major said. "Come and join us."

"How are you this morning, gentlemen?" Riker asked.

"Why, we in the cavalry are in excellent spirits," the major replied. "Say! My wife tells me that your Lurene has gone to Minnesota for the summer."

"Yes," Riker said. "She misses the children." His two sons and daughter were enrolled in a private school in Saint Paul. He could never have afforded the tuitions on his army pay, but Riker had a wealthy father-in-law who doted on his grandchildren.

"Will you walk with us, Riker?"

"That's exactly what I intend to do, sir," Riker said. "I, too, am answering a summons to General Leighton's august presence."

One of the captains remarked, "What do you suppose the general has called us together for now?"

"Perhaps he wants us to dig a ditch around the bivouac," Riker suggested. "Like those old Romans he admires so much."

The cavalry major laughed. "And put in stakes too, I warrant, hey?"

"Don't joke about it," the captain said in a sour tone. "The old man will have us each toting a sharpened log for just that purpose."

"Perhaps he thinks the cavalry have rested their mounts enough," Riker said. The halt in the march south had been called because the grain-fed horses required a resting up. Surprisingly, infantry troops traveling on foot could actually outdistance the mounted branch over a period of weeks.

"In that case," another cavalry captain said, "I suggest we parade the animals in front of the general so he can give them a damned good telling off."

"Right," Riker agreed with a grin. "By the way, in case you're interested, one of the quartermaster teamsters is peddling whiskey. My first sergeant caught a man drunk on duty early yesterday evening."

"Robertson did? I'll bet that ended up in a buck-and-gagging," the major commented.

"It did," Riker said. "It was one of my professional privates. An old soldier named Baker."

"It seems our veterans are drunkards and the rest green kids," the major said. "But that's the regular army."

"So it is," Riker agreed. He remembered the war against the South when the army was a fair representation of the nation's citizenry.

The group of officers arrived at the headquarters tent and were greeted by Leighton's adjutant-general, an energetic captain named Brooks. He wasted no time in ushering them in. The quartermaster-general of the expeditionary force was already there, enjoying a cup of coffee provided by an orderly.

"Hello, Simmons," Riker greeted him. "We hear you've got a whiskey peddler among your teamsters."

"Really?" Captain Blake commented. "Point him out, will you, old boy? I'm in the need for a bottle or two myself."

The laughter his remark produced was cut off by the arrival of Brigadier General James Leighton. The expedition commander, wearing a fresh uniform, looked as if he was still in garrison instead of out in the field. It was rumored among the other officers that the general had a trunk with no less than thirty changes of clothing in it.

Leighton waited for the headquarters orderly, dressed in a white waiter's jacket by his direct order, to serve them all coffee before beginning the staff meeting.

"Gentlemen, an inspection yesterday has caused me to reach the conclusion the cavalry mounts must be rested another two or three days," General Leighton said in a surly tone.

Feeling responsible, the cavalry major quickly spoke up. "Sir, they've not had much exercising since the spring thaw. There wasn't time before this campaign was begun. But please don't worry. The animals will shape up quick enough."

"I'm certain of that, Major," Leighton said. "But in the meantime we cannot simply sit and twiddle our thumbs. We must keep looking for those redskinned rascals. So I want you"—he pointed to Riker—"to draw rations for four days and make a foot reconnaissance down to the point where Crazy Woman River runs into the Powder."

Riker was surprised. "Sir? You want my men to go on a patrol?"

"Exactly! Your mission is to locate any Sioux camps in the vicinity and return with that information," Leighton continued.

"I beg the general's pardon," Riker said. "I don't feel a company of infantry would be particularly effective in such an undertaking."

Leighton frowned. "Explain yourself, sir!"

It seemed so obvious to Riker that he was surprised an explanation was necessary. "Well, sir, the Sioux are mounted. That makes them faster and more maneuverable than my men. And going on foot would surely invite attack."

14

"You are in the army to fight, are you not, Captain?" Leighton asked sarcastically. "And your soldiers too, correct?"

Riker's face reddened with anger. "Yes, sir! Of course. But the majority of the men are raw recruits. Of the new men, none have even fired their rifles. They've only been through dry-firing exercises."

"Your company is no different from the rest of the army," Leighton said. "Lame excuses mean nothing, Captain."

"I am not making excuses, sir," Riker said. "I merely wish to point out that—"

Leighton cut him short. "The mission is necessary, Captain. We cannot send cavalry because their damned horses are blown. So we must send L Company. I fully realize that duties of infantry in the war against the Indians is to man garrisons and provide strong defensive points during active campaigning. But we must be versatile, Captain Riker."

"Yes, sir," Riker said.

Leighton turned his attention to the cavalry officers. "I want you to take particularly good care of your mounts. I'll not tolerate more requirements for excessive resting of the animals."

"I understand, sir," the major said, feeling uncomfortable. "But after months in the stables with only parade ground exercise, one can't expect much more."

"Of course, Major," the general said in a calmer tone. "No one is claiming negligence on your part."

At that point, as far as Leighton was concerned, his part of the meeting was over. Other details to be brought up were beneath him and could easily be handled by his staff officers. The general abruptly withdrew and both the adjutant and quartermaster brought up administrative and logistical problems to be dealt with. When those matters were cleared up, the meeting was over.

Riker stepped outside, looking at his companions. "Get those horses of yours ready quickly," he said with a half-smile. "My men and I may require your sudden and timely appearance when the Sioux finally discover our presence stumbling around in the middle of their territory."

The major didn't laugh. "We'll do our best, Charlie. The best of luck to you, old boy."

"You'll need it, Riker," one of the captains said.

"Be prudent and try to avoid unnecessarily exposing yourself," the other said.

"I would stick close to the river," the major added. "The trees are generally thick there."

"Good advice. Except they will also offer excellent ambush positions for the Indians. But your thoughts are well appreciated," Riker said. He saluted, then hurried off to find First Sergeant Robertson and get the company ready for the task ahead.

Chapter Two
Captain Charles Riker

Most of the folks in Summerport, Maine were not surprised when young Charlie Riker turned his back on his family's seafaring traditions and chose to apply for admittance to the United States Military Academy at West Point, New York.

They realized it wasn't because Charlie hated the sea. And he wasn't rebelling against his father, but for all of his eighteen years, Charlie had always been one to go his own way. Not that he could have been considered peculiar; he just seemed to have his own ideas about how things should be done. One of the town wags had once said that if Charlie Riker were to construct a house, he'd do it by building the roof first, then complete the rest of the structure under it. "But," he added, "it'd turn out to be a first-rate job."

By the time Charlie was ready to attend the academy, his father—a retired ship's master who had married late in life—didn't bother to protest. After raising the boy and watching him grow, the old salt knew his son was the sort who would always chart his own course and damn the tides and the winds. Any effort to make the boy heave-to would be time-consuming and fruitless. If Charlie would go for a soldier rather than seek his fortunes on the high seas, that was the way it would be.

Thus, with the dubious blessings of his father, Cadet Charles Riker began his career at West Point in the fall of

1856.

Charlie, with a good sense of humor and a lot of enthusiasm for the difficult task ahead, moved quickly into the routine of the academy. Having a good attitude and a great deal of self-confidence, he took the hazing and discipline in stride, earning the respect of both his peers and superiors.

Many other plebes, some with fear in their eyes, were resentful and uncomfortable when braced into rigid positions of attention by upperclassmen. But Charlie took it all calmly. He endured bawlings out well, responding to them as if the episodes were somewhat harsh lessons rather than mistreatment. Like all the new cadets, he managed, bit by bit, to shape up until eventually he was well squared away into the shako, crossbelts, and gray uniform, presenting the picture of a well-trained, prepared cadet.

Charlie quickly became popular with his fellow cadets, and earned a particularly good reputation as a poker player. His dark, handsome countenance was without expression as he studied the cards and made his bets. This calmness and lack of expression made the bluffing part of the card game difficult for his opponents. Poker and history were his strong points, while mathematics and the sciences sorely tried his classroom efforts. Sometimes his marks slipped so low while he struggled with the exactness and logic of such a curriculum that he required extra tutoring. But Cadet Riker always put forth the extra effort when necessary to pass the courses.

Athletics was another area where Charlie did well. He quickly earned a place as pitcher on the baseball nine, and became the fencing master's pet as he acquired skill with saber and foil. But where he really attracted attention was in the equestrian classes, although not all of the attention was admiring. He had never ridden much before coming to the academy, and he made up for this lack of experience with boldness and a display of recklessness that dismayed the instructors and other cadets. If thrown and bruised, Charlie would brush the dirt from his britches and jump back into the saddle, daring the horse "to do that again, old fellow!"

The horse usually did.

With his inept horsemanship, poor marks in mathematics, and an unusual number of pranks, Charlie walked off plenty of demerits that he himself admitted he richly deserved. Cadets could rid their records of bad conduct marks by marching back and forth on the barracks square in the evenings after duty hours. Because Charlie wore out a lot of shoe leather in this way, he didn't make much rank in his first two years at West Point. He began as a cadet private and held that rank right up to the end of his term as a third classman. At that point, his superiors decided Charlie needed some toning down. They decided a bit of responsibility might make him a bit more serious. When he returned from furlough in September of 1858, Charlie found orders posted that appointed him to the rank of cadet corporal.

The insignia of that office was a single chevron worn on the tunic below the elbow. When the corporal became a sergeant, the chevron was moved to the upper arm. The first time Charlie put on his cadet gray with the chevron sewn firmly in place, he changed. It was not a feeling of power that moved him, nor was it a sense of superiority over the lower rankers. Instead, it was a sense of responsibility not only to those above him but to the other cadets who served in his squad.

Charlie, like most people with a natural good humor, also had a temper. When his patience finally gave way, a flash of anger would erupt like a cannonshot and the objects of his wrath had no doubt they had run afoul of him. But this generally didn't happen unless Charlie thought one of his subordinates was careless or didn't give a damn. A few sharp words from Cadet Corporal Riker and the offender was more than ready to mend his ways.

If someone was genuinely trying, however, Charlie was there to lend a helping hand. A particularly clumsy plebe had been assigned to Charlie's squad at the beginning of

19

the year. The cadet, a brainy fellow named Dickerson, had a terrible time at drill. Charlie gave him extra instruction in the intricacies of facing movements and keeping in step. One area Dickerson was especially lacking in was the manual of arms. His head bobbed, he didn't slap his musket in the movements, and his execution was far from sharp and military.

Dickerson was finally noticed by a cadet captain during a parade. He was so sloppy that it was thought the clumsy fellow was simply fooling around rather than trying. The inept marcher was given enough demerits to warrant eight hours to walk them off.

Cadet Corporal Charles Riker thought this unfair. In his own mind, it was his fault that Dickerson had not mastered the intricacies of West Point drill. If he had put in more time at special instruction, perhaps the clumsy cadet would not have gotten himself in trouble. Therefore, Charlie turned himself in and insisted that walking off the demerits was his responsibility. Dickerson was released from punishment and Charlie took his place, pacing back and forth with a musket on his shoulder in the cold evenings.

After walking the tour, Charlie was promoted to cadet sergeant. The reason given was that he had impressed his superiors with his show of leadership initiative and a willingness to take responsibility for those under his command. These were the traits he was never to lose.

Now he could move the chevron to the top of his sleeve.

Charlie was advanced one more time during his cadet days. That final promotion made him a cadet lieutenant. Now he sported two chevrons. This, and the posting as a company first lieutenant, was the highest he was to rise during his time at West Point. He continued to struggle with the sciences while excelling in athletics and pranks. His fencing improved to the point that he was regularly beating his instructor. His pitching also sharpened up quite a bit, and he kept opponents pinned down to numerous scoreless innings. Being thrown from horseback also remained a habit, and he finished equestrian activities dusty and bruised, though undaunted.

Toward the end of the fourth year, all cadets made their final choices of the branch in which they wished to be commissioned. The brainier types chose the corps of engineers. In a young nation with lots of building to do, this was considered an elite unit in which to serve. Those not quite so smart, but still with plenty of mathematical savvy, went into the artillery. Shooting the big guns required a knowledge of trigonometry and the use of angles to compute the correct combination of barrel angles and powder charges necessary for the accurate firing of cannon.

Charlie Riker's achievements in math and science did not leave him qualified for those branches of service. That was fine with Charlie. The last thing he wanted to do was spend thirty or forty years working with figures. He wanted action, and plenty of it. So he listed as his first choice the cavalry.

Unfortunately, his poor marks brought him down low in the class standings. By the time his name came up, all the openings for second lieutenant of cavalry had been filled. A few of the more humorous folks at West Point said that the situation was actually to Charlie Riker's benefit. The fact that he wouldn't be riding horses would save him countless broken bones and the government hundreds of animals over the period of his military career. Charlie, upon hearing the joke, grinned ruefully and accepted his lieutenancy of infantry.

In the fall of 1860, after a summer spent at home in Maine, the young shavetail reported to Fort Snelling, Minnesota to begin his army service. Charlie was less than happy with the assignment. As he said to his old charge Dickerson when he left West Point, "Fort Snelling is too far east for any real Indian fighting and too far west to offer an exciting social life."

He was correct about the former but mistaken in the latter. The nearby city of Saint Paul offered a social life of sorts. Even though it wasn't as fancy or up-to-date as New York or Washington, Lieutenant Charles Riker found his

21

own stimulation among the large town's gentry.

This occurred at a party in the home of one of the local well-to-dos. A blanket invitation had been issued for the attendance of Fort Snelling officers. Charlie, without much to do, accepted and went into the city. The soiree was a dinner dance held in the spacious backyard of a socialite couple who hoped their daughter might meet an eligible suitor. Charlie didn't take much notice of that particular young lady, but one did catch his eye. This was Miss Lurene Mills.

Lurene was the daughter of Silas Mills, a transplanted New Englander who had become quite a successful merchant in Saint Paul. She was a short, attractive young woman of eighteen years with light brown hair and green eyes. A graceful dancer, she possessed the great feminine talent of being able to flirt without appearing to do so. Charlie started the courtship the way he rode horses — immediately, boldly, and without hesitation. He saw to it that his name went on her dance list within a minute of being introduced to her. After that he continued to stay in her presence to the point that the other young men dancing with her began to think that quite possibly he was the one who had brought her. That was fine with Charlie.

During one of the waltzes, which Charlie had claimed as his own, Lurene's budding womanly instincts caused her to realize the handsome young officer had taken more than just a casual interest in her. And that same feminine insight made her want to tease him a bit.

"My, Mr. Riker," she said demurely. "You seem to be extraordinarily fond of dancing."

Charlie, whose nimble feet made him rather good at it, smiled. "Yes, indeed, Miss Mills. But I confess your company increased my pleasure in the pastime."

"I believe you are a flatterer, sir," Lurene said.

"Only when it is deserved, Miss Mills," Charlie replied.

After that dance Charlie offered to fetch her some punch. But Lurene, with some previous coaching from an older girl in mind, decided to let this particular fish run with the line a bit. "I'm afraid not now, Mr. Riker. Perhaps later." Then she added, "And there are other names on my dance card, sir." With that, she returned to her crowd of friends.

Feeling a bit chastened and downcast, Charlie went over to the punch bowl for his own benefit. While he was ladling a cupful, one of the local blades walked up beside him. He introduced himself with a surly "The name is Sims. Banking is my business."

Charlie, in full dress uniform, smiled at him. "Riker here. I suppose my profession is obvious."

Sims sneered. "Yes it is, Riker. And so is your unwarranted and uninvited interest in Miss Mills."

"Unwarranted, sir?" Charlie stated. He felt a hot flash of anger, but fought it down enough to control his emotions. "You speak as if I am beneath the rest of the assemblage somehow."

Sims, not wanting any trouble, backed down a bit. "Perhaps I should emphasize *uninvited,* Riker."

Charlie continued to smile. "When speaking to me, you will employ the respectful title of 'sir.' "

Sims hesitated. After all, this was probably a barracks bully. He felt like a member of the Roman senate speaking to a common centurion. Care had to be exercised, or there was every possibility of violence. "Very well, sir. We of Saint Paul are by nature a closed society. We do not welcome outsiders."

"Pardon me, Sims," Charlie said. "I would love to stand here and listen to your prattle, but I believe I have the next dance with Miss Mills."

Charlie claimed that dance, and even the last one of the evening. It was a Saturday and the young officer wanted very much to see the young lady again — soon. "May I have the honor of accompanying you to church tomorrow, Miss Mills?" he asked.

"Why thank you, Mr. Riker," Lurene replied. "But I always attend services with my parents." She smiled. "Perhaps we shall see you there."

"I believe you will," Charlie said. The music came to a halt and he walked her back to her friends. Before he left, he asked, "And what is your religious preference, Miss Mills?"

"Beg pardon?" she said.

"Which church do you attend?"

Lurene suppressed a laugh. "You have no particular one yourself, Mr. Riker?"

"At this point and time in my life, any will do," Charlie said.

"I belong to the First Methodist," Lurene said. "Services are at ten o'clock."

"Thank you, Miss Mills," Charlie said, bowing. "Until tomorrow at the First Methodist."

An hour early on that next morning, Second Lieutenant Charles Thomas Riker was standing tall by the front steps of the church. He waited patiently, nodding to other arrivals as they looked curiously at the unknown young officer loitering in front of their place of worship. When the Mills carriage arrived, Charlie performed in his usual manner. He walked rapidly up to the curb, smiling a happy greeting to the occupants.

"Good morning, Miss Mills," he said to her. "So very nice to see you."

"Good morning, Mr. Riker," Lurene replied as he helped her out of the vehicle. She introduced him to her parents when they stepped down to the curb.

Mrs. Mills, like most women, thought the young man quite attractive. But she had already heard about him the evening before when Lurene came home from the party. Mr. Silas Mills, on the other hand, was not particularly impressed. He indicated Charlie's shoulder straps with a curt nod of his head. "Don't those mean something about your title?"

"They indicate I am a second lieutenant of infantry, sir," Charlie replied.

"Then shouldn't we call you 'lieutenant'?"

"No, sir. It's quite proper to address an officer as you

24

would a civilian gentleman," Charlie said.

Silas Mills, an austere and severe member of the merchant class, considered all soldiers — officers included — barely a step or two above the status of homeless tramps. "Well, *Mister* Riker, shall we go in?"

"A capital idea, sir," Charlie said, displaying a wide grin. Being an intelligent young man, he offered his arm not to Lurene, but to her mother. "May I escort you, ma'am?"

"My, yes." Mrs. Mills said, beaming.

Mills rolled his eyes in consternation and Lurene stifled a giggle as they went into the church.

Thus, on that Sunday morning, Charlie Riker launched his attack to capture the heart of Miss Lurene Mills. Not knowing he'd already won his objective, he spent the following months plying her with flowers, letters, and visits to the home. Even howling blizzards could not deter him. His arrival on even stormy nights amazed Lurene and her parents.

Finally, it was summer. The Minnesota snow had gone away for good and the sultry evenings were well set in for the season. Now, since Charlie considered the time was right, he popped the question in the gazebo of the Mills's expansive backyard.

That was the easy part.

Next he had to get the old man's permission to marry the daughter. Lurene had already dropped some heavy hints, but it was going to be up to Charlie to make the final maneuvers in the war of love. He approached Mills later that same evening after dinner. Finding him in his study, Charlie didn't ease the conversation into the reason for his visit. He simply blurted it out.

"Mr. Mills, I would like to marry Lurene."

Mills, who had been dreading such a situation, winced openly. "God!"

Charlie wasn't discouraged. "I have already proposed to her, sir. She has accepted and I promise to be a faithful and affectionate husband."

Now it was Silas Mills's turn to be candid. "Have you

ever thought about getting out of the army?" he asked.

"No, sir, I haven't," Charlie replied cheerfully. "In fact, it is the furthest thing from my mind."

"I would prefer that my daughter wasn't married to a soldier," Mills said. His tone carried a strong hint.

"I'm afraid that's what I am, sir," Charlie said. The young man's voice echoed a tone of its own—finality on the subject under discussion.

"How would you like to get into the world of commerce, Mr. Riker?" Mills asked. "Perhaps a position with my firm would be in order under the circumstances."

Charlie became even blunter. "Mr. Mills, I would never consider leaving the army under any circumstances. I chose to attend West Point because all my life I have wanted to be a soldier. I intend to remain one, sir, until the end of my days."

Mills decided that a different approach was called for. "I had rather hoped that she would marry into the Sims family."

"I know who you mean, sir," Charlie said. "I met him at a party several months ago. In fact, it was the same one at which I was introduced to Lurene. I found Mr. Sims to be a pasty-faced fop."

Mills smiled to himself. Although not used to hearing any of the Simses of Saint Paul spoken of in such a manner, he was in complete agreement. Stifling a desire to chuckle out loud, the older man was silent for a while. "What sort of business is your family in, Mr. Riker?"

"My father is a retired sea captain," Charlie replied. "He makes modest investments in cargo now and then. We also own some unremarkable property in Maine, none of it particularly valuable, I'm afraid."

Mills, in his competitive world of business, was not used to such veracity. He looked at the young officer and realized for the first time what a serious and dedicated man he might be. "Do you think you'll go far in the army, Mr. Riker?"

"I should be a first lieutenant after ten years," Charlie

26

truthfully replied. "Then in another five or ten I could be a captain. I shall probably retire with the rank of lieutenant colonel or colonel after thirty-five years or so."

"Mmm," Mills said thoughtfully.

"Of course, one never knows," Charlie said optimistically. "Circumstances might make me a general someday."

Mills paced back and forth. "Mr. Riker, would you always entertain the thought of returning to Saint Paul if you ever found that life in the army had grown somewhat, shall we say, less than desirable?"

"Of course, sir," Charlie said without hesitation. "I promise you that, Mr. Mills."

Charlie Riker and Lurene Mills were married on January 1, 1861.

After a short honeymoon trip back to Charlie's hometown in Maine, the couple returned to live in officer's quarters at Fort Snelling. The Mills offered roomy accommodations in the family mansion and when that was refused Silas Mills offered to put them up in a house all their own in Saint Paul. But Charlie didn't want to be different from any of his fellow officers, so the couple moved on post. Lurene moved graciously into the military community. A naturally friendly young lady, she found her new friends interesting and entertaining. Charlie beamed with each compliment he received on the choice of a wife. But the happy routine came to a halt that April.

Fort Sumter was fired on down in South Carolina, and the young country went to war with itself. All the southern officers resigned their commissions and headed back for their home states as hostilities mounted. In June, Charlie's regiment was ordered to Washington, and the happy couple reluctantly parted company.

Charlie's responsibilities grew. With the departure of so many southerners, vacancies occurred in the officer cadre of the unit. Charlie was appointed commanding officer of L Company, and by the time they arrived in the nation's capital, he had been promoted to first lieutenant many years before he had expected it.

27

The regiment's main duty was to guard public property. It wasn't long before the regiments of militia and volunteers from all over the north began to flood into the city in preparation for war. Charlie was alarmed by the naive, amateur troops. They expected to have the rebel states whipped and tamed in a matter of weeks. Charlie knew what sort of soldiers came from the South. The officers were aristocratic gentlemen bred to command. The enlisted men were hard types from tough mountain environments or off dusty southern farms where life was grinding poverty. Either one—officer or soldier—was tenacious, tough, and incredibly brave.

Throughout May and June, the northern volunteers cavorted, soldiered a bit, and swaggered about in an alarming variety of colorful uniforms completely unsuited for heavy field use. In July, things turned deadly serious as the army marched out to take on the Confederates at Manassas, Virginia.

The Union troops, under the command of General Irvin McDowell, launched their attack on the Sunday morning of July 21, 1861. Charlie Riker, now a captain after his second quick promotion, was like most of the other participants—he did not know exactly what was going on. He merely followed orders, moving with his regiment from point to point either directly on or adjacent to the battlefield. Firing could be heard from different directions at different times, but Charlie and his men didn't get involved in any real fighting until late that afternoon. That was after McDowell figured he had been defeated, and decided to withdraw.

Charlie's regiment was among the first to retire. They moved toward Washington, crossing over a bridge spanning a creek called Cub Run. At this point, someone thought it prudent to have the better-disciplined regular troops hold up to cover the more disorganized militia as they retreated toward Washington. Charlie's colonel detached his company and ordered them to stay at the creek.

For a short time it was a pretty routine thing, until a

wagon was overturned on the bridge over the waterway. At that point, wild rumors caused a rout to develop. Now, instead of marching away, the Union soldiers were running away. The situation gained momentum until what had been an organized army turned into a lawless, bellowing, fleeing mob. They streamed across the bridge, trampling and jostling each other, as the Southerners closed in. Charlie, with his professional troops, stood ready to do as they had been ordered: cover the retreat.

When the first Rebel lines came into view, the jubilant Southerners were moving almost as fast as the escaping Yankees. Unless something was done, what had been a disgraceful affair could well turn into a massacre. Charlie gave the orders to form as skirmishers and move forward into harm's way. His men instantly obeyed.

Charlie ordered a volley and the muskets of his men thundered for the first time. The Southerners answered in kind. Now, receiving his baptism of fire, the young captain and his men stood fast. In a few short moments he learned of fear, fury, and grief as Confederate musketballs plowed into his men, perceptibly thinning out their ranks. But they closed up and continued to follow Charlie's orders until the final remnants of gaudy militiamen streaked past them.

Then, in an orderly withdrawal, Charlie's depleted company pulled back from the bridge. It was then the Confederates stopped firing at them. Charlie could see one of their officers giving them a salute with his saber. Charlie returned the gesture, then marched his men back to Washington.

A few days later a most distinguished visitor arrived at Charlie's regiment to interview him. It was Senator William Fessenden from his home state, Maine. The governor of the state was working frantically to build up volunteer regiments and was in dire need of qualified officers. Would Captain Charles Riker accept the position as regimental commander of one of the newly formed units, with the rank of colonel?

Smiling and thinking of his father-in-law, Charlie readily

accepted. He resigned his regular army commission on the third of August, accepting an appointment as colonel of Maine volunteers that same day.

Charlie and his regiment joined the Army of Potomac. The next four years were to be long, bloody, and unforgiving. Colonel Riker and his regiment fought in the Virginia Peninsula Campaign, the Battles of Gainesville, Antietam, Fredericksburg, Chancellorsville, Gettysburg, the Wilderness, Cold Harbor, and Petersburg. His command was filled and refilled four times over as they slogged through the most terrible war America was ever to fight. Charlie learned the agony of exchanging volley fire at close range; of having cannonball and grapeshot rip through the ranks of his men; and the terrible exhilaration of bayonet charges into enemy positions.

By the time Lee surrendered to Grant at Appomattox, Charlie Riker's Maine volunteers could muster no more than seventy-six men.

The end of the war brought the end of his colonelcy. He held a last formation of his steadfast regiment, shaking hands with each one as they boarded the train for the trip back north to the Pine Tree State. After the farewells, Charlie reapplied for his regular army commission. It was quickly activated and he returned to his regiment with the rank of first lieutenant.

He and Lurene looked forward to a return to the staid confines of Fort Snelling after the hectic, worry-filled years of the war. But instead of returning to Minnesota, the regiment went straight to the Indian Wars.

The couple's family grew to three children as they moved about from one primitive frontier post to another. Charlie, while stationed at such isolated duty stations as Fort Sill, Fort Richardson, and Fort Griffen, fought against the Kiowa and Comanche in the south. When those tribes moved onto reservations, there was more fighting to be done. Charlie and his regiment were transferred north to the wars against the Sioux at Fort Keogh, Montana.

Meanwhile, Charlie resisted entreaties from his father-in-law to leave the harsh life and join him in the family business in Saint Paul. It was tempting at times, he admitted even to himself, but the uniform he wore, the flag he served under, and the fact that Captain Riker was convinced God had put him on the earth for the sole purpose of soldiering, kept him at his postings.

He didn't seem to be destined for the high rank he'd hoped for when he'd asked old Silas Mills for Lurene's hand. The best he had been able to do after twenty years of service was the captaincy of an understrength infantry company that was now attached to an expeditionary force sent to search out and engage the Sioux.

Chapter Three
The Second Squad

Corporal Karl Schreiner had a hell of a time adapting to the United States Army. After serving as a not-too-reluctant conscript in his native Prussia's military forces and fighting against the French in the Franco-Prussian War of 1870-71, the European style of soldiering had left him with impressions of acceptable military conduct and protocol.

Or at least what he thought was acceptable.

The Americans not only demonstrated a completely different military philosophy, but they also compounded this nonconformity with a marked amount of inconsistent behavior. A procedure rigorously followed under one set of circumstances would be more than ignored in another situation; it would be completely reversed. As far as the Prussian was concerned, there was no martial norm in the field, in garrison, in the wearing of uniforms, in military courtesy and customs, or even in the conduct of war.

Schreiner had grown used to the rigid fighting of Europe, where colorfully clad armies dressed right and covered down, then squared off against each other across open fields. When the situation was right and the necessary orders issued, the sides systematically shot each other down rank by rank with deliveries of highly disciplined firepower.

This was impossible in the war against the Indians. The Native Americans refused to abide by any rules of warfare, operating in a fluid, unpredictable style. When the Sioux, for example, grew bored with a particular situation or found it to their disadvantage to continue the fight, they simply melted away into the vast wilderness of prairie and mountain. The battle came to a rather unremarkable end, without fanfare or pomp.

Yet these strange circumstances didn't bother American officers in the slightest. After taking the trouble to instruct their troops in proper battle drill — and allowing the corporals and sergeants to emphasize the finer points of the lessons with their fists and boots — they completely ignored the instructions taught. They went after the Indians in a manner the Spanish insurgents who had fought Napoleon had termed *guerrilla* — little war — a style of fighting that was unconventional and totally without an orderly pattern.

Another thing that Schreiner couldn't understand was why the American Army went to war out in the West dressed pretty much as they pleased. It wasn't unusual for buckskin to be worn by officers, and everyone had a colorful bandanna around his neck. And they all wore their headgear any damned way that suited them. Here again was an inconsistency. In garrison, strict wearing of uniform — even full dress — was observed for every formation from guard mount to formal parades on Sunday. It was enough to boggle an orderly German mind.

There was also the peculiar way the Americans showed respect for authority. After the rigid caste system of the Old World, the style of military courtesy displayed by the United States Army left Schreiner further confused. In the Prussian Army, a corporal — called an *unteroffizier* — was to be obeyed instantly under threat of dire consequences for any disobedience. The Prussian corporal did not have to be big or intimidating; his rank was enough to awe his underlings. But in the American Army there were times when, as they said, a noncommissioned officer was required to back up his stripes with his fists.

An American-born soldier in their army harbored the alarming potential of suddenly and unexpectedly exploding into a one-man rebellion by not only refusing to obey an order, but punching the corporal or sergeant who issued it. It was at times like that that Schreiner was glad he was a big man. On more than one occasion, when faced with physical insubordination, his Teutonic temper had gone wild and he'd beaten the disobedient private senseless. The most surprising thing about such situations was that the affected man rarely carried a grudge. To the Americans, such occurrences seemed to clear the air.

Corporal punishment in Europe was more severe than in the American service, but it was not necessary to employ it often, because of the built-in respect for authority most Prussians had. But bucking-and-gagging, unauthorized kicks and punches, and even spread-eagling, were nearly weekly practices in the less orderly American service.

Now, well into his second hitch, Corporal Karl Schreiner was still learning about the American character. He walked over to the squad cookfire to join his men in preparing their breakfast. Several pots of coffee, with bricklike hardtack biscuits soaking in them, boiled on the coals while the men roasted bits of salt pork stuck on the end of sticks.

Private Thomas Saxon, an Ohio farmboy, glanced up at the noncommissioned officer's arrival. "Howdy, Corp'ral Schreiner."

"Hello, Saxon," Schreiner replied in his thick German accent. He nodded to the others as he squatted down and put his own coffee on to boil.

Besides Saxon, there was Private Devlin, a former bank clerk from Massachusetts; George Hammer and Lars Larson, who had been laborers; Tim O'Brien and Tim Sweeney, both Irish immigrants out of rural communities of their native country; and Charlie O'Malley, another Irishman, but born in Pennsylvania. All the men, with the exception of O'Malley, were green recruits with less than six months of service. The man who had gotten drunk the previous day, Mack Baker, was Schreiner's only other veteran.

Saxon, only eighteen and full of enthusiasm about everything, spoke up. "Hey! Here comes Mack."

Mack Baker, released from his bucking-and-gagging,

34

walked up to the squad with a sheepish grin on his face. He still moved unsteadily, with a slight limp. "Good morning, soldiers."

Schreiner, who had turned him in for being drunk, looked up from stirring his coffee. "How are you this morning, Baker?"

"The blood's pounding through my legs, but aside from that I'm fine, I guess," Baker said. "Hell of a way to spend a night, let me tell you that, fellers."

"Where'd you get the whiskey?" O'Malley asked. As a soldier on his second enlistment, he thought the information might prove valuable, although he had no desire to experience First Sergeant Robertson's style of field punishment.

"Off one o' the quartermaster teamsters," Baker said. He looked at Schreiner. "Do I have time to eat?"

"If you hurry," Schreiner said. He looked around. One man was still back in the dog tents somewhere. "And tell Mulligan up here to get *schnell*—that is, quick."

"Right, Corp'ral," Baker said. He left them and walked back toward the orderly row of dog tents that made up the second squad's bivouac area.

Harold Devlin spooned out some of the soggy hardtack from his coffee and took a bite of the hot, spongy mass. Chewing thoughtfully, he asked, "I wonder what they'll have us do today?"

Schreiner shrugged. "I saw the captain to a meeting going at the general's tent. I am sure he will come back with some news."

"Thank God for cavalry horses," Devlin said sardonically. Like the others, he'd grown so used to the way Schreiner sometimes mangled English sentences that he scarcely noticed it. "If it wasn't for those poor suffering brutes they would walk us to death."

"Even a plow horse needs rest," Tommy Saxon pointed out.

Devlin slowly shook his head. "I never thought I would be in a position where more consideration would be shown

35

animals than men."

Old soldier Charlie O'Malley laughed. "That's what happens when you go for a soldier, Harold. No one made you 'list, did they?"

"No," he admitted.

"In Prussia," Schreiner said, "they make every able-bodied man in the army go to put in time. They conscript them."

"They did that in the war here," Devlin said. "But rich men could hire substitutes."

The sound of a scuffle broke out in the tents. They all stood up to see Mack Baker and another member of the squad, named Michael Mulligan, engaged in a fistfight. By the time they all ran over, Baker was on top of Mulligan, pounding his head on the ground.

Schreiner, disgusted, dragged him off. "What between you two is going on?" he demanded.

Baker's face was livid with rage. "I caught this son of a bitch in my tent!" He reached into Mulligan's shirt and pulled out a pocket watch. "See? This is mine. It's got my name engraved on it."

Schreiner glared at Mulligan through his cold blue eyes. "Get on your feet."

Mulligan, his face expressionless, stood up, brushing bits of grass off his uniform.

"That watch is the only thing I got that's worth anything," Baker said to the others. "I seen him pulling it outta my haversack."

Lars Larson grabbed Mulligan's shirt front. *"Tyv!* Were you the one that took the dollar from my tent?"

Mulligan maintained his silence.

Schreiner grabbed him by the arm. "Come wit' me, Mulligan. It's off to the first sergeant to see. Move!" He pointed to Baker. "And you too come."

"Shit!" Baker complained. "I ain't gonna get any hot coffee this morning!"

Schreiner and Baker both held onto Mulligan as they marched and pushed him through the company bivouac to the dog tents where the sergeants lived. They walked to where the two noncommissioned officers were consuming their own breakfast.

"Sergeant McCarey," Schreiner said.

McCarey, recently returned from his duty as sergeant of the guard, groaned. "Now what? Is Baker in more trouble? Christ, he's only gotten out of a bucking-and-gagging not an hour ago. Sure, and even he ain't capable o' finding more whiskey this fast."

"No, Sergeant," Schreiner said. "Mulligan it is who is in trouble. He is a t'ief. We ask from you permission to the first sergeant to take him."

"Goddamn yer Dutch eyes, Schreiner!" McCarey complained. "I wish ye'd learn the English language better. Are ye asking me permission to take Mulligan to the first sergeant? If so, go right ahead, with me blessings."

Schreiner and Baker propelled the accused man to the large tent that served First Sergeant Robertson as both an office and living quarters. When they arrived, Robertson was seated inside at his field table, bringing his duty roster up to date. He was not pleased with the interruption.

"What the hell's with you three?"

"We caught a t'ief," Schreiner announced.

"Who's a thicf?" Robertson asked.

"Mulligan, Sergeant," Baker interjected. "I caught him in my tent pulling my watch outta my haversack."

Robertson only shrugged. "He don't look like a thief to me."

Schreiner was astounded. "But in the act he was caught by Baker. He stole—"

Robertson leaned forward. "Listen to me, Schreiner. Mulligan don't look like a thief to me. Thieves got black eyes and busted noses and busted jaws. That's how a thief looks. So don't bring no healthy-looking son of a bitch over here and tell me he's a thief."

Schreiner was confused at first. Then he realized that once again he was dealing with an American idiosyncrasy—the art of saying something in a most roundabout

37

manner. "Come on," he said to Baker. "To those trees over there we will take him."

"With pleasure!" Baker said.

Mulligan allowed himself to be dragged to the inevitable beating. It was nothing new to him. He'd endured such treatment all his life. It had been his father at first. Later on he'd been knocked around in the streets as his life evolved into professional thievery. The police had done their share of pounding on him. Physical batterings were a way of life for Mike Mulligan. He was already mentally prepared when Schreiner and Baker dragged him inside the tree line.

The first punch was to the back of his head.

Mulligan figured Schreiner must have done that. He was big and strong enough to knock a man down with one blow. The next was a kick to the ribs. That was Baker's style. He tried to cover up, but the beating grew more intense, until he was unable to protect himself properly.

Mack Baker grabbed him and dragged him to his feet. When Mulligan covered up his face, Baker punched him hard in the stomach. The thief doubled over in pain and got another rabbit punch from Schreiner. He went down again.

"Get up!" Baker snarled, kicking him until Mulligan struggled back to an erect position. Baker unleashed a series of hard punches that dumped the man onto the seat of his pants in the grass. Mulligan was in pain, but there was still some defiance in him.

"Ah!" he exclaimed, looking up at his tormentors. "The two o' you bastards together can't hit as hard as one Irish copper."

That earned him a more intense thrashing, until he felt his consciousness start to slip away. Finally it stopped.

Schreiner and Baker grabbed Mulligan's arms and dragged him from the trees and over the open field back to Robertson's tent, depositing him on the ground.

Robertson looked over the table that served as his desk. He noted the barely conscious, badly beaten soldier in front of him. Robertson grinned. "Now that," he an-

38

nounced, "is a thief!"

"Thank you, Sergeant," Schreiner said. "Now back to our squad we go."

Leaving Mulligan in the less-than-tender care of First Sergeant Robertson, the two returned to the squad fire and were met with a barrage of questions from the others. Baker, as the fluent native speaker of English, told how Robertson had failed to recognize Mulligan as a thief because he hadn't been beaten up. Everyone but Harold Devlin thought it funny.

"Barbaric," he said. "We're supposed to be living under conditions governed by military regulations set by the law-makers of a civilized land. Yet we beat up thieves and tie up drunkards."

"I ain't mad about being bucked-and-gagged," Baker said. "I got drunk and was caught at it."

Devlin sighed. "Never mind."

"And Mulligan has been stealing from us for quite a while," Tommy Saxon said. "A lot of money has turned up missing. It was just a matter of time before we caught him."

"Yeah," George Hammer added. "A feller that steals from his friends ought to get beat up."

"Right," Tim O'Brien agreed. "And beat up bad!"

"I said to never mind," Devlin said.

"You'll have to learn a hell of a lot more before you're a real soldier," O'Malley, the veteran, told him.

"I'll never be a real soldier," Devlin said with a hint of superiority in his voice.

"That's for damned sure," Baker said.

Further conversation was interrupted by the company bugler sounding Assembly. The different bugles within the command had subtle differences. Over a period of time, each company was able to recognize their own trumpeter.

"The rifles grab them," Schreiner commanded. "Fall in!"

The squad quickly assembled and was marched up in front of First Sergeant Robertson's tent. There they fell in with the other squad of the first section.

The haste with which Robertson took over the formation

was ample proof that something unusual was up. His announcement confirmed the suspicions.

"We've been ordered to a four-day foot patrol," the first sergeant announced. "General Leighton wants to see if we can locate any camps of Sioux war parties between here and where the Crazy Woman River joins the Powder."

The eager young recruits like Tommy Saxon felt a surge of excitement. The older soldiers groaned inaudibly.

"We'll strike the dog tents and go in light marching gear of haversacks and shoulder rolls," Robertson continued. "Store all other equipment in the quartermaster wagon." He turned toward his tent and barked, "Mulligan! Get out here!"

Visibly bruised and battered, the thief appeared. He walked up to the noncommissioned officer and halted.

"Private Mulligan has been put under field arrest by order of the comp'ny commander," Robertson announced. "For you rookies, that means he'll stay with his squad during the day and report to me each evening. He'll also draw a spade outta the comp'ny supplies and carry it with him on the march."

The men grinned openly at Mulligan, who seemed unconcerned about the whole affair.

Robertson continued, "We'll fall back in at eight o'clock. That gives you a half hour to strike tents and take care of your equipment. Section leaders take charge and dismiss your men."

Within moments, second squad was marching back to ready themselves for the job ahead. Tommy Saxon, excited and eager, could hardly wait for the adventure to start.

Chapter Four
Private Tommy Saxon

An Ohio farm is not a very interesting place, especially to an eighteen-year-old boy like energetic Tommy Saxon, who had grown up on tales of derring-do and glory experienced by his uncles in the Civil War. The drudgery of daily, never-changing chores was amplified when Tommy compared his life with what he imagined a soldier experienced.

The boy's mother, the sister of the two veterans, used to complain about the tales they told the youngster. "You're going to have the boy thinking that being a soldier is the best thing in the world."

"In a way it is," one of them retorted. As with all veterans, his memories of service had begun to match the stories he spun in a combination of bragging and exaggeration.

The two uncles had served in the 92nd Ohio Volunteer Infantry Regiment as part of Sherman's March-to-the-Sea. They had seen some action, but actually spent most of the war away from their unit on detached service with the provost guard. They did sentry duty at road junctions, bridges, and other military facilities. The pair, in spite of protests from Tommy's mother, continued to talk incessantly about their war experiences. The adventure and bravado increased with each telling. Tommy loved hearing the war stories more than anything else.

He even badgered his uncles for them, and as he grew older, his concept of army service was largely shaped by their tales.

In the spring of 1880, with the planting almost due to start, Tommy made a momentous decision. The hard work ahead seemed disheartening to him, and he couldn't face up to the yearly routine one more time. So he decided to run away to enlist in the army, and go west for some real adventure. If there weren't any more Johnny Rebs around to whip, he'd do it to the Indians.

With plenty of manpower on the Saxon farm, he wasn't an essential member of the work force. Though he was handy to have around, as the youngest male in the family the boy was given menial jobs anyway. So, shortly after everyone in the large farmhouse retired on a late April evening, the boy slipped out his bedroom window with some bread, cheese, and apples stuffed into a cloth flour sack. He sneaked across the farmyard and struck out over the fields until he reached the county road. Then, walking rapidly, he headed for the nearest big city—Akron—where he knew an army recruiting office was located.

Tommy had left a note stating his intentions, and he was afraid that his father, uncles, and brothers would soon be bearing down on him. He walked all that night and through the next day until late evening, when he was finally so exhausted he had to rest. He left the road and concealed himself in a grove of trees. After a few hours of sleep, he went back to the road, keeping a lookout behind him in case his family was closing in. But no one had come after him, and on the third day of his journey he crossed the city limits of Akron. Wasting no time, he went directly to the U.S. Post Office and found the army recruiter's office.

A large, friendly sergeant manned the station. A bit paunchy, he sported a large moustache and an extremely friendly smile. When Tommy walked in, he looked up with beaming eyes and a hearty greeting.

"Well, a good morning to you, young fellow. What might I do for you?" he asked, rubbing his hands together in anticipation of a warm body to be clothed in army blue.

Tommy felt slightly self-conscious, as if he were about to ask for a great favor. "Well, sir, I reckon I'd be pleased to join the army."

"Now that sounds like a fine idea to me." The sergeant looked him over. "Why, boy, I can tell by looking at you that you'd make a crackerjack soldier. That's what I think."

"Really?" Tommy answered, flattered.

"Sure." He offered his hand. "Sergeant Sanders is my name. And I'm proud to tell you that I'm known throughout the army as the recruit's best friend."

"Is that right?" Tommy asked, feeling better.

"You bet. You can ask any fellow that I've enlisted," Sanders said. "I get my boys in the best regiments. That's something you can depend on. And what's your name, young man?"

"My name is Tommy, er, that is—Thomas Saxon."

"Tell me, Thomas," Sanders said, with a grin that was very close to a leer. "How old are you?"

"Eighteen, sir."

"Mmm," Sanders said thoughtfully. "You'll need your parents' permission, Thomas. Do you have that?"

Tommy's heart fell down to the bottom of his clodhopping shoes. "Well . . . I didn't know—"

"But your pa wouldn't mind if you enlisted, would he?" Sanders asked with a wink.

"I'm not sure," Tommy answered. He could see his scheme for military glory slipping quickly away.

Sanders sensed his disappointment. "Don't get down in the dumps, Thomas," he said, keeping his tone cheerful. "Wouldn't your dear old dad think that army service was a patriotic thing to do?"

Tommy shrugged. "I reckon."

Sanders slipped an official printed form across the desk along with an inkwell and pen. "Sure he would! Why, as for myself, I figure your pa wouldn't mind a bit, boy. So why don't you save him and you both a lot of trouble and fill in the blanks on that paper with the information asked for?"

"I reckon I could do that, sir," Tommy said.

"And sign your pa's name," Sanders added with one eyebrow raised.

"Yes, sir." Tommy settled down and filled out the form. When he'd finished, it read: "I do certify that I am the father of Thomas Saxon; that the said Thomas Saxon is eighteen years of age; and I do hereby freely give my consent to his enlistment as a soldier in the Army of the United States for the period of five years. Given at Akron, Ohio this Seventh Day of April of Eighteen Hundred and Eighty."

Tommy carefully read it over, then signed his father's name.

Sanders took it and carefully read the statement to make sure it was correct. "This will look fine with your packet of papers, Thomas." He got another printed form and scribbled on it. "Now you take this down to the doctor. He's a civilian contract surgeon the army pays to look at recruits. He's six blocks straight down the street there. His shingle is out in front of his office with his name on it. He's Dr. Gomper."

Tommy didn't care much for doctors. They were called only as a last resort or in case of very unpleasant circumstances like fractured bones.

Sanders understood. "It won't hurt a bit, Thomas. He's just going to make sure you're breathing and have all your limbs," he explained with a good-natured wink. "A strong young feller like you don't have no worries with physical examinations. Go on and don't worry."

"Yes, sir," Tommy said. He took the form and hurried

down the street until he found the physician's office. The MD, who was paid a dollar and a half per examination, made quick work of the job.

"You want to join the army, do you, boy?" he asked.

"Yes, sir," Tommy answered.

"What in the hell for?" the doctor asked. "Things can't be that bad in your life."

"Things are fine, sir," Tommy replied, a bit confused by the physician's attitude toward military service.

"Then suit yourself."

After examining Tommy's throat and listening to his heart, he quickly filled out the form and handed it back. "Are you sure you wouldn't rather dig ditches for a living?"

"No, sir, I don't think I'd like that," Tommy answered.

Within a half hour, Tommy had returned to the sly recruiter's office.

"This is fine, Thomas," Sergeant Sanders said. He had a quota for the infantry that needed filling. "I suppose you're in a hurry to get into that fancy uniform, hey?"

"Oh, yes, sir!"

"I think I can arrange something here for you, Thomas," Sergeant Sanders said. He shuffled some papers, creating the impression he was studying them, finally pulling one out. "Mmm! It looks like if you sign up for the infantry, I can have you on the next train to Columbus Barracks. Why, you'd be sleeping in an army bed this very night. What would you think of that?"

"I reckon that would be fine," Tommy said. "But I don't quite understand what the infantry is."

"The best dang soldiers in Uncle Sam's army!" Sanders said. "That's who they are, by God! They look the best and have more fun than any ten cavalrymen or artillerymen.

"Why is that, sir?"

"Because they ain't got any horses or cannons to take

care of in the evenings," Sanders said, stroking his moustache. "Why, them infantrymen are in town dancing with the pretty girls while the poor jaspers in the cavalry and artillery is cleaning up stables and swabbing out cannon barrels."

Tommy was grateful. "Then sign me up for the infantry, Sergeant Sanders!"

Sanders grinned out of the side of his mouth. "You're the kind of fellow I like, Thomas. I already made out the intent-to-enlist papers. You'll sign the final official form after you been swore in." He laid the papers on the table and pointed to a line at the bottom of the document. "Sign here."

Tommy dutifully scrawled his signature as instructed. "Now what do I do?"

"Well, young fellow, I'm going to put you on a train for Columbus Barracks with that packet of papers we just got ready," Sanders said. "When you get there, go into the depot and you'll find a desk where an army corporal is sitting. He's easy to locate; don't worry about that. And he's wearing stripes on his arms, see?" Sanders patted his own chevrons. "Except he's got two instead o' three of 'em. Understand?"

"Yes, sir."

"He'll take you out to the post. Tomorrow you'll be properly sworn in by a commissioned officer and you'll be a bonafied soldier of the United States Army," Sanders said.

Tommy smiled. "When do I get my uniform?"

"Why, I'll wager that by this time tomorrow you'll be parading around in army blue just like me," Sanders said. "Your train won't leave 'til later this afternoon. Are you hungry, young soldier?"

"Yes, sir," Tommy admitted. He'd already consumed all the bread and cheese he'd brought from home.

"Then you're about to get your first meal at government expense," Sanders said. "C'mon, Private Saxon."

46

Tommy liked the sound of that. He followed the sergeant out the door and together they went down the street to a small eatery. Inside, Tommy noticed the smell of hot grease. The owner, behind the counter smoking a cigar, gave Sanders a wave.

"How're you doing, John?"

"Just fine, Phil," Sanders answered. He pulled a slip of paper from his pocket and signed it. "Here's a chit for another new soldier."

"I'll fix him right up," the owner said. His ease at accepting the form showed he'd done it many times before.

Within moments he produced a plate of runny fried eggs and a couple of slices of bacon. A hunk of stale bread lay on top of the mess.

"Thank you kindly," Tommy said, sitting down. He was so hungry he didn't care what condition the food was in. The boy consumed the meal with gusto.

The owner slowly shook his head. "I reckon a feller's got to be pretty damn hungry to go for a soldier."

Sanders laughed. "This boy wants to fight Indians."

"So you're sending him west, are you?" Phil asked. He turned to prepare another meal.

"You bet," Sanders said. "There's regiments out there that are just crying for a fine young fellow like Thomas, here."

The café owner turned back to work and quickly prepared a plate for the sergeant. The eggs were scrambled and plentiful. There were two pieces of bread and potatoes with the bacon.

Tommy finished and glanced at the sergeant.

Sanders looked back. "Want some of my taters?"

"If it ain't any trouble," Tommy said.

Sanders laughed and shoved some of them off his plate and onto the youngster's. "Eat up, soldier."

"Thank you," Tommy said. He noticed that Sanders didn't give over any chits for his own meal.

47

After eating, the two returned to the post office to wait an hour for train time. Sanders got him down to the station a bit ahead of time. He handed the packet of Tommy's papers to him. "Now don't lose these, whatever you do," he cautioned the young man. "It's your intent-to-enlist papers, physical examination, permission from your pa, and a statement on your moral character. I done that myself. I could tell by looking at you that you was just the sort of fellow we're looking for."

"I'll be careful with, 'em, sir," Tommy promised, again feeling flattered.

"Remember. If you don't have these when you get on post, they'll just make you do all this over again."

"I'll hang on to 'em, sir," Tommy said.

"And here's your ticket," Sanders said. "Give it to the conductor when he asks for it."

"Yes, sir."

"You reckon you might have any pals that would want to enlist?" Sanders asked.

"There could be one or two," Tommy answered.

"Well, write to 'em and tell 'em Sergeant John Sanders is the recruit's best friend."

"I sure will," Tommy said.

"And tell 'em to come to the Akron post office," Sanders added. "You'll remember that, won't you?"

"Yes, sir."

When the train arrived, Tommy's excitement grew. He had never ridden one before. The decision to join the army looked better and better.

The sergeant accompanied him out to the platform and offered his hand. "Best of luck to you, Thomas."

"Thank you," Tommy said, getting aboard.

Tommy gingerly walked down the narrow aisle and found a seat, waiting in excited agitation for the trip to begin. When the train pulled out, the noise and rattling unnerved him some, but he braced up by reminding himself that a soldier has to be brave at all times. By the time they reached Columbus two hours later, he had grown quite used to it.

Tommy found the corporal. The man, a short, stocky, surly individual barked, "Gimme your papers!" Then he pointed to a bench at the side of the waiting room. Two other young men were seated there. "Now go over and park your ass with them recruits. There's one more train coming in."

Tommy did as he was told. Nodding greetings to the others, he sat down on the bench. "Did you fellers join up?"

"We sure did," one replied. He offered his hand. "I'm George Hammer."

Tommy smiled. "I'm Tommy Saxon. The sergeant in Akron said I was going in the infantry."

"Me, too," George said. "This here's Charlie O'Malley."

O'Malley, an older-looking fellow, shook hands. "Nice to know you."

"Charlie's been in the army before," George explained. "He's reenlisting."

O'Malley snorted a sardonic laugh. "Yeah. When it comes to starving and soldiering, I figgered soldiering was better. My old first sergeant was right. I couldn't make it on the outside."

"Are you going in the infantry too?" Tommy asked.

"Yeah. But not my old regiment," O'Malley said. "The sergeant major is the meanest son of a bitch in the world. The old bastard would love to see me again."

"What's a regimental sergeant major?" Tommy inquired.

"You know about God, don't you?" O'Malley asked.

"Certainly!" Tommy answered.

O'Malley grinned. "Well, as long as you're in the army, God comes second after the sergeant major."

Tommy was a bit disturbed by the minor blasphemy, but he made up his mind he would avoid any individuals

49

identified as sergeant major.

A train hissed into the station, coming to a noisy halt. A couple of minutes later two more men approached the corporal. He took their papers and brought them over to the three on the bench.

"Awright. Let's go."

They walked through the streets for four blocks, finally turning down a bricked lane that ran along the river. When they reached the barracks gate, the corporal stepped back and motioned them through. The guard at the gate grinned and shook his head ruefully as the new men entered the post proper.

"This way," the corporal said, stepping ahead of them once more.

They were led to a building marked with a sign that identified it as POST HEADQUARTERS After ushering them into a bare outer office, the corporal left. A minute later he returned with a man wearing a well-cut uniform with shoulder straps. He had a friendly, intelligent face. "Good evening, men," he said in a pleasant tone of voice. "My name is Lieutenant Parker. I'm going to administer the oath of enlistment to you, then ask you to sign the final form of enlistment that was sent with you from the recruiting office where you joined up."

The corporal pushed and shoved them into a line. "Raise your right hands and repeat after the lieutenant," he intoned, "using your own name where he uses his."

Tommy proudly repeated the solemn words after the officer as he had been instructed: "I, Thomas Saxon, have voluntarily enlisted as a soldier in the Army of the United States of America for a period of five years, unless sooner discharged by proper authority; and do also agree to accept from the United States such bounty, pay, rations, and clothing as are or may be established by law. And I do solemnly swear that I will bear true faith and allegiance to the United States of America; that I will serve them honestly and faithfully against all their enemies whomsoever; and that I will obey the orders of the President of the United States, and the orders of the officers appointed over me, according to the Rules and Articles of War."

After that brief ceremony they stepped forward one by one to sign the actual enlistment papers. When that task was finished, the corporal ushered them outside. As they walked down the street, other young men, all wearing rather baggy uniforms, watched them from barracks windows. The gawkers shouted out at them.

"Hey, you strawfeet. Get in step!"

"Smarten up there, Johnny Raw!"

"You'll be sorr-ee!"

"Go on back to your mamas!"

The corporal sneered. "Listen to the veterans. They been in the army two whole days now."

Tommy felt justifiably put in his place. After all, they at least had been issued their uniforms. He and his companions were still wearing their civilian clothing.

A sergeant waited for them by a barracks door. The corporal led them up to him and said, "Here they are, Sergeant Duncan." With that, he abruptly left, as if glad to be freed of the recruits.

Duncan was decidedly unfriendly. "Get your blowzey butts inside the barracks and grab a bunk!" he bellowed.

All, except for the veteran Charlie O'Malley, were startled. They rushed inside and went to individual bunks. Dirty sack mattresses filled with straw were stretched across the small beds.

Duncan followed them in. "The first thing I'm telling you is not to try to run away. Your asses belong to the army for the next five years. If any o' you babies change your minds and decide to go on back home, then we'll come and get you. And then, by God, we'll put you up against a goddamned wall and shoot you!" He glared at each as if they were all serious potential deserters. "Now. Any old soldiers here?" When nobody answered, Ser-

51

geant Duncan slowly walked around the barrack room studying their faces. When he reached Charlie O'Malley, he stopped. "If I look up your packets and see that any o' you served before and didn't tell me, I'll have him on kitchen police ever'day that he's here."

O'Malley smiled. "I pulled a hitch in the Fifth Infantry."

"You're an acting corp'ral," Duncan said. "Keep an eye on these baby boys 'til I get back to take you to mess call."

"Yes, Sergeant."

Duncan left them and the men settled down on their bunks. A couple pounded the sacks, making dust fly out of the straw ticking.

"These things are dirty," Tommy Saxon said.

O'Malley lay down on his own mattress. "Relax, boys. You're in a recruit depot. This here is hell on earth. You'll get yelled out, punched, kicked, and fed pure shit. But don't worry, eventually you'll be transferred out to a reg'lar unit."

"You been through this before, right, Charlie?" George Hammer asked.

"Sure," O'Malley answered. "Back in '74. I remember telling myself during them days to cheer up, things could be worse."

"What happened?" Tommy asked.

"I cheered up and, sure enough, things got worse," O'Malley said, repeating the old joke.

Nervous laughter filled the barrack room as the new soldiers settled down to see what would happen next.

An hour later, Sergeant Duncan reappeared. This time he took them outside and bullied them down the street to a large building filled with wooden tables and benches. A simple kitchen was located at one end of the place. After being shoved into line with some uniformed recruits, Tommy and his companions were given tin plates, cups, and a spoon each. They continued on their way until harried kitchen police served them fried mush and coffee. Allowed ten minutes to consume the awful-tasting meal, the new men were soon back outside and returned to their barracks.

Duncan deposited them back in the same room with another warning about running away. This time, however, he added, "You're confined to barracks. Don't go through that door for any reason. Even if the place catches afire, you're to stay in here and die. That way we'll have no trouble gathering up the bodies. Good night, soldier lads."

A bit shaken, Tommy and his new friends passed the evening in the faint light of a single lantern. O'Malley, the old soldier, knew what to do when a post bugler sounded Taps. He turned out the light with a warning. "Don't let the sergeant of the guard catch you outta bed until the morning unless you're making latrine call."

"What's latrine call?" George Hammer asked.

"You went and pissed in that outhouse to the back of the barracks already, haven't you?" O'Malley asked.

"Sure," George replied.

"That's making latrine call," the older soldier said.

"What time are we supposed to get up, Charlie?" Tommy asked him.

O'Malley grinned. "Saxon, old son, knowing when to get up will be the least of your worries for the next five years. There'll always be somebody around to wake you."

The new men settled down on the filthy mattresses without covers and one by one drifted off to sleep. Tommy awoke once in the chilly night. Noting there was nobody awake, he got up and went to the window to look out into the barracks yard. A lone sentry, his rifle across his shoulder, paced slowly across the stone surface, his heavy army shoes making a distinct thud with each step. He disappeared from view as he walked past the limit of light thrown out by a lantern hanging on a nearby door. A few moments later he reappeared, coming back in the opposite direction. It all looked a bit foreboding and melancholy.

Now feeling homesick, Tommy went back to the bunk and lay down. He hugged himself and drew up his legs for warmth.

The night was short. Sergeant Duncan appeared in the doorway, bellowing for them to get up. Still dressed and with no blankets, the men simply stood up. They were taken down to the mess hall for more mush and coffee, then returned to the barracks and told to wait. Once again, Tommy went to the window. It seemed more cheerful then, with the sunshine streaming down on the scene. Groups of new soldiers were at drill as sergeants and corporals yelled and cursed at them. They might have been clumsy and inept, but to Tommy the sight was more stirring than the best Fourth of July parade back in Columbiana County.

An hour later, under Duncan's harsh authority, they were taken to the quartermaster stores building to draw the initial issue of uniforms. Tommy hardly noticed the sarcastic treatment given him by the clerks as his martial clothing was thrown at him. He received a kepi, campaign hat, a light-blue caped overcoat, dark-blue blouse with shiny brass buttons, two wool shirts of the same color, two pair of light-blue trousers, a pair of brogans, socks, two sets of long underwear, and a black leather belt with an oval buckle bearing the letters *US*. The last item they received was a padlock and locker box.

Next, stumbling along with the lockers filled with the uniforms, they returned to the barracks. Now Tommy's impatience was almost unbearable. At Duncan's command, the men slipped into the uniforms. Most were disappointed with the terrible fits.

"Stop your bellyaching!" Duncan yelled. "Trade around 'til you look halfway decent!"

Although the trading made them look a bit better, it

54

was still far from satisfactory. Tommy, wearing a full army uniform for the first time, wished there was a mirror available so he could see himself. The best he could do was look at his reflection in the panes of the barracks windows. This pleasant pastime was interrupted when they were instructed how to properly fold and place the unworn items of clothing in the lockers.

"When you get to your regular unit, you'll hang most o' this stuff up," Duncan told them. "But here in the recruit depot there's too damn many thieves, so you'll lock 'em away safe and sound."

As they performed the task, Tommy whispered to O'Malley. "What do we do next?"

"Get ready to spend your hard-earned money, bucko," the veteran replied with a wink.

"Outside!" Duncan roared when everyone was dressed and ready. When they were outside, he yelled again. "Now get in one bloody line!" It took them a bit of doing. Duncan pointed. "Go that way and stay in line or I'll kick the ass of any wanderer. And keep your goddamned eyes straight ahead. You're gawking like a bunch o' schoolgirls!"

The next trip was to the post sutler. The civilian contract merchant had a store located in the garrison. When they arrived there, Duncan took them inside to purchase cleaning kits.

Tommy was worried. "I ain't got any money," he said, horribly embarrassed.

"Don't worry about it, Johnny Raw," Duncan said. "Whatever you get in there—and I'll tell you what to buy—will be deducted from your first pay and given to the good sutler."

"Thank you very much," Tommy said.

"You're very welcome," Duncan replied in a mild tone. Then his voice exploded, "Get inside, goddamn your eyes! And be quick about it!"

The men purchased shoe polish, razors, soap, soap

cups, combs, hair brushes, shoe brushes, sewing kits, metal polish, and other items already laid out for them.

"I don't need no toothbrush or comb or nothing," George Hammer said. "I brung my own."

Duncan walked up close to him. "You'll buy new ones here—now—today."

"But I don't want to spend the money," George protested.

Duncan grabbed him by the front of his newly issued tunic and shook him so hard that George's kepi fell off. "I said you'll buy 'em here!"

"The prices is too high," George insisted. "We can get 'em cheaper—"

Duncan slapped him hard with an open hand. "Don't you ever, ever, ever argue with a sergeant! Particular yours truly!"

"Yes, sir," George said.

"And don't call me 'sir'! Duncan growled. "My parents was married. Only officers is called 'sir'. You call me 'sergeant,' understood?"

"Yes, Sergeant."

They went from the sutler back to the barracks, where the newly purchased items were deposited in the locker boxes with the uniforms. "Take out your other pair o' trousers," Duncan ordered. "We're going down to the post tailor to see if the poor man can do something with the fit."

It took them the rest of the day to have blouses and trousers cut and resewn to fit better. The man doing this, though a soldier, also charged for his services. He began by making a few suggestions about trading around a bit more for better fit. Then he set to work. He was fast and professional, having had plenty of experience with the cut and style of uniforms. When he'd finished, the recruits had to admit they looked a lot better.

Another meal of mush and coffee ended the day's activities, and they were once again in the barracks for the evening. They all followed O'Malley's example by using their new overcoats as blankets as they lay down on the dirty mattresses. The recruits were able to strip down to underwear and socks and spend a more comfortable night.

The following morning put them under the full, unrelenting weight of Sergeant Duncan's tyranny as he introduced them to the mysteries of the drill. O'Malley, already an expert, acted as an assistant instructor as the men began the lesson by learning to stand properly in the positions of attention and parade rest. Facing movements followed this, and each mistake made was brutally corrected with curses, punches, and kicks.

By the time they progressed to actual marching, Tommy and the others had large bruises on the backs of their calves and thighs where Duncan had kicked them hard. Now really scared, they progressed to learning column and flanking maneuvers.

Drill was interrupted only by work details in the kitchen or cleanup of the garrison. Another break in the activities and bullying came when the same officer who had sworn them in read the Articles of War to the new men. These rules—all one hundred and twenty-eight of them—were the basis for army law and regulations. Crimes and the punishments thereof were clearly listed there so that even the densest soldier understood what was expected of him.

That first day of drill was the beginning of a routine they were to follow. The only difference was that Duncan was able to drill them with less bullying as their proficiency in the movements continued to improve.

After three weeks, they were good enough at drill to be assigned to a regular recruit company. Tommy and his friends began to feel more like soldiers then. The drill continued to grow easier for them, although they still got a few kicks and punches when they forgot recently learned lessons.

They were even allowed a few hours in town. Tommy, thinking he was impressing all the civilians, swaggered around the streets of Columbus under the impression that everyone—particularly the girls—were giving him admiring glances. This attitude was dashed somewhat when some local boys suddenly chanted at him and his friends:

"Soldier, soldier, will you work?"
"No, sir! No, sir! I'll sell my shirt!"

Charlie O'Malley and some of the older men got drunk and visited a brothel. Tommy and George Hammer were too timid to go that far, so they contented themselves with simply walking around the town and taking in the sights. The next day, the two youngsters were fresh and enthusiastic while Charlie suffered from the effects of having been totally intoxicated.

The routine in the barracks now included teasing the new men arriving daily in civilian clothing. They jeered them with pleasure, making sure the newcomers understood the lowly positions they occupied in the military hierarchy.

By the time Tommy and the others became aware of the open secret that Duncan and the other depot noncommissioned officers were getting fees from the sutler and post tailor, they were cynical enough not to be surprised.

Finally, six weeks after they had arrived at Columbus Barracks, orders sent the older recruits out in levees to the active regiments.

Tommy and his group found they were slated for an infantry outfit stationed at Fort Keogh in Montana Territory.

Chapter Five
The First Day

Trumpeter Uziel Melech stood with his bugle in front of the large tent occupied by Captain Riker and Lieutenant Worthington. The two officers, in deep conference with First Sergeant Robertson, bent over a map as they decided on the exact route to be followed during the patrol.

Melech, called Mournful Melech by the other men of the company, was a sad-looking individual. Short, dark, and thin, he had stoop shoulders and did not look particularly martial. One of the more literate men, a private named Harold Devlin, said that Melech reminded him of how Ichabod Crane of Washington Irving's story *Sleepy Hollow* must look. No one knew the taciturn Melech's background except that he was a Jew and his accent showed he was not a native-born American.

His musical ability was so good that the regimental band's principal musician had tried to induce him to transfer into his unit, but Melech refused That added to his reputation as being somewhat weird. What man in his right mind would remain as a bugler with a line company when he could easily go into a much softer life at higher pay in a headquarters unit?

With no friends and showing little inclination to have

any, Trumpeter Uziel Melech was left to himself. Whatever the man's background, everyone—officers included—surmised it must have been filled with grief and trouble.

L Company's camp, formerly made up of neat rows of the dog tents, had completely disappeared. Only the flattened grass and the newly formed paths showed evidence that soldiers had once occupied the area. Now the men, their excess gear in the supply wagon, lounged about the area, ready to don their light marching equipment of blanket roll and haversack when given the word. The early morning sun was pleasantly warm and it was nice to loll about with nothing particular to do. They passed the time dozing or lethargically watching the activities of the cavalrymen tending to their horses.

The officers and first sergeant finally stepped from the tent. Worthington, the company's lieutenant, laughed. "Well, at least we shouldn't get lost, should we?"

"I would say we're safe in regard to knowing our location at all times," Riker agreed.

"Following the trees on the riverbank is not only safer, it makes more sense in a lot of ways," Robertson said.

Mournful Melech came to attention and waited for his instructions.

"Sound Assembly," Robertson ordered. The little trumpeter quickly obeyed.

Sergeants Donahue and McCarey, standing off to one side of the waiting men, barked at their corporals. Those junior noncommissioned officers leaped into action, yelling at their charges and forming them up into an orderly, two-row formation for each section. Only after that had been completed did the sergeants deign to join the troops.

First Sergeant Robertson marched to a spot in front

60

of the company. "Section leaders, report!" he barked.

"First Section all present 'n' accounted for!" Sergeant McCarey reported.

"Second Section all present 'n' accounted for!" Sergeant Donahue yelled.

Robertson performed a faultless, snappy about-face and waited for Captain Riker to appear. When the officer strode up to a spot in front of him, the sergeant saluted. "Sir! L Comp'ny all present 'n' accounted for!"

"Take your post, Sergeant," Captain Charles Riker said.

Robertson saluted again, then marched to the rear of the formation where Lieutenant Worthington stood.

"Right, face!" Riker commanded. "Right shoulder, arms! For'd, march!"

L Company paraded out of their former bivouac area and marched sharply past the tents of the cavalry squadron. They continued on to the horse picket line where the troopers were grooming their mounts. The cavalrymen stopped their work to shout at the foot soldiers in the time-honored tradition of the army.

"Ho! There they go! The walking marvels!"

"The doughboys are on the march!"

"Look at the shoe leather burn!"

But an Irish horse soldier, watching the small parade go by, summed it up best by muttering to himself, "Sure, and it's the poor bluddy infantry."

The column continued on its way out into the open country. Finally, after traveling far enough to be out of sight of the camp, Riker ordered, "Sling arms! Route step, march!"

The men relaxed a bit and slung their rifles over their shoulders, breaking step and settling in for the foot soldier's main job—putting one government-issue shoe after the other as the first mile slowly slipped beneath them.

61

The first stint of marching was for forty-five minutes. At that point, Riker ordered a fifteen-minute halt. The men took advantage of this to make whatever adjustments they wanted to on their equipment. But after being out in the field for a month, most had already become expert at the cross-country movements.

Charlie Riker and Lieutenant Fred Worthington stood together and watched as First Sergeant Robertson went to each of the men to make sure there were no physical problems to deal with. If so, the affected man would have to return to the main camp. In Indian campaigning, a physically disabled soldier would be at a grim disadvantage.

"He's a fine NCO," Worthington said absentmindedly.

"Indeed," Riker agreed. "He's a bit quick on corporal punishment, but I hesitate to interfere with his running of the company."

Worthington shrugged. "It's good for those fellows. The common lot needs to be slapped down hard in order to keep them effective. Leave them alone and they're nothing but a mob."

"You haven't a very high opinion of enlisted men, do you," Fred?" Riker asked.

"Not really," Worthington admitted. "No private has proven himself until he's earned some chevrons. And even some of the noncoms have to be kept up to snuff." He quickly added, "Except those like Sergeant Robertson, of course."

"Of course," Riker said. He didn't like Fred Worthington very much. For his own part, the captain had often wondered what it would be like to serve in the enlisted ranks. His cadet days gave a hint of sorts, but no member of the corps was ever bucked-and-gagged or beaten to a pulp by a noncommissioned officer. "Perhaps the army should require a bit more of recruits," he said thoughtfully.

Worthington laughed. "And only pay them thirteen dollars a month, Charlie? We're lucky to get what we do. And it takes strong sergeants like Robertson to make them toe the line."

"Perhaps," Riker said.

Robertson strode rapidly from the column over to the officers. He saluted. "Sir, the men are in fine fettle. We can keep 'em all."

"Thank you, Sergeant Robertson," Riker said. He checked his pocket watch. "Form 'em up, Sergeant. And put out flankers."

"Yes, sir!" Robertson replied. He turned back toward the men, bellowing loudly, "On your feet and fall in! Sergeant McCarey! One squad for flankers!"

"Yes, Sergeant!" McCarey replied. "Corp'ral Schreiner! Put out flankers!"

"Yes, Sergeant!" Schreiner barked. "Baker, Larson, Mulligan, Sweeney, O'Brien! On the right flank! Saxon, Devlin, O'Malley, Hammer! On the left flank! Move out!"

Riker watched the company quickly form up under the prodding of the sergeants and corporals. He looked at Worthington. "Care to take the point, Fred?"

Worthington smiled and saluted. "My pleasure, sir." He waved at Robertson. "Give me a couple of men for the point, Sergeant!"

"Yes, sir!" Robertson replied. "Sergeant Donahue! Two men for the point!"

"Yes, Sergeant!" Donahue said. He turned. "Corp'ral Marteau! Two men for the point! Report to Lieutenant Worthington!"

"Yes, Sergeant! Carpenter! Asztalos! Report to the lieutenant on the point!"

L Company was formed up with the flankers and point men in their proper positions. All this was accomplished in less than a minute as orders and instruc-

63

tions were properly passed down the chain of command.

When Robertson noted that everyone was in readiness, including Lieutenant Worthington and the two men up ahead, he turned and saluted Riker. "The comp'ny is ready, sir!"

Normally the first sergeant would give the order to move out, but with Worthington out in front it would have been improper for him to issue such an order to an officer. Such protocol was very important to the first sergeant. Therefore it was Riker who bellowed, "Sling arms! Route step, march!"

Tommy Saxon and his friend Harold Devlin walked together on the flank. The two, like the others charged with security on that side of the column, marched twenty yards on the right of the main body. Tommy's enthusiasm practically bubbled over.

"Ain't this something though, Harold?" he asked. Holding his rifle at the high port position, he hefted it as if an attack by Indians was imminent.

Harold Devlin, who at the age of twenty-five was seven years older, glanced back at the youngster and slowly shook his head. "You're really enjoying this, aren't you, Tommy?"

"This is soldiering, Harold!" Tommy exclaimed. "Ain't this why we joined up?"

Harold smiled. "Perhaps."

"It sure beats working the farm, let me tell you," Tommy said. "They're getting ready to plant back on the farm. I'm glad I ain't there."

Harold thought about his old job in the hometown bank. Although he missed it terribly, he would not have gone back to it for anything.

"What do you think we're going to be doing out here, Harold? Do you think we'll finally see some Indians? Maybe we'll have a battle, huh?"

"Listen, Tommy," Harold said. "What we're doing is the same thing that's been going on ever since we marched out of Fort Keogh a month ago. We're going through another miserable, pointless job thought up by some narrow-minded martinet."

Tommy liked Harold, but the older soldier sometimes dampened his spirits. "What's a martinet, Harold?"

"He was a French drillmaster from very long ago, Tommy. He loved senseless marching about and the wearing of uniforms. But never you mind; just enjoy this soldiering," Harold said. "You can forget that farm of yours for at least another four and a half years."

"Sure, Harold," Tommy said He was thoughtful for a few moments. "You know a lot. You're a real smart feller. I reckon you're the smartest soldier in the com-p'ny," Tommy said. "Ever'body says so. You're always reading books. I'll bet you got one in your haversack right now."

"Actually, I have three," Harold replied with an amused smile. "I would like to have more since it appears we're to be out here for quite a while. But I hadn't the room."

"Maybe you should try to be an officer. Would you like that, Harold?"

"Hell, no! I'll put in my five years and get out."

"How come you 'listed, Harold?"

"Hurt pride drove me here. And it's that same pride that's going to make me do my duty and see my hitch all the way through instead of running off like some of the other fellows," Harold said.

"You have lots o' schooling, Harold," Tommy said. "I'll bet you even have a trade. Do you?"

"My education isn't what I would like to have, but I do have experience as a bank teller," Harold said.

"A bank teller!" Tommy exclaimed. "Why in the world—"

"We'd better quiet down and keep a lookout for Indians or Sergeant Robertson is going to come out here and give us a kick," Harold said.

"Sure," Tommy said. He shifted his Springfield rifle again and shook his head. "Imagine that. A bank teller marching along out here in the wilderness."

"Don't remind me," Harold Devlin said. He chuckled, but there was no mirth in it.

The march continued through the rest of the morning. Riker kept them moving for fifty minutes, then called ten-minute rest breaks. By midday the column had traveled twelve miles over the rolling, dipping terrain.

An hour was allotted for the noonday meal, and those men not detailed on picket duty immediately set to building fires and heating water for coffee. By staying close to the river, they had no problem with keeping their canteens filled with cool, fresh water.

The one exception to the activities was Private Michael Mulligan.

As per the first sergeant's instructions, he reported to the senior noncommissioned officer at each break. Most of the time he was required to remain standing in one place and not given permission to remove his haversack or blanket roll. But the midday routine was different.

Robertson, gnawing on a piece of salt pork, gave his instructions. "You're gonna dig a hole six feet long, six feet wide, and six feet deep."

Mulligan's battered features assumed an expression of indignation. "Just when am I supposed to eat?"

"In the mornings and evenings," Robertson said. "Thieves in my outfit don't answer three mess calls a day." Then he added ominously, "And them that complain only make one."

"I ain't got nothing but that little spade to dig holes with," Mulligan said with a complaining tone in his

66

voice. "We throwed the big shovels in the quartermaster wagon back at the bivouac."

"You don't need a big shovel," Robertson said. "And I was worried about you having to tote one anyhow. That's why I picked out a little spade. Ain't I nice? So you can use that."

"I ain't gonna use that!" Mulligan protested. "It'll take a long time to dig any kind o' hole with it."

Robertson stepped forward and delivered a solid punch straight to the soldier's chest. He waited while Mulligan, fear and anger in his gaze, struggled back to his feet. "And before you start digging, I want you to scout around here for rocks. Gather up a load of 'em."

"Can I take off my haversack and blanket roll?" Mulligan asked.

"Hell no, you thieving son of a bitch," Robertson hissed. "Now get to work!"

Mulligan, fearful of a real beating, got quickly to the task. It took him a half hour to gather up a pile of stones that he stacked in front of the first sergeant.

"That's enough," Robertson said. He chose one of the larger rocks. "Put that in your haversack."

Mulligan did as he was told.

"And that one. That one and the other there. Quickly! Quickly!"

Now Mulligan stood with the overloaded pack pulling him down on one side. He knew better than to complain. Numbly, knowing the suffering was really only starting, he waited for his next orders.

"Get out that spade and start digging."

Mulligan shifted through the stone-laden haversack and retrieved the digging implement strapped to it. Sinking to his knees, he began to make the hole, scooping out the dirt with the small tool.

The other troops, sipping coffee and eating, watched in interest the thief's punishment. All were happy to see the unpopular man catching hell from the first sergeant.

Baker, the old soldier, leaned toward O'Malley, the other veteran. "Mulligan will be a wreck in three more days."

O'Malley shook his head. "He'll be doing good if he can crawl by tomorrow night."

In spite of working fast under Robertson's less-than-gentle supervision, when the order was given to fall back in to continue the day's march, Mulligan had managed to work his way down only a couple of feet.

"Don't worry," Robertson said with a wry grin. "You'll get better at it."

The afternoon was a repetition of the morning, with one exciting exception. During the second break, Captain Riker gathered the men around him for a little talk.

"The first thing I'd like to say is that I've been very pleased with your performance during all the time we've been out on this expedition," Riker said in a cheerful tone. "I realize that most of you are new soldiers, and I must compliment you on the fine job you've been doing. No veteran outfit ever performed better."

The recruits' chests puffed out a bit at the white lie. The veterans, knowing that no one had really been under much of a test, took it as just one more condescending remark from an officer, though they truly liked and respected Captain Riker.

"Now we're a long way from civilization and there's a pretty good chance we just might run into a few hostile Sioux," Riker said. "And we sure want to be ready for that, don't we?"

"Yes, sir!" Tommy Saxon shouted. Then his face reddened as the others laughed at him.

"Good attitude, Private Saxon," Riker said with a smile. "So, since we're on active campaign right now, I

68

thought it might be a good idea for each of you to fire a round through your rifles. None of you new men have ever fired the Springfield, and if you must in battle, we want you to have more than some dry-firing experience with the rifles. Any questions?"

George Hammer raised his hand. "Sir, if we shoot at Indians, where are we supposed to aim? At their heads?"

"Aim right at their chests here," Riker said tapping himself on the solar plexus. "A head shot is difficult. But if you happen to shoot low while trying to hit them in the chest, your bullet will strike their bellies. If you go a bit high you'll blow their brains out. In case that happens, we'll send 'em to serve in the cavalry."

The men laughed at the joke, greatly appreciating it.

"Now, a squad at a time, let's line up and face the river," Riker said. "We'll pretend there are Sioux in the trees there."

The first squad, under Corporal Raymond Marteau, marched up on line as skirmishers. Following Riker's orders, they blasted a volley toward the trees. Several spurts of dirt erupted yards short of the target, and some leaves in the top of the trees were clipped by others.

First Sergeant Robertson hung his head and groaned.

"Second Squad!" Riker barked.

Corporal Karl Schreiner brought his men up on line.

"Squad, load!" Riker ordered.

Tommy Saxon, like the others, brought his rifle up from the order arms position and opened the breech. He pulled one of the fat .45 caliber bullets from the loop in his canvas cartridge belt and inserted it into the chamber. Then he locked the breech down.

"Squad, aim!"

He'd done this many times in the dry firing. He lined his sight up on an imaginary Indian, playing as if the

69

warrior was also aiming at him.

"Squad, fire!"

The Springfield exploded and slammed back into his shoulder so hard it took his breath away. The pain brought tears to his eyes.

"Open breeches!"

Now barely able to move his arm because of the sore shoulder, he popped the breech open again. Corporal Schreiner checked them all to make sure no rounds were still in the weapons. Then he marched them away as the Third Squad came onto line.

After the firing, the hike south resumed. It continued until early evening, when a halt was called. The men prepared to go through the complicated tent-pitching routine in which the canvas shelters would be perfectly aligned and dressed down in a strictly defined pattern. But Captain Riker surprised them.

"There will be no more dog tents used until we return to the main column," the captain said. "You'll maintain squad integrity, but you'll make bedrolls and sleep on your tent halves. Spread out a bit and keep in mind that we are in a territory that is effectively controlled by hostile Indians. Sleep with one eye open and remember that those on guard duty are our first line of defense in the event of attack."

The first sergeant immediately took over and the night's camp, informal and untidy in appearance, was organized. It was another of those American eccentricities that baffled Corporal Karl Schreiner, ex-Prussian noncommissioned officer.

Afterward, the fires were lit and they had more roasted salt pork and hardtack in coffee. Even Mulligan was allowed to eat, but when the meal was finished, Schreiner sent him over to report to Robertson.

Tommy Saxon and Harold Devlin were detailed for the first relief of guard. Picking up their rifles, they followed Schreiner out to where they would be posted. Tommy glanced over and saw Mulligan in the twilight, digging away at the ground with his little spade.

Tommy thought it justice. "That will teach him to steal, huh, Harold?"

Harold Devlin looked at the field prisoner laboring at the make-work task. "Barbarians," he said under his breath. "Damned philistines!"

Chapter Six
First Blood

Now that they were separated from the main column under General Leighton's command, the men of L Company saw a different side of Captain Charles Riker's character.

Riker's battle experience, both in the Civil War and the Indian Wars, had made a practical military leader out of him. A battle leader could not have survived the murderous fighting of the war against the Confederacy and the countless bloody clashes in Indian fighting without becoming adaptable and practical. The mindless following of spit-and-polish ritual was not part of the commanding officer's procedures.

The first example the soldiers experienced of this officer's pragmatism was his announcement that no tents were to be pitched. Most commanders in the field, particularly the priggish sort, would have insisted that a proper bivouac be organized with the men's shelter halves buttoned together to form the dog tents. This would include having them set at the proper intervals in squad and section formations.

Instead, the captain personally addressed his small column and gave instructions to spread the tents out on the prairie grass and use them as ground sheets. The soldiers were to sleep in blankets on top of them. Riker followed this course of action for two reasons.

First, it made the camp less visible and harder to locate during the hours of twilight, darkness, and dawn. He'd known instances in the past when marauding Indians easily slipped through even the most alert sentries and found no difficulty at all in finding the places where soldiers slept. The thud of a tomahawk or the slice of a knife had taken many a slumbering trooper's life in such instances.

The second reason was that in responding to trouble the troops could roll out of blankets in the open a lot more quickly than if they had to struggle through the small opening of dog tents to meet an attack. They also had a full view of the situation by simply raising their heads and looking around. That saved the time of having to assemble the individual squads and send them off in the right direction.

Another martial custom that Riker ignored was the use of bugle calls. Trumpeter Melech, instead of blowing notes through his instrument, was sent scurrying from place to place to deliver verbal messages. Bugle calls worked well with great masses of troops, but to a small, isolated unit on its own in hostile territory, they did nothing but let the Sioux know that soldiers were close at hand.

Thus, at dawn on the second day of the patrol, the sergeants and corporals shook the men awake rather than yelling at them through the openings of dog tents. The soldiers responded quickly, knowing that First Sergeant Robertson would soon be on the scene looking for lazy bodies that would be exposed for an easy kicking to full wakefulness.

Breakfast fires sprang up and the inevitable water for coffee began to boil. Even Mike Mulligan was left in peace as he prepared and ate his breakfast. The only harassment he received from Robertson came as they formed up to begin the day's march. The first sergeant

73

made sure the thief still had the heavy rocks in his haversack, with the spade strapped into place. At that point, even the small extra weight of the tool added perceptibly to the thief's burden.

Riker, waiting until the flankers and point detail were set, started the day rolling with his now familiar command of "Sling arms! Route step, march!"

It was the third squad's turn for flanker duty that day. Tommy Saxon and his bunkies Harold Devlin and George Hammer stayed in the main column. Except for the physical fatigue, it was rather pleasant. They were able to walk along, heads down if they wished, lost in their own private thoughts.

George Hammer concentrated on what he would buy from the sutler's store when they returned to Fort Keogh. He'd developed a taste for canned sardines and soda crackers. The combination made a dandy snack during an evening in the barracks.

Harold Devlin, on the other hand, mentally glossed over the chapter of the book he was now reading. Written by Frank Stockton and published the previous year, it was called *Rudder Grange* and was about the adventures of a family who lived on a boat. When Harold finished that one he still had Thomas Hardy's *The Return of The Native* to read. He'd read the brand new *Ben Hur* by Lew Wallace during the first part of the expedition. It now nestled in the bottom of his haversack.

While his friends daydreamed, Tommy Saxon enjoyed his own reveries. He thought about his return from the army to Columbiana County and what a hero he was going to be to everybody. Tommy figured he'd have some pretty good Indian-fighting stories to match those of his uncles by the time his five-year hitch was up. Then, of course, there was Rose Becker. He'd harbored a secret crush on her for as long as he could remember. Tommy loved to picture her admiring reaction at seeing

74

him in uniform. He always imagined the scene with him in his full-dress outfit complete with helmet, ignoring the fact that discharged soldiers did not take the fancy clothing with them when they left the service.

Mike Mulligan walked ahead of them in the column. He was beginning to stagger a bit as the weight of the stones in his haversack pulled down cruelly on his shoulder. No matter how many times he shifted the weight, it always ended up giving him a severe muscle ache on the right side of his neck. The handle of the spade slapped against the side of his leg with every step. He hadn't noticed it before, but now the sensation was beginning to be painful. Getting the hell beat out of you was bad enough, but at least it was over in a relatively short time. Enduring long hours of torment was something else. He glanced back at Tommy, Harold, and George, wanting some sympathy, if nothing else.

"It's hurting me, boys."

They looked at him but said nothing.

"I done wrong and I paid for it, din't I? I got whipped by two other fellahs." He wheezed. "I'm telling you, boys, I'm dying. This extra weight is pulling me down."

Mack Baker overheard from the rear of the squad. He hurried forward. "Don't listen to the son of a bitch," he told the recruits. "There ain't nothing lower'n a barracks-room thief that'd steal from other poor soldiers that ain't got no more than he has."

Charlie O'Malley, up ahead, glanced back. "Maybe somebody oughta whip your ass again, Mulligan."

"You're lucky you got caught in the army," Baker said. "This here treatment is gonna save you from prison. If you'd stole a watch on the outside, the judge would put you in jail for two or three years." He spat at Mulligan's feet. "The army's too good for you, you bastard! We oughta leave your ass out here for the Sioux to

75

chop up or burn up."

"Yeah," O'Malley agreed. "You ain't a real Irishman, are you, Mulligan?"

Mulligan gritted his teeth through the pain and didn't answer.

O'Malley continued. "Maybe us Irishmen ought to put you through a special session to set you right. That'd teach you not to shame the race. You prob'ly got English blood in you, anyhow."

Suddenly Mulligan staggered to the side and fell down. He sat up, moaning. "I can't go no further, boys."

Baker and O'Malley ran over to him and jerked him to his feet, giving him a shove. Mulligan stumbled forward and started to fall again, but Sergeant Robertson, who had been watching from the side of the column, rushed over and grabbed him.

"Keep going, Mulligan," Robertson hissed. "Or, so help me God, I'll leave you here for the damn Indians."

"You wouldn't do that!" Mulligan cried. "For the love of God, Sergeant Robertson, leave me take these damn rocks outta me haversack. Please!"

Tommy, watching, swallowed hard. He felt sorry for the other youngster, thief or not. George Hammer looked the other way. Harold Devlin started to say something, but changed his mind. Any protest he made might cause his own haversack to be filled with rocks.

Robertson gave a convincing demonstration of his own attitude toward thieves in his company by delivering a hard kick to the soldier's buttocks. "Move! Goddamn your eyes, Mulligan! Move! Or the Sioux are gonna find you here and roast you alive over a fire!"

Mulligan, frightened he would indeed be abandoned to a hideous fate, controlled his desire to weep. Although his legs were wobbly, the fear gave him the strength he needed to keep moving.

Robertson went back to his place next to Captain Riker. Riker, who had watched the episode, was worried. "What's Mulligan's condition, Sergeant Robertson?"

"He's about done for, sir," Robertson admitted.

"I want those rocks taken out of his haversack after we break for the midday meal," Riker said sternly.

"Yes, sir," Robertson said. Then he asked, "Do I have to let him eat?"

"Give him a half hour of digging, then allow the man to take some sustenance," Riker said. "And let me impress on you that I'll expect Private Mulligan to be an effective soldier in case of attack."

Robertson knew what the captain meant. "Yes, sir."

"And I want him to have three meals a day every day from now on," Riker added.

"Yes, sir."

"You can give him extra duties in the evening until dark," Riker said, relenting a bit.

"Yes, sir."

The little column struggled on through a large patch of thick buffalo grass, keeping close to the banks of the Powder River. Riker maintained a distance from the trees along the bank, in order to keep the column far enough away to prevent a devastating ambush from hitting them out of the woods. The thick foliage there offered excellent concealment to any hiding Indians. On the other hand, he wanted the narrow stretch of trees to be close enough to be easily accessible in case they were attacked from the open country.

The flankers, though new soldiers, were well aware of the danger they faced. Their squad leader, Corporal Bakker, had to yell at them only a couple of times to keep them on the alert. On the point, Lieutenant Worthington trudged on, hoping like hell he was leading the company into some sort of action. He had the flap of his holster undone in case the excitement he hoped

77

for actually occurred. Mumbling to himself in impatience, the officer trudged on, his eyes darting back and forth between the river and the open country.

Riker pulled his watch from his blouse pocket and checked the time. "Sergeant Robertson, we'll stop for mess call." He turned toward the column and yelled, "Comp'ny, atten-hut!"

The men went from route step to a regular march, falling into step as they straightened up.

"Comp'ny, halt!" Riker commanded.

The outfit abruptly stopped and formed up properly except for the third squad who, as flankers, stayed out on picket duty. Robertson marched to the front of the formation, saluting the captain.

"Take charge of the company for mess call," Riker instructed.

"Yes, sir." Robertson saluted. He made an about-face and set the midday routine into action.

The men settled into their little groups, getting the fires going. Mulligan limped up to Robertson. His face was red from exertion and his uniform was sopping wet with perspiration.

Robertson studied the soldier, staring into his sweating, pain-wracked face. "Take them rocks outta your haversack, Mulligan."

Mulligan quickly obeyed, throwing the stones to the ground. When he finished he looked hopefully at the sergeant.

Robertson sneered. "You're a lousy Mick son of a bitch, Mulligan. I'd like to leave you here for the Sioux to play their games with you. But I reckon you've heard that from the others too, ain't you? Too bad the Articles of War keep me from doing that."

Mulligan's experience in punishment was varied and substantial. He knew things were now going to get a bit better, so he grimaced a bit to give the impression he was expecting worse.

"You won't have to dig no more holes during mess call," Robertson said. "The commanding officer said I could make you shovel away for a half hour, but I don't think you're man enough to even keep that up. So you'll eat like the others and dig at night instead. Fix yourself some chow."

"Yes, Sergeant!" Mulligan quickly turned and raced back toward the squad. He felt as if he could fly, with the horrible weight now gone from the haversack. He walked up to the fire, but before he could squat down, Baker pushed him back. Mulligan was angry. "Sergeant Robertson said I could eat."

"We took a vote in the squad, Mulligan," Baker said. "You cook and eat by yourself."

Mulligan shrugged his indifference. He didn't give a damn what they thought of him. He walked away a few paces and settled down to roast his own dried meat. He was just glad to be rid of the rocks and able now to eat three times a day.

The meal break was a short one. Riker, eager to keep things moving, had the men up and marching again within the hour. The sun was hotter now, and they settled down into a mind-numbing routine of hiking slowly but steadily across the wild country.

Tommy Saxon, Harold Devlin, and George Hammer once more sank into their daydreaming as they shuffled along in the column. Mulligan, refreshed and feeling better, kept to himself but was noticeably jauntier. The old soldiers Baker and O'Malley, along with Corporal Schreiner, endured as old soldiers will, simply going through the day if for no other reason than to get it over with.

"Enemy sighted! Left flank!"

All flankers and the men on point closed back into the column. Riker, with Robertson close by, waited for

Corporal Bakker to make a proper report.

"Sioux, sir," the corporal said with a flourishing salute. "A small war party of a dozen."

"At least we outnumber them," Riker said.

Lieutenant Worthington, who had arrived in time to hear the report, was jubilant. "I'll take some men and make fast work of the redskin bastards, sir."

"Stand fast, Mr. Worthington," Riker said coldly.

Worthington was persistent. "Sir, I can—"

"Goddamn it, Mr. Worthington!" Riker snapped. "I gave you an order, if I'm not mistaken."

Worthington wisely shut up and waited for orders.

Riker wasted no time in forming the company into a square. Lieutenant Worthington, the three section sergeants, and Trumpeter Melech formed up as a fifth squad stationed in the middle of the formation.

The Indians came into view, slowing their horses to a walk. From the way they lined up, the veterans knew the Sioux would not simply stand there and watch for very long.

"Company load!" Riker commanded.

The infantrymen chambered a round in their Springfields and waited to see what was going to happen.

Now the Sioux went into action, galloping back and forth a bit to check out the situation for themselves. Several of the younger and brasher of the warriors made feints toward the soldiers, gesturing and yelling at them.

On the second squad's side of the square, Tommy Saxon nervously licked his lips. "Shouldn't we shoot?" he asked of no one in particular.

Schreiner glanced down his line of soldiers. "If shoot any of you do," the Prussian warned, "I'll have him digging holes wit' Mulligan."

Riker noticed the agitated movements among the green soldiers of the company. "Stand steady!" he yelled.

"And wait for orders!"

The Sioux withdrew from sight. For five minutes there was nothing except silence. Now the soldiers fidgeted worse as the quiet slowly continued. But that was abruptly changed when the sound of pounding hooves could be heard and felt in the trembling ground. The Indians burst into view over the rolling horizon, charging straight at the company. Then they pulled off to one side, finally turning and riding back out of sight.

Lieutenant Worthington, angrily clutching his Colt pistol in both hands, muttered to himself, "Come on, you sons of bitches! Come on!"

A full quarter hour went by with nothing happening. Then, as before, the Sioux made a sudden appearance. This time the charge kept coming, headed straight for the second squad. Lieutenant Worthington and the others of the temporary fifth squad moved into position. They each placed themselves in an advantageous firing position beside one of Schreiner's men.

"Squad, aim!" Riker bellowed.

Now the Indians cut loose with some ragged shooting, their bullets popping and buzzing overhead. George Hammer inexplicably walked forward a few steps and lay down.

"Fire!"

The volley roared, the soldiers pushed back by the violent recoil of the weapons. No Indians fell, but the hostiles turned away and went back out of sight.

The Sioux made two more half-hearted rushes, but kept their distance, then disappeared from view again. After a half hour passed, it was obvious they had gone away. "Fall in!" Riker commanded.

The men began to move back into column formation. Tommy yelled out at George, who still lay peacefully in front of the group. "George! What're you doing? C'mon, George. We're forming up."

Robertson, still standing with the second squad, walked over to the young soldier lying in the grass and turned him over. "Sir," he yelled at Riker. "We've had a man killed."

Tommy lost his head and ran out to his friend. He knelt down and looked into his face. George's eyes were open, but his face was a pasty gray color and there was no color in his lips.

Robertson gave Tommy a shove. "Fall back in, soldier! Move it!"

Tommy started to sob. He stood up and broke into tears. "George! George!"

Robertson's voice was uncharacteristically soft. "You'll see plenty of more dead bunkies before your hitch is up, son."

Tommy wiped at his tear-streaked face. "Yes — yes, Sergeant."

"Be a good soldier," Robertson said quietly. "Be a brave soldier."

"Yes, Sergeant."

"There's a good soldier lad," Robertson said, keeping his voice calm. "Go back and report to Corp'ral Schreiner."

Tommy nodded and went to his squad.

An hour later Mulligan and his little spade had scooped out a shallow grave for young George Hammer. The dead soldier's friends in the second squad pulled the blanket roll from the corpse. They undid it and rolled it out, making up a bedroll by combining it with the shelter half of the dog tent.

"His last bivouac," Harold Devlin said, helping to fold George's hands across his chest.

Tommy wasn't crying anymore, but he snuffled a bit as he straightened out George's legs. A single, not too bloody, wound showed in the chest. First Sergeant Robertson explained that most of the damage done by the bullet was out of sight inside the body.

They finally folded the blanket roll over the corpse and carried it to the grave; George was laid to rest. The other members of the company, who had been detailed to pick up three stones each, put the rocks down over the corpse; this would keep wolves from digging him up.

When it was done, Mulligan filled in the remains of the excavation with dirt, tamping it down. Baker watched, remarking, "A hell of a way to go to your Maker, after having a thief stamp on you."

Mulligan ignored the gibe. He finished the work and stepped aside. Captain Riker came forward. With the third squad posted as pickets, he gathered the other men around.

"I have done this many times," Riker said. "And it never gets easier to bid farewell to a brave soldier who has died for his country. We didn't know Private George Hammer very long, yet I believe no faster bond can be created between men than in a war. None can grieve for him more than us, not even his family—for we loved him as a comrade-in-arms and shared the danger and hardship of soldiering with him."

The men kept their hats on per army protocol, because they were all armed.

Riker went on. "Bow your heads and we'll pray." He waited a moment for the men to comply. "Lord, we ask you to accept this American soldier into the Kingdom of Heaven. He was a fine lad, true to his cause and deserving of a better end than he received. We ask you in Jesus' name, amen."

"Amen!"

"All right!" Robertson yelled. "Fall in!"

After the company was formed, Riker moved them out for the rest of the day's march. He watched his green men, visibly shaken by the death of Private Hammer, as they stepped out across the wild country. The captain knew there would be no more need for the noncommissioned officers to constantly harangue the soldiers to stay alert. After the attack, they would be expecting the worst — and probably getting it before the patrol was over.

Riker turned his gaze from the main column to the point where Lieutenant Frederick Worthington led the way. Although only recently promoted from second lieutenant, Worthington was an experienced officer with ten years of service. Yet at times he displayed an alarming tendency to become uncontrollably excited. Riker knew he would have to keep an eye on his second-in-command.

The column reached their objective early that evening. They stood on the banks where the Crazy Woman River flowed into the Powder River, the water veering sharply southward. With no enemy camps sighted, the patrol had been a bust.

The men moved quickly into their bivouac routine. Harold Devlin, scheduled for picket duty with Charlie O'Malley, had quickly consumed his supper. He picked up his rifle from where it was laid across his gear. He noticed Tommy Saxon sitting by the fire, staring into it with a sad expression on his face. Harold walked over and put his hand on the younger soldier's shoulder.

"We'll be starting the return trip to the main column in the morning, Tommy. Then it won't be long until we're back at Fort Keogh," Harold said. "Why don't we plan on going fishing the first chance we get?"

"Sure, Harold. I'd like that," Tommy replied.

"I miss our squadmate too," Harold said.

Tommy sadly nodded his agreement. "I really liked ol' George," he said sadly. "Right off when I met him at the recruit depot in Columbus Barracks we was friends. He was a good feller. Too good to be put in a little

84

grave so far from his home. I hope that don't happen to no more of us."

"Me, too," Harold said.

He left his friend and walked out to join O'Malley. The long summer evening eased toward a close as the sun reluctantly began to give up its place in the sky. Harold glanced out over the open country, wondering if any more Sioux were nearby.

"Good Lord," he said softly. "What have I gotten myself into?"

Chapter Seven
Private Harold Devlin

For the most part, the economic classes of the town of Drury Falls, Massachusetts were neatly divided into two sections. This distinction had been in effect almost since its establishment as a village back in 1702.

The finest homes of the community could be found on the west side of the Taunton River, which flowed through the center of the town. That section, known as Riverview, contained the domiciles of the better merchant class as well as those of the Grange family, owners of the large Grange Mill whose hundreds of looms were the backbone of Drury Falls's economy.

Across the river, in an area given the unambiguous name of the East Side, lived the workers who manned the cloth-weaving machinery. Underpaid and forced to work long hours in a dangerous environment, most were recent Irish immigrants. The laborers knew only the horrible poverty of their homeland. The mere fact that they could now get enough to eat without starving, and have a dollar left over for whiskey, gave them the impression that America was, indeed, the Promised Land. These people—men, women, and children alike—worked hard, played hard, and drank hard while brawling and blustering their way through their arduous lives. Yet even the toughest man always stopped to tip his derby respectfully when any of the Granges walked by, be it on the street or in the workplace. The mill workers knew when to be deferential. Even the hovels they lived in were owned by the mill.

One family, however, didn't seem to fit either of the town's categories. The Devlins hovered between the two classes, depending on the conduct and fortunes of the father, Norman. He and his wife Elaine had moved to Drury Falls a year after their only son, Harold, was born. Devlin had received a small inheritance when his father died and had invested it in a drygoods store on the East Side. The business, located on a street that ran along the riverbank, was stocked with good merchandise and soon attracted even customers from Riverview. Devlin flourished in a limited way, but was able eventually to purchase a modest but spacious home down the street from his commercial enterprise.

Elaine Devlin was a quiet, intelligent, and refined woman educated in a Catholic girls' academy in Brockton. Like all the students, she was given an education that the good sisters considered proper for girls destined to be fine Christian wives. Elaine could cook, sew, keep house, and play the piano. The latter she did quite well, and she was sought out for weddings and other special occasions. Norman Devlin never allowed his wife to accept payment for the musical service, and his ego would not permit her to bring any money into the home. That, as far as Devlin was concerned, was the job of the man of the house. Also, he considered it beneath their dignity for her to perform for money. It didn't make any difference to Elaine one way or the other. She enjoyed playing, especially for an appreciative audience.

87

Devlin's business continued to make money for several years. He had always been a bit of a tippler, and the habit grew as time went by. He did his drinking at home, but eventually he began to enjoy hitting the bottle a bit at the store during slow times. It relaxed him to withdraw back to the storeroom and imbibe a bit to relieve the pressures of the business.

But that practice continued to grow until drinking was a big part of his day and he was intoxicated most of the time. The customers from Riverview thought it appalling to be waited on by a man reeking of liquor, while the East Siders thought it amusing. Either way, it wasn't good for business.

Finally the store went broke and he was forced to clerk in other town businesses. He lost those jobs one by one for drunkenness, until he sank to the level of working at a low-paying, unskilled job at the mill.

During the periods of brief sobriety that occurred occasionally between bouts of lengthy drunkenness, Devlin was ashamed and angry. But he blamed all his troubles on everyone but himself. The family finally lost their nice house. Bitter and morose, Devlin drifted away from town for months on end, only to return to the various homes that grew poorer and poorer with the passage of time. Elaine was forced to give music lessons for a living. The little money she earned barely kept her and Harold fed and clothed, but the boy never missed school and was always present for class in worn, but clean and mended, clothing.

Harold Devlin was a bright boy; the mother had passed her intellect and sensitivity down to the son. He did well in school, working hard and applying himself to his studies. At the end of his eighth year of study—the last school he was to attend—Harold had won the scholastic prizes in literature, mathematics, and history.

Elaine Devlin beamed with pride at the ceremonies when Harold marched up to the front of the room to accept the grand prize of them all — a plaque with his name engraved on it. The faculty had chosen him as the outstanding student of his entire class.

The event was marred somewhat by the unexpected appearance of Norman Devlin, who staggered into the auditorium in the middle of the presentation. Drunk and loud, he pushed and bumped his way down a row of seats. He was politely but firmly escorted outside after taking a noisy, cursing fall.

The next day, armed with several letters of recommendation from his teachers, fifteen-year-old Harold presented himself at the Drury Falls Bank and formally applied for a position as office boy. The president of the institution, a blustering but efficient manager named Erastus Brucker, accepted the keen young man without hesitation.

Harold went to work with the same drive and determination he exhibited in school. Always arriving on time when Ferguson, the old guard, opened the front door, he would have the fire going and all pens, pencils, forms, and inkwells prepared for tellers and at the customer service desk as well. He was quick-witted and intelligent, his eagerness to please making him much more useful than most youngsters in similar jobs. Harold had worked for three years without missing a single day's work when, at the age of eighteen, he was promoted to teller and given a salary of fifteen dollars a week. Since he was still living at home with his mother, he was able to add quite a bit to the family income. As a result, they were able to leave their home and move closer to the riverbank. In Drury Falls, this was a most visible and meaningful step up in one's standard of living.

Although they were never able to get a home as nice as the one the family had had when they first moved to Drury Falls, the house was comfortable and Elaine furnished it as best she could. During those times, Norman returned home less and less frequently. His times with his wife and son were made unpleasant with his drunken rages and their embarrassment. The father finally announced on a spring morning that he was leaving for good, and wandered off to destinations only he was to know.

Harold grew into a fine-looking young man. Forced to wear glasses, he appeared a bit bookish because of his slight build and gentle way of speaking. But in the banking business, that was a plus for him. Elaine's pride in her son grew with each passing year. Sensitive and attentive, Harold was a good son. He was also progressing well at the bank. Every day his books tallied and he made no mistakes in his accounting or when dealing with customers. At twenty-one, Harold Devlin was promoted to the prestigious position of chief teller. With a salary of twenty dollars a week, he supervised the other tellers and handled any difficulties that arose in the day's business. Things could hardly have been better for Harold and his mother.

But Norman made one more appearance at the family home.

Harold always worked late on Saturdays. It was payday at the mill and the farmers of the area came in to conduct their business on that day. On that particular evening, Harold had gone from cage to cage, checking the proceedings and helping with any problems in the handling of customers and their accounts. From time to time, he was called into Mr. Brucker's office to tend to various points of business that kept popping up. It wasn't until seven o'clock that the last customer was

90

dealt with. That meant Harold didn't get out of the building until after eight. He had to make his inspections and write up the daily balances to be put on Brucker's desk so the bank president could see them first thing Monday morning.

When Harold walked across the bridge into the East Side that evening, he was tired, hungry, and cross. His mood plummeted further when he walked through the door and found his mother sitting on the sofa weeping.

Norman, weaving slightly, stood in the middle of the living room. He glanced over at Harold's entrance, then turned his attention back to his wife. "I got the law on my side, Elaine," he slurred. "So there's no sense in arguing 'bout it."

"What's the matter?" Harold asked.

Elaine was crying so hard she could do no more than shake her head to indicate that Norman was causing a problem.

"Gimme the money," Norman said. He turned, stumbling a bit, and looked at Harold. "I got a bus'ness deal going and I come home to get the finances I need."

"Mother doesn't handle the money," Harold said coldly. "I do."

Norman squinted and stared at his son. "Well! Bless my soul, maybe you do, boy." He grinned and staggered over, throwing an arm around Harold's bony shoulders. "How'd ya like to 'vest some o' 'at money, boy? I got a real good bus'ness arrangement with a fellow up at Haverhill."

"What sort of business?" Harold asked.

Elaine was finally able to speak. "Don't listen to him, Harold! You've worked too hard—"

"Shut up!" Norman bellowed. He looked back at Harold. "A man's got to keep women in their places,

91

huh? Haw! Huh? We got to do that, boy." He reached in his back pocket and pulled out a pint bottle. After tipping it up and finishing it, he tossed it on the sofa. "Speaking of investing, it looks like I gotta put some money into another o' them whiskeys, huh?" He laughed again. "I'm going back into the merchandising business. I'm gonna open a store with a fellow up in Haverhill."

Harold felt cold rage. "I'm not giving you any money."

"Goddamn! You're my son," Norman said. "This here's a business deal—with a fellow up in Haverhill."

"You ran the store here into the ground," Harold said. "I certainly cannot imagine you doing any better in the future."

"Hey! You just hold up there, boy!"

"Get out of here," Harold said.

"What?"

"The family money is mostly mine. Mother has agreed that I have all the say in how it is handled." Harold's anger, like all his emotions, was controlled. "I said get out of here. You're nothing but grief. We don't want you coming around anymore."

"Why, goddamn!" Norman's anger welled up. He drew back his hand and slapped Harold hard across the face. "Don't talk t' me like 'at. I'm your father."

Harold rubbed his face and bent down to pick up the glasses that had fallen off. He stood up and looked at his father, saying nothing.

Norman glared at him; then his gaze softened. The drunkard swung his eyes to his wife, then back to his son. He started to sober up so fast, with realization of what he'd done, that it was almost visible. Then he started to weep. "I'm sorry, Harold. I'm—" He looked at his wife. "I'm sorry, Elaine. God above, what am I doing? I shouldn't have come back here and bothered you. I don't know what made me do it." He went to the door and stopped, turning back to his family. "I don't know why I'm like this. I wish I knew." He shrugged. "But I don't know; I just am. And I'm sorry as hell. I won't be back. I promise." He lurched through the door and clomped across the porch on down to the sidewalk.

They never saw him again.

Harold worked in the bank for nine years. His life revolved around the sixty-hour weeks he put in on his job. His only diversion was renting a buggy on Sundays and taking his mother for a ride after Mass. Elaine appreciated Harold's attention and the way his hard work had improved their lives, but she was a practical woman and knew that she hampered his life. Elaine wanted Harold to find a nice girl and settle down to raise a family. She realized he would be sorely pressed to do so as long as she lived with him. Being an unselfish woman, when she had a chance to leave, she did just that.

Her sister Madelyn, who lived in Brockton, had married quite well; her husband ran a cartage company in the city. A much older man, he had had a stroke and died several weeks after the episode of Norman's final departure. The two sisters had always been close, and when Madelyn asked Elaine to come live with her, she didn't hesitate. Harold argued with his mother, but there was no changing her mind. Even when he kept badgering her to stay while they stood on the depot platform waiting for the train, Elaine would have none of it.

"That's enough, Harold," she said firmly. "I'm going to live with Aunt Madelyn and that's the end of it."

He finally relented. "All right, Mother. But I'll send

93

you money—"

"You'll do nothing of the kind!" Elaine snapped. "Madelyn has promised I would have no need for it. Besides, since you began to support us, I've managed to save up a bit from the music lessons and sewing work, so I should have enough pin money to last me my life."

"Yes, Mother."

"I want you to start seeing young people your own age, Harold," Elaine said. "You're twenty-four years old and have a fine, steady job. You should be thinking of marriage."

"Mother!"

When the train arrived, Elaine got aboard, but not before eliciting one more time a promise from Harold to start branching his life out from his work at the bank. And once more, Harold promised.

Even portly Erastus Brucker, president of the bank, thought Harold was evolving into a stuffy old man before his time. And he did more than talk about it. One Friday afternoon the blustery but kindly banker called his chief teller into his office for a one-sided conversation.

"Now see here, Harold. You're getting to be a bit of a wet blanket. We can't have that, can we? What would this bank's reputation be if everyone in Drury Falls thought its chief teller was a gloomy Gus? That wouldn't do. No, sir! That wouldn't do at all."

Harold, knowing the old man was leading up to something, simply nodded and waited to hear what was going to be said.

"I want you to get out more, Harold. You represent this institution and people have got to know you. Now, there is a soiree over at the Reardons' home this Saturday. It is being hosted by the daughter, who is about your age, I believe. George Reardon is a great friend of mine and I've arranged to have you invited. I want you to go and have a good time. And keep in mind that those young people are future customers with whom you will be dealing someday."

"Yes, sir," Harold said.

"George married one of the Grange sisters," Brucker explained. "So you'll be meeting the crème de la cremè of Drury Falls society, Harold." Then he added with a wink, "So behave yourself. I've been told that several of the young ladies who come in here think you're a handsome fellow! Don't break any hearts." He winked. "That wouldn't be good for business, either."

Harold, his face reddening, feared what he might face in an unaccustomed social situation, but he accepted his employer's instructions as readily as he would have orders dealing with work.

Harold's fears about feeling awkward and alone were dispelled when he arrived at the party that following Saturday night. Everyone there was his age and, although many of them had attended private schools while he was receiving a public education, he knew most of them through dealings with their families at the bank. The greetings he received were reserved in some quarters, but several of the young people were quite friendly.

Particularly Nancy Reardon.

The young lady, a very pretty honey-blonde with bright blue eyes and a petite figure, was a vivacious and attentive hostess. When she noticed that Harold Devlin had not joined in the dancing, she walked up to him and asked why, in a manner of frank curiosity.

Harold smiled shyly. "I'm afraid, Miss Reardon, that I do not know how to dance."

"Then I shall teach you, Mr. Devlin," Nancy said.

"In front of everybody?" he asked with dread.

"And why not? If they don't like it, then pooh on them!" She took him by the arm before he could offer any further protests, and led him out while a waltz was playing. He stumbled a bit at first, but quickly picked up the rhythm. With Nancy guiding him along, by the time he finished the dance he was performing rather acceptably.

"Well!" he said. "I didn't know I could do that!"

"You must dance with me more than any of the other girls," Nancy told him. "You owe me that, Mr. Devlin." Again leading him, she took him to several of the other young ladies and explained he had just danced for the first time. This led to the other girls also wanting to teach him. Even after old Brucker's statement, he still didn't realize that he was the sort considered by women to be rather good-looking. Harold thought they were just showing him some extra kindness.

He had a grand time at the party. When it came time to leave, he made his good-byes with a bold invitation to Nancy to accompany him on a buggy ride.

"We can't go alone, silly," she said, smiling. "So you won't mind if my cousin Philomena Grange comes along, will you?"

"Of course not, Miss Reardon," he replied, happy she was accepting.

"Then we shall meet you at the ice cream parlor Sunday afternoon at two o'clock," Nancy promised.

For the first time since he had begun working at the bank, the week seemed to drag by. His job was tedious at times, but Harold's devotion to his duties was more than enough to keep his usual efficiency at a high level.

The Sunday buggy ride with the two girls was filled with good humor and a lot of laughter. That happy occasion ended with another invitation from Harold.

This time he wished to escort Nancy to a party at the home of his employer Erastus Brucker. Harold's heart leaped for joy when Nancy accepted.

That week seemed even slower than the first. Now deeply infatuated with the attractive young woman, Harold swore there were extra days thrown into the schedule as time slowed between Monday and Saturday. Closing out the tellers' books was pure agony, but he managed to finish the task in record time. At six o' clock he was already at home, bathing and getting dressed for the festive occasion.

When Harold arrived at the Reardon residence, he was met at the door by her father. The young man, gingerly cradling a box of chocolates under his arm, smiled broadly at Mr. Reardon. "Good evening, sir!"

"And a good evening to you, Mr. Devlin," Reardon said. He stepped out onto the porch, gently took Harold by the arm, and walked with him to one side of the house. "I say, young man, may I have a word with you?"

"Of course, sir," Harold replied.

"Now listen, Mr. Devlin," Reardon said when they were standing in the shadows. "You're a good sort, you know. You have an excellent reputation down at the bank and, by golly, I respect that. I truly do."

Harold was pleased. "Thank you very much, sir.

"You know your duties and you perform them admirably," Reardon went on. "Why, Brucker brags you up constantly. Did you know that?"

"No, sir, I didn't," Harold said. "But I'm pleased to hear about it."

"Of course," Reardon said. He cleared his throat. "So I know that you are a man of responsibility. And I must ask you to meet another set of obligations."

"I'd be happy to, sir," Harold said, becoming a bit

puzzled by what seemed to be a rather pointless conversation.

"I'm going to ask a big favor of you, Harold," Reardon said, using his first name. "I am going to ask you not to take Nancy to the party tonight."

"Sir?"

"In fact, I am going to ask that you not see her again, Harold," Reardon said.

"I don't understand, Mr. Reardon."

"I just don't think it would be a good idea if you and my daughter became friendlier," Reardon said. "There is a great deal of difference in your social standings. I'm afraid that dissimilarity is so great that it cannot be surmounted. You wouldn't want to create any awkward situations, would you, Harold?" Reardon asked. "Not an intelligent, hardworking fellow like you."

Harold recognized the contempt and insult hidden in the condescending tone of Reardon's voice.

"You understand, do you not?"

"Yes, sir," Harold said softly. "I understand." He realized, in cold, emotional pain, that Reardon hadn't wormed his way into the good graces of the Grange family to have his daughter marry the lowly bank teller son of a drunkard.

Harold turned and walked across the porch and down the steps, still carrying the chocolates.

Monday morning Harold reported to the bank and drew out his entire savings. He put most of it into a bank draft that he sent to his mother in Brockton. Then, with a few dollars in his pocket, he went into Mr. Brucker's office and informed the shocked president that he was resigning his position immediately.

"I say, Harold!" Brucker said. "Is this a joke?"

"No, sir," Harold answered. "Not in the slightest. I

am leaving the bank immediately. I apologize if my departure creates an awkward situation, but I can no longer tolerate my existence in this town."

"Let's have a long talk, Harold!" Brucker begged.

"No, sir. I must leave here as quickly as possible. I need time to gather my thoughts and decide which way I wish my life to go. Good-bye, Mr. Brucker. I thank you for all the kindness and confidence you've shown me.

Leaving the sputtering old man at his desk, Harold walked out of the bank and went down the street, where he immediately enlisted in the army.

He wanted to forget everything — Drury Falls, his father, the bank, and most of all Nancy Reardon.

The army sent Harold to the David's Island, New York, recruit depot. He endured the usual bullying from the drill sergeant and fleecing by the sutler and post tailor. Bitter and quiet, he kept to himself, not offering friendship nor seeking any. After a few weeks he and the others were given orders transferring them to an infantry regiment at Fort Keogh in the Montana Territory.

They traveled by train in a primitive car. The benches were hard and scarred by levees of previous recruits who had used the vehicle. A barrel of tepid water, with but one ladle, stood at one end of the conveyance. The trip wasn't so bad until they reached Cincinnati, Ohio. There recruits sent down from Columbus Barracks joined them. From that point on, the trip was uncomfortable and so crowded that the soldiers had to take turns using the benches. Meals were no more than stale bread and coffee as they rolled slowly westward.

The one bright spot was when Harold met a younger soldier who bubbled with enthusiasm. He was an Ohio farm boy named Tommy Saxon. Harold's bad humor

99

eased up a bit in conversations with the light-hearted and merry youngster who looked on the miserable journey as a fantastic adventure.

The train trip ended at Fort Meade, Dakota Territory. Here the neophyte soldiers disembarked and were met by an officer and two sergeants from Fort Keogh. Herded together after a quick feed of salt pork and hardtack, they hiked overland to the Powder River. At that point the best part of the entire trip took place. They boarded a roomy steamboat and traveled the rest of the way to Fort Keogh aboard the airy vessel.

The arrival at their destination was the herald of busy days ahead. Several of the new men, Harold and Tommy Saxon included, were assigned to Captain Riker's L Company. After being issued rifles and field gear, they went through four weeks of detailed training. Following that, their outfit was put on detached duty and assigned to be part of Brigadier General James Leighton's expeditionary force into the Sioux country.

They then began a march south along the Powder River on a hike that led them down into Wyoming Territory. Now, a bit more than a month later, the young infantrymen, separated from their main command and on foot in a territory under the complete control of hostile Indians, bivouacked where the Crazy Woman River flows into the Powder.

As Harold asked himself when he went on guard duty that evening, "What have I gotten myself into?"

Chapter Eight
The Return

Captain Charles Riker and Lieutenant Fred Worthington stood together sipping their coffee while viewing the early morning scene of the bivouac. A slight mist rose off the river and drifted through the trees. The sky was overcast, giving an impression of grayness to the scene. Even the men's voices and the banging of rifles and equipment seemed muted.

Pickets on the alert had been positioned out on all sides while the other troops boiled their coffee and hardtack. Sergeant Robertson was a distance away, having some word or two with Mulligan the thief. The senior noncommissioned officer emphasized whatever he was saying with sharp jabs of his finger into the soldier's shoulder.

Worthington chuckled deeply in his throat. "I don't think Mulligan is going to be returning on his feet. From the way Sergeant Robertson is riding him, he'll be lucky if he can crawl back into the main camp."

Captain Charles Riker was not amused. Sometimes he thought the lieutenant got some sort of pleasure when he witnessed some enlisted man's discomfort. "I told him to back off a bit. The man won't be worth a damn in a battle if he's exhausted to the point of collapsing."

"He's a thief, Charlie," Worthington reminded him. "You must remember that life in the barracks isn't the same as it was for us at West Point. There is no honor code among the enlisted men. Harsh physical punishment is the only method we have to protect the honest soldier from his unscrupulous mates. We're dealing with simple fellows who need the basest and most primitive discipline to get them to behave in an acceptable manner." He yelled to Trumpeter Melech by the fire. "Bring the pot over here."

The little man immediately obeyed. He quickly refilled the officers' cups and returned to his position.

"I know Mulligan is a thief," Riker said. "And I also know that as an officer I shouldn't interfere in something that concerns the enlisted men."

"That's right," Worthington said. "There's such a thing as the unwritten regulations pertaining to soldiers' business among themselves. That is the sole reason for having noncommissioned officers. If we dealt personally with the enlisted men's lives, we wouldn't need sergeants and corporals."

"But I'm beginning to feel that the efficiency of my company may be at stake," Riker said.

"Over one man?" the lieutenant asked.

"That's right, Fred," Riker said. "One man means one rifle. Have you given any serious thought to the predicament we're in out here?"

"You know me, Charlie," Worthington said. "My motto is 'damn their eyes, shoot 'em down!' "

"A bit of inappropriate bravado," Riker said. "We're on foot, two days away from the main body, and the damned Sioux not only know how many there are of us, they also know exactly where we're located at all

102

times."

"They've been scouting us, all right," Worthington agreed. "That war party we faced up to yesterday has more than likely spread the story of the fight throughout several Sioux villages."

"It didn't take you ten years out here to figure that out, did it?" Riker asked.

Worthington smiled and shook his head. "I suppose it didn't, Charlie. And I'm well aware we're under the gun—literally."

"I was afraid you really didn't appreciate the situation," Riker said seriously. "On the way back, I don't want any flankers out, and no point. We'll keep together to be able to get the most weaponry on target in the least amount of time."

"Good idea, Charlie."

"You lead the column, but only to show the way. I don't want you getting too far in front of the company yourself," Riker said.

"Right," Worthington said. "I presume that the sergeants and myself—with Melech, of course—will still act as a fifth squad."

"Correct, Fred. And I'll expect you to do a good corporal's job," Riker said with a wink. "Now give Robertson the word to get things packed up. The sooner we start, the sooner we get back."

"Or the sooner we die," Worthington said.

Riker again was not amused. "You worry me, Fred."

Worthington laughed. "You're so serious sometimes, Charlie. It's just that I like a damned good fight. And I'm no baby-faced second lieutenant either. I've been under fire plenty of times, so don't bother to preach to me."

"I won't preach, Fred," Riker said coldly. "But I'm not George Armstrong Custer who will charge with

103

blaring bugles into the unknown. So I'll goddamned sure give you precise orders that I expect to be carried out to the letter."

"Yes, sir!"

In the middle of the small camp, Tommy Saxon sat cross-legged on the ground, pensively sipping his coffee. He could see the ostracized Mulligan sitting by his own fire doing the same thing. Harold Devlin, packing his belongings into his haversack, looked at his younger friend. He'd become a bit concerned about Tommy's periods of quiet since George Hammer's death. "A penny for your thoughts, Tommy."

"I was just wondering why God let Mulligan live and made George die," Tommy said.

Harold shrugged. "They say everthing that happens is part of a divine plan."

"That's what I was taught in Sunday school," Tommy said. "But it don't make any sense. George was a nice feller. Ever'body liked him, too. Mulligan steals from folks and he goes right on living. So why would God take George away from us and leave Mulligan?"

"It's confusing, all right," Harold said. "Maybe you should talk to the post chaplain about it when we get back to Fort Keogh."

"I don't like him," Tommy said. "I think he drinks."

"He does," Harold said. "Anyway, are you feeling any better, Tommy?"

"Nope," Tommy responded. "My mind keeps churning up thoughts on George. I never thought when I met him at Columbus Barracks that he'd die in a battle so damn quick."

"I'm certain he didn't think so, either," Harold remarked.

Mack Baker had been listening to the conversation

104

while wrapping his blanket roll. "It's tough to lose a bunky, but in war that's just part o' the game."

"Sure is," Charlie O'Malley agreed. "We was in a fight against Kiowas down on the Washita and there was five fellers in my comp'ny killed in a space of two or three minutes."

"I've heard soldiers who fought in the Civil War talk about thousands dying in a matter of minutes," Harold said. "A fellow I know back in Drury Falls, Massachusetts, once told me that he'd seen fields where you couldn't take more than two steps without walking on a corpse."

"My uncles used to talk about that war a lot," Tommy said. "But they never said much about the killing part of it."

"Then they didn't see much of that," Baker said.

"Maybe not," Tommy said. "I think they was on detached service with the provost guard or something."

"That means they stayed behind the fighting," O'Malley said.

"Yeah," Baker said. "They must've pulled a hell of a lot o' guard duty, though."

"It's better'n dying," O'Malley pointed out.

"I think getting hurt and crippled up is worser than dying," Baker said.

"I've heard o' fellers that's been hit in the face so bad that if they lived they'd look like monsters," O'Malley said.

"Yeah! Me, too!" Baker said. "And I heard that the surgeons let 'em die."

"Or give 'em extry chloroform to let 'em croak easy," O'Malley added.

"For the love of God!" Harold exclaimed. "Can't we change the subject?"

Baker shrugged. "Anyhow, Tommy's uncles was

105

more'n likely just doing sentry duty through the war."

"They sure had some fun, though," Tommy said. "They even seen General U.S. Grant a coupla times."

"Ain't that a hell of a name?" O'Malley remarked with a laugh. "Imagine anyone named United States."

"The U.S. stands for Ulysses Simpson," Harold said.

"The hell it does!" O'Malley snapped. "His name is General United States Grant." He looked for support to Baker. "Wasn't it, Mack?"

"Shit, I don't know," Baker admitted.

"Well, it is," O'Malley insisted. He glared at Harold. "Just 'cause you read books don't mean you know ever'thing, Devlin."

"Forget it," Harold said.

O'Malley pressed his point. "You can learn a hell of a lot more about life by getting out and living and seeing things."

"I'm sorry I brought it up," Harold mumbled.

"And you can learn by hearing stuff too," O'Malley said. "Like General United States Grant's name."

Further argument was impossible when Corporal Schreiner walked up to the fire. "Put it on your gear!" he snapped. "We're moving out."

Now Robertson's bellowing voice sounded over the scene. "Fall in, L Comp'ny!"

Harold laughed as he slung his blanket roll over his shoulder. "Who else is out here?"

"That's the army way of calling a formation, Devlin," O'Malley said angrily. He was beginning to doubt he was right about Grant's name and it upset him.

Devlin, who had been in difficult moments before with other bigger and stronger men not as bright as himself, let it pass. He joined the others as they fell into formation to be marched into the first section's

106

place by Schreiner.

The entire company, with the exception of a couple of lookouts, were drawn up with as much precision as if they were in a formal garrison back east. Robertson faced Captain Riker, saluting and reporting:

"Sir! L Comp'ny all present 'n' accounted for!"

"Take your post, Sergeant," Riker said. He waited until the noncommissioned officer went to the back of the formation. Then he ordered, "Parade, rest! Men, we are two days away from the main column. I need not emphasize the importance of keeping up a continuous, vigorous pace. The war party of Indians who attacked us are but a small part of a much larger force. There is no doubt they will return in larger numbers to seek us out. We will post no flankers nor a formal point. Each and every man will stay within the formation and maintain an intense state of alertness to avoid a surprise attack. Lieutenant Worthington will lead the way. It is a simple matter of following him and keeping a sharp eye out at all times. Do as you're told and we'll get safely back without any trouble." He smiled. "You'll have some fine stories to tell your grandchildren when you're old and gray." He turned serious again. "Company, atten-hut! Sling arms! Left face! For'd, march! Route step, march!"

They moved out as the lieutenant trotted to a position in front of them. The men settled into their march routine, although this time there was very little listlessness. The proximity of hostiles and the probability of an attack swept away any casual drowsiness they might have felt. They constantly looked up and scanned the far horizon on one side while the squads nearest the river peered into the dense vegetation there for any sign of ambush.

The morning passed fretfully for the column. Riker decided that stopping for a noonday meal was a luxury far more dangerous than beneficial, so he kept the men pressing on. No one complained as the march routine was altered to five-minute breathers every two hours. Even then, the sergeants and corporals did not have to remind the company to keep a sharp lookout for marauding Sioux.

The Indians did not arrive until mid-afternoon.

Uncontrolled shouting heralded the Sioux appearance and it took Robertson's infuriated bellowing to bring order back to the column. Riker had more time to react this time than during the previous encounter.

He moved the men toward the protection of the riverbank and formed them up in two lines. The first section knelt in front of the second while Lieutenant Worthington, Trumpeter Mournful Melech, and the sergeants arranged themselves as they saw fit.

The Indians stayed out of range, however, simply galloping back and forth and shouting unintelligible taunts at the soldiers. They brandished their weapons, and several rode forward, trying to egg the white men into shooting at them.

"Nobody fires!" Riker barked. "They want to check out the range of your rifles. We'll save that as a great big surprise for them."

One of the soldiers in the second section nervously brought his Springfield up to his shoulder. Luckily, First Sergeant Robertson stood close by him. "Put that weapon back at high port, you bastard!" Robertson hissed. "Or I'll cram it up your ass sideways."

The young soldier, having no doubt that Robertson would do exactly what he said, swallowed nervously as he lowered the rifle. "Yes, Sergeant!"

Tommy Saxon, Harold Devlin, Mack Baker, and

Charlie O'Malley knelt together in a row. Harold was fascinated at the sight of the Indians in their war regalia.

"Just think of it," he said. "We're among the last white people ever to see those magnificent aborigines as God made them."

Tommy licked his lips. "What're you talking about, Harold?"

"They and their way of life are going to be destroyed," Harold explained. "It happened to the Indians in the East and it's as inevitable out here as it was back there." He shook his head ruefully. "It's a shame."

Mack Baker spat. "You're crazier'n hell, Devlin! I hope to God we don't never see no more of 'em."

"That's exactly what's going to happen to them," Harold said. "And we are all instruments of their destruction."

"Jesus!" Charlie O'Malley exclaimed. "Will you listen to him?"

"You read too damn many books, Devlin," Baker said. "If anybody is going to get destructed around here, it's prob'ly going to be us."

"Yeah," O'Malley said.

Tommy didn't like the way the two were talking to his friend Harold. "There's more of us than there are of them," he pointed out.

"Sure," Baker said. "Maybe here. Maybe now. But them bucks can go back to their village and bring three or four hunnerd warriors whenever they want to."

"Quiet in the ranks!" Sergeant McCarey yelled.

All talking ceased. The Indians continued to mill about and shout. Then suddenly, as if by a signal, they broke away and left the scene.

109

Riker waited fifteen minutes; then he ordered, "Fall in!"

The column moved out again; slogging on through the deep grass the rest of the afternoon and into the evening. Finally, as dusk swept down over the open country, Riker called a halt for the night. He wanted to get a good defensive camp organized before complete darkness settled in.

The men arranged themselves in a square to pass the night. As before, half would sleep while half guarded. This time, however, they didn't spread out their shelter halves. They piled up the haversacks and blanket rolls as rifle rests. The long night would be spent in the wet grass.

Mack Baker, wishing like hell he had a tall bottle of whiskey to nip at, adjusted his rifle on his pack. "Well, boys, there ain't none of us gonna have sweet dreams this night!"

Chapter Nine
Moonlight and Shadow Warriors

First Lieutenant Frederick Worthington walked the square formed by the men of L Company. The short, husky officer stopped here and there to adjust a soldier's position or to make sure he had a good field of fire.

"You have that bush directly in front of you," he said to Tommy Saxon. "That will keep you from being able to shoot at anything farther out. Shift to the right a bit."

"Yes, sir," Tommy said. He was glad for the move. It put him closer to his good friend Harold.

Worthington hurried to the next squad. He had to work fast in the gloomy twilight to be certain that each rifleman was fully prepared for the hours of darkness. When he had completed his inspection, he reported back to Captain Riker.

"Everything is as good as it can be, Charlie," he said. Then he added with a wink, "We can be thankful the Sioux don't have artillery."

"What are you talking about?" Riker asked.

"We're violating military doctrine," Worthington explained. "The men are so close together that one shell

111

could wipe out the entire company." He chuckled.

Riker didn't appreciate the humor. He had experienced the flesh-shredding force of fused cannon rounds during the war against the South. At one point in the Battle of Antietam, a Confederate barrage hit the regiment ahead of his on the line. The men there had evaporated in the detonating hell of the shells' impacts and explosive fury. The soldiers were there one instant and gone the next.

"We've plenty of trouble as it is," Riker said dryly. "Goddamn that Leighton for sending us on such a foolhardy mission."

"The general was concerned about the horses," Worthington said.

"Well, thanks to his kind attitude toward animals, we're on foot, surrounded by a stronger enemy, and still a day's march from our main force. Frankly, I can't figure out what's keeping the Sioux from launching a massive attack and wiping us out in one fell swoop."

"Perhaps they're scattered, Charlie," Worthington suggested. "After all, we didn't spot any camps along the river."

"Could be," Riker allowed. "But it won't be long before they gather together when the news about us is spread through the council fires."

The conversation was interrupted when Sergeant Robertson presented himself with a sharp salute. "The men are well situated for the night, sir. They're formed into a square with a squad on each side."

Riker knew that Robertson was aware Worthington had already made an inspection and report. But in the first sergeant's mind, that was his responsibility, too. The noncommisioned officer damned common sense, as he often did, and followed the book.

112

"Thank you, Sergeant," Riker replied.

"The men are close enough that even in the dark they can deliver some pretty solid volleys if need be. But it'll still be far from a regimental front like we had in the war," Robertson said.

"Indeed it will," Riker agreed.

Worthington, who had entered the service after his graduation from West Point in 1870, had missed the war. He envied the two their experience, saying, "By God, I would have loved to see fighting like that. Corporal Schreiner was in the Franco-Prussian War and he told me of massed infantry fire against rank after rank of charging enemy. It must have been magnificent!"

"It was hell on earth," Riker said.

"That it was, sir," Robertson added.

"Have you passed the word on guard duty and fires?" Riker asked.

"Yes, sir. We'll be on fifty percent alert and no fires allowed," Robertson said. "After the long march today, even a cold meal of hardtack and water will taste good to the men."

"I doubt that" Riker said. "But it's the best they're going to get."

"Any special orders for the noncommissioned officers, sir?" Robertson asked.

"Yes, Sergeant Robertson," Riker answered. "Mr. Worthington and yourselves will continue to act as a fifth squad. In the event any side of our little square needs reinforcing, you shall do the honors." He looked around for Melech. "Trumpeter!"

The little bugler, in his position behind the first squad, stood up and trotted over. He reported in with his usual unmilitary salute. "Trumpeter Melech reporting as ordered, sir," he said in his heavy accent.

"In the case of a pitched battle, we'll use your bu-

113

gling skills," Riker said. "I'll have you simply sound Charge on my command to keep the men's spirits up. There's no sense in noise discipline in a close-packed fight as we'll have."

"Yes, sir."

"How are you holding up under all this, Trumpeter?" Worthington asked.

"I am fine, sir."

Worthington gazed thoughtfully at the smaller man. It was hard to guess his age, but there was gray in his hair. His face seemed worn, but not so much with age as with strife. "Someone told me you turned down a chance to transfer to the regimental band. Is that right?"

"Yes, sir," Melech said.

"Are you really that fond of L Company that you can't stand the thought of leaving?" Worthington inquired.

"I don't care to serve in the regimental band," Melech stated. His English was fairly good, much better than Schreiner's, but he had a heavy accent.

"You play the bugle quite well," Worthington said. "I've heard plenty of trumpeters but you're the best, in my book."

"Thank you, sir."

"So you prefer to be posted as a field musician rather than the more challenging position in the band, hey?"

"Yes, sir," Melech said doggedly.

"I don't understand that, but carry on," the lieutenant said.

Melech went back to his gear and retrieved his instrument, slipping the mouthpiece into place.

Worthington watched him for a few moments. "He's a prime example of the simple fellows who serve in the

114

ranks."

"I'm sure every man has a unique past all his own," Riker said. "And, consequently, his own reasons for enlisting."

In less than ten minutes after Melech's bugle was readied, a deep darkness settled over the scene of the camp. The Wyoming sky was heavy with clouds obscuring the moon most of the time. But from time to time, the aerial vapor drifted enough to allow brilliant light to show through for a few moments at irregular intervals.

It was quiet on the side of the square occupied by the second squad. Tommy Saxon and Harold Devlin were so close to each other they were practically huddled. They stared out into the inky blackness, able to see nothing past the front sights of their Springfield rifles. As with all the weapons in the company, a .45-caliber round was locked and loaded in the chamber for immediate firing in the event of an attack.

"You want to sleep first, Harold?" Tommy asked.

"I'm not tired right now," Harold replied. "Go ahead if you want. I'll take the first relief."

"I can't sleep neither," Tommy said. "Maybe we'll both just stay awake all night."

"If we do, we'll be pretty miserable tomorrow when our strength gives out," Harold said. "Are you sure you don't feel at least a little sleepy?"

"I sure don't," Tommy said. "Why don't you close your eyes and try to nod off."

Harold grinned, shaking his head. "It wouldn't do a bit of good. Knowing there are Indians out there that can pounce on us at any time is not conducive to sound slumber."

"Yeah," Tommy said. He was silent for a while. "I'll be glad when we're back with the main column tomorrow night."

"Me, too," Harold said.

A muffled snort sounded off to their immediate right. It was Mack Baker, two scant yards away. He had been listening to them. "I wouldn't be so damn sure we're gonna make it."

"Why?" Tommy asked.

"For one thing," Baker said, "we're outnumbered about a hunnerd or two hunnerd to one. Did that ever occur to you? We're out here in the middle of Sioux country with nobody else around."

"God!" Harold moaned.

"And not only that," Baker continued. "Them Injuns got horses and we ain't. They can ride circles around us—which they been doing if you ain't noticed—and they can sweep over us any time they want to."

"Then why ain't they?" Tommy angrily demanded to know.

"Who knows?" Baker replied. "I've fought Kiowas, Comanches, and Cheyenne besides the Sioux. They all got one thing in common. None of 'em make a lick o' sense in their decisions. That's why nobody can figger out what they'll do. You just got to wait and see."

"Maybe you're wrong about how many there are and what their intentions are," Harold suggested.

"No, I ain't!" Baker snapped. "And O'Malley knows it, too."

Tommy tried to see O'Malley but it was too dark to see past Baker. "Hey, O'Malley. Do you really think Mack is right?"

"He's asleep," Baker said.

"How can he sleep if there is such a strong possibility of a disastrous attack?" Harold asked.

"Because he's an old soldier and knows how important rest is," Baker said. "And you Johnny Raws better

116

do the same. Tomorrow is gonna be a hell of a day."

There was a rustling in the grass behind them and Corporal Schreiner's angry whisper interrupted them. "It is not allowed talking!" he hissed at them. "On the alert stay and the mouths keep shut!"

Harold nudged Tommy. "Go to sleep."

Tommy nodded and laid his head down on his arms. For almost a half hour his mind was filled with either agitated thoughts of the present situation or a fond remembering of the farm back in Ohio. But eventually he drifted off into a light slumber.

After thinking so much about home, he dreamed about it. The mental images were confusing and non-sensical. He was in the barn pitching hay, but wore an army uniform. First Sergeant Robertson and Sergeant Duncan from Columbus Barracks were both there egging him on to work faster. Finally they inexplicably disappeared, and he lay down on the soft hay to rest and take a nap. But somebody started shaking him. He tried to resist, but they were persistent.

"Tommy!"

Finally he realized it was Harold Devlin. "Huh?"

"It's your relief," Harold said. "Are you awake?"

Tommy rubbed his eyes and yawned. "Yeah."

"Sure?"

"Yeah," Tommy said, becoming fully alert as the realization of his physical surroundings drove away the last vestiges of sleep. "Go ahead and get some rest," Tommy said. "Are you tired now?"

"I sure am," Harold said with a yawn. "A few winks is exactly what I need now."

Tommy reached up to check the position of his rifle and the web cartridge belt. Then he settled down to wait, listen, and stare out into the darkness. Within a few moments, Harold's regular breathing sounded softly

117

beside him. He was glad Harold was there. He found comfort in the older friend's company and quickness of mind. He was also glad that Captain Riker and Sergeant Robertson were close at hand too. Tommy was frightened of them in a way, but he had every confidence in their ability to deal with a bad situation. He just wished that Mack Baker would keep his mouth shut. The old soldier could make him extremely nervous with all his talk of the Indians being able to massacre them.

A depressing wave of homesickness swept over Tommy. At that particular moment, as the penetrating cool of the night made him draw his arms around him, he wished like hell he had never joined the army. He wanted to be back in the house, seated around the big kitchen table with his family, listening to the hearty, humorous talk as they sipped coffee in the light of a kerosene lamp. His room, with its comfortable feather bed, was always close by and waiting for him. Tommy sighed and mentally calculated that he had a grand total of fifty-six months—four years and four months— left to do on his army hitch. At that moment, he swore that if he ever again walked into that farmyard, he would never go out of it except to work the fields or go into town on market day.

Tommy stared out into the inky blackness. The more he stared, the more confused the sight became. It seemed little dots of dim light sprouted up and quickly drifted away. He blinked hard and kept up the vigil.

Then fear rushed through him.

He could easily see an Indian's head, complete with a war bonnet, a few yards to the front. Tommy thought of waking up Harold, but his friend's deep breathing showed it would take too much time. Tommy grabbed his rifle, aimed as best he could, and jerked

118

the trigger. The butt slammed back in his shoulder as it always did when he fired. He quickly pulled another bullet from the web belt and inserted it.

Now firing exploded on all sides of the square. Brilliant flashes of light illuminated the open country for quick instances as the soldiers cut loose. Within moments, those who had been sleeping joined in the battle.

"Cease fire!" Captain Riker's voice sounded over the shooting. "Cease fire! Cease fire!"

Tommy could hear footsteps behind him. Robertson's voice was full of anger. "Who started the shooting over here?"

"Me, Sergeant," Tommy answered. "I seen an Indian out there. He was crawling toward me."

Now Lieutenant Worthington had joined them. "Where was he, soldier?"

"Straight ahead, sir."

"Hold your fire, men," the lieutenant said. "I'm going out there for a look-see." Carrying his pistol, Worthington dropped down on all fours and crawled out into the grass.

The men could hear the officer scurrying about. Captain Riker arrived on that side of the line. "What the hell is going on?"

"Private Saxon seen an Indian, sir," Robertson reported. "The lieutenant went out to take a look around."

Riker was angry and surprised. "He did *what?*"

Robertson shrugged. "That's what he done, sir."

Finally, after fifteen minutes, Worthington returned.

"Anything out there, Mr. Worthington?" Riker asked. He wanted to scream in the lieutenant's face about acting like an idiot, but he controlled his temper because of the proximity of the enlisted men.

119

"No, sir. I didn't find a thing," the lieutenant replied.

Riker nodded. "All right, men. Let's quiet down. Stay on the alert."

After a few moments of excited whispering, the soldiers settled back to the routine they were following. Harold again drifted off to sleep, while Tommy continued his stint on sentry duty. He rubbed his sore shoulder, cursing the Sioux and the inventor of the Springfield rifle, while he scanned the black nothingness out in front of him.

Then the Indian returned.

The feathers on the bonnet danced with movement. Tommy, panicking again, fired. Once more a rapid, uneven staccato of shooting erupted.

"Cease fire! Cease fire!" Riker commanded.

Robertson returned to the second squad. "Saxon! Was that you again?"

"Yes, Sergeant," Tommy replied. "That Indian came back."

"I'll take a look this time," Robertson said. "Where was that Sioux?"

"Straight ahead," Tommy said, pointing.

"Hold your fire, second squad," Robertson said. The first sergeant, walking at a crouch and holding his rifle ready, stalked silently out into the night. He was back in five minutes. "I don't know if you seen an Injun or not, Saxon. But if you did, the son of a bitch is gone now."

"Nothing out there, Sergeant?" Riker asked.

"No, sir," Robertson said.

Riker, who had more faith in the first sergeant's scouting abilities than he did in his lieutenant's, began to doubt that there were Indians close by at all. "You men be damned careful that you can see something before you start shooting again," he warned them.

120

"Did you hear that, Saxon?" Robertson asked.

"I seen an Indian out there, Sergeant. Honest!" Tommy exclaimed.

"I'm sure you did, soldier," Riker said. "But be very sure you do before you shoot again."

"Yes, sir."

By then it was time for the first relief to come back on duty. Harold took Tommy's place and the youngster, now tired and sleepy, was glad for a chance to doze for a couple of hours.

Silence dominated the scene for a long time. Then a distant sound, so far away it drifted away when the breeze kicked up a bit, could barely be heard. Eventually, Tommy, like all the others, was awakened by it.

A dull, rhythmic thud and high-pitched chanting sounded from the east a long way off. Mack Baker and Charlie O'Malley, the veterans, knew what it was.

"Sioux drums," O'Malley said. "They're getting ready for something."

"They're singing their war songs," Baker said.

"And we're the fellers they're getting ready for," O'Malley said. Then he spat and said, "Shit!"

121

Chapter Ten
The Thin Blue Line

"Hannah!"

Trumpeter Uziel Melech spoke his wife's name so loud that he woke himself. He sat up abruptly on his blankets, fully alert although he'd just come out of a deep sleep. He looked around the little camp. The forms of the men, some sleeping and others on guard duty, were barely visible in the pre-dawn darkness.

Melech sighed sadly, then lay down and rolled over on his stomach, putting his face down into the warmth of his crude pallet. He could never decide if dreaming of her was a torture or a delight. He said the name again, this time in a barely audible whisper, the grief evident even in his quiet voice.

"Hannah!"

Her memory flooded into his mind in an unbroken tide of sweet pain.

Most men would not have considered Hannah beautiful. She was small and thin with a funny little face crowned by the full black tresses of her hair. Prone to be a bit sickly, she walked with an awkward, almost boyish, gait, without grace or style. Melech loved her passionately and deeply, not in spite of her physical appearance, but rather because of her spiritual sensitivity and the beauty it caused to shine from those over-large dark eyes.

They had met through a matchmaker who had almost given up getting the girl paired with the right man. But a friend, also in the same business, had a male counterpart of the problem. Her particular client was Uziel Melech.

Thus, what might have been Rabbi Sawinsky's lucky chance at marrying off a homely daughter in a logically and carefully contrived arrangement, turned into a passionate love match. Melech was a professional musician even then. He played second French horn in the Warsaw *Simponia Orkestre*. Although this was a national orchestra, Melech barely made a living. Melech's matchmaker was faced with a multitude of problems about him. The young man wasn't good-looking, either, and his economic condition certainly didn't make him much of a catch. The fact that the rabbi agreed to the marriage was ample evidence of the difficulty he was having in getting a husband for his plain daughter.

Later, Melech and Hannah decided that must have been what eventually drew them so close together in the marriage.

"Opposites don't always attract, do they, my beloved Uziel," Hannah had said on many occasions. "Here we are, two bad catches for anybody else, yet we have found a complete happiness in each other that even other people in love rarely attain."

Melech always replied, "My darling wife, why do you refer to yourself as a bad catch? You are the most beautiful woman in the entire world!"

"And you, my darling husband, are the handsomest man!"

"We are liars, Hannah," he used to say, laughing.

123

"But we are loving liars, Uziel," Hannah would reply.

The country in which they lived, Poland, was under the thumb of czarist Russia in those days. Polish Christians were treated harshly, forbidden to speak their own language in schools or other parts of public life. Under those conditions, a poor little Jewish French horn player didn't stand much of a chance of earning stature in the national symphony. In fact, it was Melech's great talent that allowed him to win a spot in the orchestra at all. And it was to his great credit that he eventually worked his way up to the position of second French horn. But he wanted more from his professional life. Melech's desire was to be able to progress as far as he could with his art. His ultimate goal was to be a conductor, something absolutely out of the question in Russian-dominated Warsaw.

These desires were not all egotistical or the results of a creative man's vainglory. More than anything in the world, Melech wanted Hannah to be proud of him and to live in a grand home, as she deserved.

That was the reason for the decision to emigrate to America.

Hannah didn't want to go. She could not stand the thought of being torn from her parents and friends. "I don't care if you are a famous musician or not, Uziel," she said while begging him to change his mind. "Nor am I concerned with riches and a big house. I will remain in love with you, and ecstatic, right here in Warsaw.

But Melech was determined to follow his plan. Although realizing that it was breaking her heart, he stood firm in the matter. They would leave Poland and go to America. They sold what they had, borrowed what they could, and accepted what was given them as gifts until enough money was gathered for two passages. They sailed out of Gdansk on a gray spring morning and endured a month-long voyage before reaching New York.

But Melech's hoped-for favorable reception in the United States was not to be. Non-English-speaking players of French horns — or other instruments — were not in great demand in the New World. The best orchestras were already well manned and looked for talent only at specific times and places. Becoming a conductor of any musical organization of any import was next to impossible. Instead of practicing his art, Uziel Melech ended up wrestling a handcart around New York's east side. He sold secondhand clothing from the mobile business. And that business definitely was not good. If Melech had been poor in Poland, he was an absolute pauper in America.

Melech and Hannah lived in a tenement with no inside plumbing, or even stoves for heat. The outhouses in the back served the entire building, and the broken panes in the windows stayed that way, as the place was largely neglected by its owner, who sent a burly rent collector around on the first day of every month. No delay in payment was tolerated. It was "fork over or get out." This situation humiliated an artistic man with talent, adding to his frustrations.

Melech's persistence in spending his spare time chasing after music jobs finally bore fruit. He got a job in a band that played in a beer garden. Although it didn't pay well, the salary was going to be enough eventually to get them out of that awful neighborhood.

But the good luck came too late to hold off the bad. It was typhoid that killed poor, fragile Hannah. It swept through the slums in a three-month orgy of killing that took away the old, the weak, the very young, and the unlucky. When Hannah died, Melech felt the

125

weight of unbearable guilt and grief settle over him.

It was his fault they had come to America, and his fault that he hadn't made enough money for a decent place to live, so all logic dictated it was his fault that Hannah was dead.

Uziel Melech didn't have the physical courage to commit suicide. He almost hanged himself twice, but couldn't do it. He finally figured it was a message from the Lord God of Israel that he was surviving in order to suffer. If that was what his punishment was, Melech was more than eager to accept it. He sought out the most miserable existence he could find. After weeks of pondering what he must do, he almost decided on giving up music as the worst thing that could possibly happen to him after Hannah's death. But before returning to the handcart, Melech remembered seeing a poster at an army recruiting center during his days in the streets. It pictured a soldier blowing a bugle. At the time, Melech had thought it the worst thing in the world—even worse than being a peddler of secondhand clothing—to take the great art of music and reduce it to military signals. He thought it so debasing that he found the lithograph repugnant.

Melech went down to the building and enlisted in the army.

Now, stuck in the wilderness with an infantry unit after ten years, Melech was into his third hitch of playing music that was reduced to simple bugle calls telling soldiers when to awaken, eat, sleep, or even when to enter battle.

Robertson's voice broke through his sad reverie: "Melech!"

Melech rolled over and sat up. "Yes, Sergeant?"

"Go wake Sergeant McCarey and Sergeant Donahue," Robertson said. "Tell 'em to get their men up and mov-

126

ing. We'll be leaving immediately without eating."

"Yes, Sergeant!"

The noncommisioned officers wasted no time in getting their sections and squads up on their feet. Since the soldiers had spent the night fully dressed, all they had to do was don their blanket rolls and haversacks.

When Tommy Saxon stood up, he glanced out to where he had seen the Indian trying to sneak up on him. He peered out into the flat terrain. Suddenly his eyes caught sight of a slight mount with a clump of grass growing out of it. It was the same one that Lieutenant Worthington had made him move away from because it blocked his line of sight.

Tommy squatted down and peered at it. There was his Indian. In the dark it had looked like a war bonnet. His face reddened and he decided not to mention it to anybody.

"What for are you looking?" Schreiner asked him. "It is time for to fall in. Move, Saxon!"

"Yes, Corp'ral," Tommy said, going over to join the squad.

In five minutes the entire company was drawn up in two ranks. After the inevitable report by First Sergeant Robertson to Captain Riker, the commander put the men at ease to give them a talk.

"Today is going to be a crucial one, men," Riker said. "I believe every soldier can understand how important it is for us to rejoin the main column. If we push on, we should make it early this afternoon. I won't fool you men. There is a good chance we'll be under fire again today. You all know about the Indians that tried to sneak up to the second squad during the night."

Tommy lowered his head and looked at the ground.

"And we all heard the drums and chanting off in the distance last night," Riker continued. "I am sure the veterans in the company informed you newer men that meant the Sioux have some big plans afoot. There can be no doubt we are included in their war-making scheme. Therefore, we will remain in a tight two-column formation during the day's march. The first section will be on the left and the second on the right. Lieutenant Worthington will take the point and set the pace. We will stick close to the river and use it to guard our backs in case of attack. If there is trouble, stay calm and follow orders without hesitation. I must emphasize that last point. It is of utmost importance that you obey the noncommissioped officers, Lieutenant Worthington, and me in a quick, vigorous manner.

The men, their empty bellies growling, were eager to start the day's activities. Hot meals and rest waited for them when they reached the main bivouac.

"Remember," Riker said. "We whipped the Indians once and we can sure as hell do it again." He paused and gave his command a careful but quick gaze to gauge their mood. He knew the rapid marching was going to take its toll soon. "Comp'ny, atten-hut!" he commanded. "Left face! Sling arms! For'd, march! Route step, march!"

The day warmed and brightened perceptibly as the sun climbed in the broad Wyoming sky. The weather, which had been temperate and comfortable, showed an inclination to become hotter and dryer. The men lowered the brims of their field hats to protect their faces from getting burned. Those who hadn't put bandannas around their necks did so when their bunkies warned them that their necks were reddening. By ten o'clock, the heavy blue army shirts were soaked in perspiration. With the river close by, water discipline wasn't necessary, so the contents of canteens were consumed with gusto.

Although Riker's plan was to keep moving without stopping, he was forced to allow a couple of breaks for the men to refill their water supply. This was done a section at a time, with one of the units always standing guard in case of a surprise attack. There would be no mess call, and the troops consumed hardtack crackers while on the move, even though the brick-hard squares were difficult to bite into without being soaked in coffee. The soldiers broke off bits and laboriously chewed on them as they would have hard sugar candy.

The morning passed uneventfully except for an alarming tendency for the columns to spread out as fatigue set in. Riker was forced to slow the eager Worthington's pace and to put the shorter men at the front so the longer strides of the taller troops wouldn't force them to trot to keep up. The day grew hotter, beating down on the struggling little unit like a blast furnace. Dog-tired and not talking, the infantrymen slogged on, enduring the discomfort in numb patience.

"Enemy to the right!" Robertson's voice exploded.

All eyes snapped in that direction as a half dozen Sioux warriors rode into view. They were soon joined by others. The Indians made no overt moves, only riding slowly along, keeping pace with the walking troops.

"Close it up!" Riker commanded. "The command to halt has not been given. Keep moving!"

Robertson joined him. "It looks like them Sioux are on the way somewhere, sir," he remarked.

"I was getting that impression, too," Riker said. "They're not behaving as if they came out here looking for us in particular."

Robertson shrugged. "It won't make any differ'nce one way or the other. They found us whether they meant to or not."

Riker looked at his men. They were spread out again.

"Mr. Worthington!" he bellowed. "Slow the goddamned pace!"

Robertson knew that the lieutenant had a wild side to him. "Should I take the point, sir?" he asked. Then the sergeant added diplomatically, "I figger you and the lieutenant would want to have a conference.

"Yes, Sergeant Robertson. Thank you," Riker said.

Robertson ran up to the front of the column. Worthington left his post and walked over to where Riker strode along. "Did you want to speak to me, Charlie?" he asked.

"Yes!" Riker whispered furiously. "What the hell's the idea of running these men?"

"What are you talking about?" Worthington asked, surprised. "You told me to take—"

"I told you to set a pace," Riker said: "I didn't tell you to go so fast the column would break up."

"Charlie—"

"Use your goddamned head, Fred," Riker said. "You have a tendency to act without thinking. And I'm getting damned sick and tired of it."

Worthington wisely said nothing else.

Riker went on. "It doesn't appear this bunch was out looking for us. But here we are and there they are."

"Well, they were going somewhere in that war paint," Worthington said. "Now that they're here, we'll just have to wait in order to see what they'll do."

The Indians reversed their direction of travel, going back a bit. Then they turned around and maintained their horses at a walk, keeping pace with the infantry. Riker knew they were warming for an attack.

"Company, halt!" he commanded. "Right, face! Company, load! First rank, kneel!"

Now L Company was formed in two ranks with the first kneeling in front of the second. With their backs close to the trees along the river, they were in a defensive position in which they faced danger from three sides. The nature of the trees along the bank precluded the Sioux from surrounding them.

Suddenly a couple of the warriors kicked their horses' flanks and charged forward, galloping toward the troops.

"Hold steady!" Riker hollered. "Do not *aim* without the order being given! Do not *fire* without the order being given!"

The soldiers stood fast as the Indians who advanced came to a stop. One cupped his hands around his mouth and shouted, "Soldiers, you die!" Then he and his friends turned and went back to join the others.

Robertson, standing in the middle of the rear rank, hollered out, "If they make a run at us, remember to aim for the horses' chests!"

A couple of minutes passed, then suddenly the group of warriors exploded into action. Shouting, they all charged forward in a tight mass.

"Steady," Riker said. "Steady! Steady!" He waited as the warriors closed in. "Company, aim!"

A few more seconds passed. Now the troops could make out the facial characteristics of the Indians and note the individual patterns of war paint.

"Fire!"

The Springfields belched smoke and .45-caliber slugs zipped across the open space and smashed into the line of attacking Indians. Three of the horses went down, tossing their riders to the ground, and two other Indians fell from their mounts. One of the warriors who had lost his horse was able to get to his feet and leap up behind a friend as the attackers drew off out of range.

"There, by God!" Riker shouted, pleasantly surprised

131

that the men were showing more accuracy. "You've let 'em know they're up against the United States Infantry."

The men cheered and quickly reacted to the order to once again load. Feeling confident, they waited for the next charge. In less than a minute, the Sioux tried again. The results were the same. A crashing volley knocked down some more Indians and horses, and they again pulled back out of harm's way.

"That's doing it, men!" Riker yelled.

Worthington, standing next to the captain, leaned close to his ear and spoke softly. "Our ammunition is going to go after a while. We can't keep this up forever."

Riker nodded. Once more he shouted a command. "Fix bayonets!"

The men pulled the edged weapons from their scabbards and attached them to the ends of their rifles.

"Be brave and fight hard," Riker said.

"No one has even shown them how to use those goddamned things," Worthington said.

"They'll have to rely on instinct," Riker said. "But it won't matter much one way or the other."

"I guess not," the lieutenant said. "But I'm going to take a lot of those heathen sons of bitches with me."

For one wild moment, Riker thought of making a break for the cover of the trees. But he realized it would do no good. The Sioux would simply split the company farther apart and kill the men piecemeal. It was better to stand together and deliver deadly, coordinated fusillades for as long as possible.

Now the Sioux were completely out of sight. A quarter of an hour passed with nothing else happening. Worthington, fidgeting, scanned the horizon for some sign of the Indians. "Should I go take a look out there, Charlie?"

The last thing Riker wanted was for Worthington to pull some rash act that might bring certain ruin down on them. "Stand fast, Fred. I want you here with the troops." He looked over at Robertson. "Sergeant Robertson! Take two experienced men and make a scout forward.

"Yes, sir! Baker! Donegan! Front and center, move!"

The three, in a pathetically small skirmish line, advanced out from the main group. They moved slowly, gingerly, anticipating the sudden appearance of the Indians. The trio went a hundred yards before turning and coming back.

"Sir," Robertson said reporting in. "The Indians are gone. They've pulled out."

"That doesn't make sense," Riker said.

"I know, sir," Robertson said. "There was enough of 'em to eventually wear us down." He shrugged. "Maybe they had something more important to do someplace else."

"Just like us," Riker said. "Let's form back up and keep this march on the move. The main column is only two hours away.

"Pardon me for saying so, sir," Robertson, said. "But in this situation, they might just as well be on the moon."

Chapter Eleven
A Grim Discovery

Whatever fatigue the men had been feeling earlier was completely dissipated by the battle. The overwhelming fear and excitement of the fighting, combined with the noise and slamming recoil of the Springfield rifles, invigorated Company L both spiritually and physically. When they formed up to continue their march back to the main column, they were as talkative as excited schoolgirls, although there was no gaiety in their chatter—only a sense of relief that they were still alive.

"We whipped 'em!" was the statement voiced more often by the excited young soldiers.

"Ain't no damn Indian gonna stand up against disciplined infantry," veteran Corporal Jim O'Rourke of the fourth squad said. "But it still makes me wonder why the bastards run off like that."

His good friend Sergeant Tom McCarey was equally confused. "They coulda wore us down after a while. There really wasn't no reason a'tall fer 'em to skidaddle."

Private Daniel Black of the fourth squad thought he had it all figured out. "We whipped em good and proper. That's the plain truth of it, and that's exactly

134

why they run off."

Mack Baker called over from the second squad. "They just stopped fighting, Johnny Raw. Them damned Sioux wasn't whipped by a long shot."

"Yes, they was!" Black yelled back.

"What the hell do you know about it?" Baker sneered in anger over a recruit disagreeing with him.

Others voiced their opinions and an argument ranged up and down the column, with the veterans insisting the Indians were not defeated and the younger men arguing they'd been given a good hiding.

Sergeant Robertson did nothing about the excited talking in the ranks for a while. But after allowing ten minutes of the chattering, he bellowed:

"Shut your yaps! You're at route step and the enemy is still close by!"

The men quickly obeyed, their nervously darting eyes the only sign of their physical agitation. This extra energy generated by the fighting was also reflected in the increase of their rate of march. They pressed on across the rolling countryside in quick, distance-eating strides. Lieutenant Worthington, specifically ordered by Riker to keep a careful, measured pace, was constantly feeling pressure from the column behind him.

Toward the late afternoon they began to recognize landmarks that showed them they were very close to the main column. The thoughts of hot food and rest raised spirits. It made the jobs of the noncommissioned officers a bit more difficult in maintaining discipline, but even they laughed at the absurd joking and bantering while doing some unnecessary chattering of their own.

The general mood in the company continued to improve and the pace stepped up even more, until a cry came from the front of the column:

"Oh, God!"

Large birds could be seen in the short distance, circling and diving toward the ground out of sight behind a large section of woods. The veterans knew the meaning of the ominous sight.

"As skirmishers!" Riker yelled. "Two ranks!"

The men quickly obeyed with drill-like precision. They'd done this particular maneuver countless times while in training back at Fort Keogh, and the short spates of Indian fighting had increased their skill in the movement.

Tommy Saxon, confused, leaned toward Mack Baker. "How come we're doing this?" he asked.

Mack spat. "You see them crows and buzzards, Saxon? That means there's dead folks on the other side o' them woods. And from the numbers o' them feathered bastards, we're gonna find a whole lot o' corpses."

Charlie O'Malley, listening in, said, "And we don't know for sure who they are."

"Could be Indians or could be soldiers," Baker remarked.

"Yeah," O'Malley said. "But we got a pretty good idea, don't we?"

"In the ranks, shut up!" Corporal Schreiner hissed.

The skirmish line grew a bit ragged as they continued forward toward a thick grove of trees. Riker ordered a halt at that point.

"Sergeant Robertson," he called. "Take two men and scout those woods."

Robertson signaled to Mack Baker and Al Franklin. "Let's go, you two."

"Damn!" Baker said under his breath as he left the squad to join the other two.

Keeping their weapons ready, the men watched the trio approach the trees. Moving slowly, the small scouting party reached the copse and moved inside. In only

136

a matter of moments, they reappeared. Sergeant Robertson signaled for the others to join them.

Tommy Saxon and Harold Devlin instinctively drew closer together. Although there seemed to be no danger from Indians, there was something foreboding in the atmosphere. Though the exact reason for the uneasiness was not identifiable, it was still strong. When they reached the trees, a stench assailed their nostrils from the other side of the woods. It grew more intense as they advanced.

When the company stepped out on the other side, there was a noticeable gasp from all the men — veteran, and recruit alike.

A strange sight greeted them. Mounds of pale globs were scattered around the area. These looked as if dozens of thin sticks were sticking out of them. As the company moved closer, the new soldiers could see what the old troops already knew — these were dead men, sprawled naked on the ground.

After another dozen yards, they also realized that what they looked at were not whole bodies, but hunks and pieces of corpses shot full of arrows.

The cadavers had been horribly mutilated. Blood that had gushed from deep gashes slashed in legs and torsos had now dried into brown blotches. Arms and legs were severed in many cases, and a few heads had also been chopped from the bodies and allowed to roll a few feet. The genitalia had also been sliced away and skulls bashed in with the brains spilled out in the grass.

Riker cursed. "Goddamn it to hell! The column!"

"All dead," Worthington said grimly.

A soldier vomited, and this seemed to be an example for several others to follow. Gagging and spitting grew more noticeable, and several younger soldiers wept with their hands pressed close to their faces.

137

One recruit stared in horrified silence at the awful carnage. Then he suddenly cried out and turned around. He started to run away back into the woods. A corporal, catching sight of him, gave chase and grabbed the horrified boy, dragging him back.

Now Tommy realized the full implication of what had happened. "Oh my Lord save us! This is our old camp, Harold!" he gasped, grabbing onto his friend's arm.

Harold, unable to speak, stared with a horrid fascination at the scene. He wanted more than anything to close his eyes, but it was if he had no control over them. Finally, he turned around and faced the other way. He fought the sobs, then gave in as his emotions took over.

"They were all killed!" he gasped.

"It's ever'body that stayed back," Tommy added.

Robertson, walking past the two shocked soldiers, joined the two officers. "We'll need to do something, sir," he said. "The men can't just stand there and look at all this shit."

Worthington, visibly pale, licked his lips with a dry tongue. "Are we going to be able to bury them?"

Riker shook his head. "Under the circumstances—no. We can't stay here that long." He looked at Robertson. "You know what to do, Sergeant. Carry on."

"Yes, sir," Robertson said. He turned around and walked over to the edge of the camp. "L Comp'ny! Fall in!"

The first men came over, relieved that there was something to do. They tried to form up on the near side of the first sergeant.

"Over there!" Robertson barked. He wanted them to look past him at the scene. When both sections were aligned, he asked for a report, to give some sort of normalcy to the situation.

138

"First Section all present 'n' accounted for," Sergeant McCarey said.

Sergeant Donahue echoed with, "Second Section all present 'n' accounted for."

"Stand at ease," Robertson commanded. He glared at the men, seeing the horror and revulsion in their eyes. Someone vomited again. "Well?" the first sergeant bellowed. "What the hell did you think soldiering was about, anyhow?" He paced up and down in front of the company. "This is the regular army in a real war against Indians. Not a fancy-pants rich man's militia out parading around the town square of a Sunday back in some dreamy eastern town!"

Now someone finally fainted, his body thudding to the ground. His squadmates left him alone, envying him his unconsciousness.

"This is real!" Robertson continued. "Men die! When they die because they was massacred by Indians, they get cut up and butchered. If we hadn't been out on that scout, it would have happened to us." He let the last bit of enlightenment sink in for a couple of minutes. "And it could still happen if things go bad for the comp'ny. So you're all gonna have to stay on the alert and obey orders proper and quick."

Mike Mulligan, the thief, had shown no emotional reaction whatsoever. Even now, he looked on the scene with a detached calmness. He'd seen dead men before. Corpses that had been stabbed, shot, and beaten to death were common in the Bowery. Although none had been mutilated, he didn't find the situation that much different. But he didn't like the smell that seemed to grow denser and more obnoxious with the increase in the day's warmth.

Robertson gestured to the dead behind him. "We ain't gonna be able to bury these poor soldiers 'cause there

139

ain't time. But we can honor 'em and respect 'em. We owe 'em that 'cause they were our friends and comrades-in-arms."

Every man—rookie and veteran alike—was glad he wouldn't be required to pick up and put the hunks of humanity into graves.

"So you'll go out there and walk among 'em. If you recognize somebody, give his name to your squad leader," Robertson said. "We'll make up a list for the official report. Their families can be notified that way. You'd expect the same consideration showed you. Comp'ny, atten-hut. Move out! Now!"

Tommy and Harold looked at each other in a silent invitation for company. They walked slowly among the scattered dead, not really looking at any of them.

Mack Baker and Charlie O'Malley, on the other hand, were pointing out various cadavers.

"Ain't that Dempsey?" Baker asked.

"Kinda looks like him," O'Malley mused. "But I ain't sure. Didn't Dempsey's ears stick out?"

"Yeah. Come to think of it, he was a real jug-eared son of a bitch," Baker said.

Devlin glanced at them. His stomach churned with horror and revulsion. "Is that the way you old soldiers honor your dead comrades? Call them jug-eared sons of bitches?"

"Only if they got big ears," Baker said with a grin.

"Hey." Tommy exclaimed. Although he tried to avoid looking directly at any of the corpses, he thought he recognized one. "That's Red. Remember him, Harold? The feller from the cavalry we talked to a couple o' times. We called him Red, didn't we?"

Harold forced himself to look at the naked, pulverized remains. "Yes. But I don't remember his name."

O'Malley looked. "His last name was Scott." He

called out the name to Corporal Schreiner, who dutifully recorded it in the small notebook he carried.

They approached the charred remnants of a quartermaster wagon. When they walked around it, they saw a blackened corpse that had burned with the vehicle.

O'Malley slowly shook his head. "I hope the poor devil was already dead when they throwed him on the fire."

Harold Devlin was shocked. "They wouldn't burn a man alive, would they?" He'd read of such things in books before, but he couldn't accept the horrible reality of it.

"Sure they would," Mack said. "You know why they chop up dead folks, don't you? It's on account o' pure hatred, boys. Them Sioux think you'll spend eternity in the same condition your corpse is in."

"That's why they're so respectful to their dead and put 'em in trees all wrapped in hides, with bows and arrows and other things they'll need in the happy hunting grounds," O'Malley added.

"You mean they want us to be in heaven or hell like—like *that?*" Tommy asked, pointing around.

"God! They must really hate us," Harold said.

"They do, young soldier," Baker said. "They truly do."

"That's why the boys sometimes do terrible things to dead Injuns," Baker said. "On account o' they know it really makes their friends and relatives feel bad to find 'em all cut up into hunks."

When the company reached the other side of the former bivouac, Robertson turned them around for another walk through the area. This second trip went much faster than the first. When that was done, the entire company moved into the cover of the trees while Robertson picked up the lists of names of the identified dead from the sergeants and corporals.

After settling the men down, the first sergeant sought out the officers. All three withdrew for a conference. Riker, though trying to keep a nonchalant expression on his face for the benefit of the men, made no attempt to hide the pessimism in his voice.

"We're really cut off now," the captain said.

Worthington nodded his head. "Now we know why the Sioux didn't spend the time or effort to wipe us out. They had something bigger going here."

Robertson tried to look on what bit of brightness there was in the situation. "They'll be off celebrating a victory this big for a while. It gives us a chance to make some tracks."

But Riker was not optimistic. "There are one hundred and fifty miles of wide-open country between us and Fort Keogh," he pointed out. "We're short of ammunition and rations. Even if we manage twenty miles a day, that's—" Never very good at mathematics, Riker struggled with the equation.

"That'll take a bit more than a week," Worthington said helpfully.

"And we've no maps of the country," Riker said.

"All we got to do is head north, right, sir?" Robertson asked.

"We could wander right past the post," Riker said. "If that happened and we did manage to last that week, we'd eventually get caught on the other side of Keogh." He was thoughtful for a few moments. "We'll have to go northeast until we hit the Tongue River. We can follow that to our destination."

"We sure been following lots o' rivers, lately," Robertson remarked. "But they been good to us."

Riker was silent once more for a minute. Finally he said, "You two realize, of course, that our chances of

142

making it are nil."

Worthington was not bothered by the thought. "If they catch us, we'll take ten apiece with us before we die."

"If you're looking for a glorious death, Fred, you're certainly going to get it," Riker remarked.

Robertson nodded his agreement. "Yes, sir. You'll die, one way or the other."

"Let's call the troops together and get this show on the road—again," Riker said. "It goes without saying that I want to see a display of complete confidence and optimism."

"Of course," Worthington said.

"I'll talk to the NCOs, sir," Robertson said.

"Excellent, Sergeant," Riker said. "Tell them if I catch any sergeant or corporal making discouraging remarks, I'll break him down on the spot."

"Yes, sir."

Riker turned to Worthington as Robertson walked off. "Fred," he said to his second-in-command, "this is the worst situation I've ever been in during the twenty years of my commissioned service."

Worthington knew the captain had something to say to him. "Yes, sir."

"I'm expecting you to be prudent and cool," Riker said. "You've gotten away with things in the past because of blind luck. That won't do out here now. Do you understand?"

"Of course, Charlie," Worthington said.

"Good. Now let's see to the men," Riker said.

Within moments the company was drawn up and Riker stood in front of them. "This has been a terrible setback, men," he said, trying to keep his voice enthusiastic. "But we've still got a damned good chance. Our plan is to cut cross-country to the Tongue River and

143

follow it straight up to Fort Keogh."

The old soldiers listened with a numb realization of the real situation, while the Johnny Raws grasped at the straw of hope the captain cast out to them.

Riker went on. "We can make it if every man does as he is told and doesn't waste ammunition. We cannot afford that." He paused, then suddenly hollered, "Are you with me?"

"Yes, sir!" they answered.

"There're my good soldiers," Riker said. "Comp'ny, atten-hut! Fix bayonets!" He waited until the sharp instruments were locked onto the muzzles of the rifles. "Sling arms! Right, face! For'd march! Route step, march!"

As they moved out, Harold Devlin noted the glint of the sun on the bayonet blades. He was not a stupid man. He knew they had no more ammo once the cartridge belts were empty. That was why the captain had them attach the bayonets before any trouble started. Any future battles with Indians would be a primitive fight to the death. He glanced at Tommy Saxon. The young soldier's face was strained and serious. Harold grinned sardonically.

The fun of soldiering was over.

Chapter Twelve
Riker's Scout

Now moving northwest, L Company realized, less than a half a day's march after leaving the scene of the massacre, that they were not the only men in that wide expanse of wilderness.

"Enemy right!" someone hollered on that side of their formation.

"Enemy front!" Lieutenant Frederick Worthington quickly echoed.

"Company, form a square!" Riker ordered, knowing there was no time to waste. He wished his command was back by the river where it would be possible to use the natural terrain features as part of a defense. Being in the open as they were, the boxlike infantry formation was the only tactic he could follow. "Load!"

A couple of small groups of Indians rode into view, approaching from the horizon, showing no inclination to rush things. When they came in closer, they began to canter almost lazily to and fro. The casual riding about caused the bands to intermix and split up several times. Finally, after several minutes, they calmed down and hovered nearby.

The men in the company could easily see the Sioux

talking to one another. Now and then one would point at them and gesture in some manner, as if giving orders or suggestions to his fellow warriors. Periodic shouts were exchanged between the two bunches of Indians.

"Maintain the square," Riker said. "But keep moving." He didn't like the idea of remaining stationary. As the men renewed their march in the awkward formation, both Riker and Robertson kept anxious eyes on the horizon all around to watch out for any hostile reinforcements.

Fewer than a dozen warriors rode in each group, and they made no attempts to link up into one large war party. Remaining calm, the Sioux traveled with the soldiers. They seemed to be more curious than warlike as they observed the blue-uniformed troops for more than an hour.

Angry and nervous muttering broke out periodically in the ranks while the soldiers kept a vigil on their unwanted company. The NCOs barked short, explicit instructions to shut up as the war of nerves edged on.

Finally a quartet of young braves broke loose from one war party and mounted a small but thundering charge toward the company.

"Halt!" Riker commanded. He hollered to the unit on that side of the line. "Second squad, aim!"

The four warriors continued toward the soldiers, shouting in defiance and bravado.

"Steady, now!" Riker cautioned them.

Robertson joined the second squad, bringing the enemy into his own Springfield's sights. "Remember to go for them horses' chests, boys!"

Riker waited until the last minute. "Fire!"

The small line belched smoke and flame. One of the Indians twisted and tried to hang on to his rawhide bridle. But he finally fell over to the ground. His three

146

friends, spreading out, turned and galloped away.

An abrupt outbreak of shouts sounded from the front of the column where the first squad held their part of the square. A dozen Indians, who made up the entirety of one of the groups, galloped toward them in a loose, strung-out formation.

"Fifth squad, into position!" Riker yelled.

Worthington, Robertson, and the two sergeants, with Melech, joined the squad to add their firepower to the defensive efforts. Although Worthington normally carried only a pistol, he had taken the dead George Hammer's Springfield rifle, glad to have the long arm for its superior range and accuracy.

This time the Indians fired first. Although their shooting was uncoordinated and ragged, the fusillade proved lucky for them. Private Dulgher flipped over on his back and Private Anderson spun around and dropped to his knees before falling face-first to the ground.

"Fire!"

Eleven .45-caliber slugs exploded out of the formation and flew at the Indians. Three of the Sioux were blasted from the backs of their horses, their bodies kicking up small clouds of dust as they bounced off the dry grassland.

"Second squad, Fifth squad, load!"

The surviving warriors wisely made a sharp turn, galloping away from the formation of soldiers. But ten more of the Indians charged from another side, putting Second squad under attack once again. Like the others, they also combined their running attack with firing at the soldiers. But this time the incoming bullets were more numerous because of the rapid shooting accompanying the charge.

Tim Sweeney yelled, "Oof!" He put his hands to his

147

chest and pulled them back bloody. "Sure now, and I'm shot," he said rather calmly. Then he staggered backward. "Oh, boys, take care o' me," he said, before collapsing a few paces behind his messmates.

Lars Larson stared down at Sweeney. After a few seconds he realized the man had died. Larson, his face contorted with horror and fear, looked wildly about. Suddenly he threw down his rifle and bolted out of the formation, running in a panic for the open country.

"Larson!" Corporal Schreiner shouted. "Come back! Come back!"

But the man was beyond taking orders, or even thinking clearly. The blind, unthinking instinct to get away from the scene of death and roaring noise drove him on as he ran wildly across the grassland. He sobbed and wailed to himself in his deranged flight to nowhere.

Now the Indians spotted him. Instantly and mutually abandoning the idea of their charge, all ten rode hard after the running soldier. Yelling in a happy rage, they closed in on him.

Larson glanced over his shoulder and saw the ten Sioux riders closing in fast and furiously. Now screaming insanely, he tried to run faster.

The first Indian, wanting to count a war coup, rode up beside the fleeing rifleman and slapped him hard on the shoulder with his open hand. Yelling in triumph at the honor he had garnered for himself, he turned to make sure his friends had seen the deed.

The blow knocked Larson to the ground, but he was immediately on his feet again. Something in his fear-crazed mind now told him to get back to his unit. Reversing his direction, he now ran toward the Indians, who were almost on top of him. They thought it all was a great game as they pulled on the rawhide reins and spun their mounts.

Another Sioux counted coup, sending Larson to the ground again. But this time as he got up, the third Indian to reach him swung a tomahawk that hit him with a violent blow between his shoulder blades. Larson went down, wiggling and thrashing in his death throes, with a broken neck.

Back in the formation, the men watched as the Indian stopped his horse and dismounted. Quickly and expertly, he scalped the soldier, holding up the bloody trophy with a howl of triumph.

The men had but a few seconds before another Indian charge occupied their attention. This time, the fourth squad came under fire. Luckily, they sustained no casualties as the Sioux turned back again after this fourth assault.

The squad reloaded, the clicks and clacks of the receivers slamming shut sounding flat and loud in the late afternoon. Riker kept turning as he watched for the next attack. The fifth squad, ready at a moment's notice to reinforce any side of the square, also surveyed the distant horizons.

But the Indians had pulled back.

Leaving the four dead men sprawled where they fell, Riker got his men moving again in the original northwesterly direction. Maintaining the square, they marched nervously and agitatedly, waiting for more Indians to appear. Time meant nothing to them; they all were consumed with fearful anticipation of the next attack. Even their hunger and thirst went unnoticed in the anxiety of the moment.

The sunset was forming in the west when Riker caught sight of a thick copse of trees to their immediate front. Knowing the Indians would not occupy it for an ambush in wide-open terrain, he ordered the men to move toward it. Traveling in the dark was dangerous. It would be almost impossible to maintain any sort of contact or unit cohesiveness at night. And the men needed a rest desperately.

"Mr. Worthington!" Riker called out. "Take the point, please. We'll bivouac in those woods."

"Yes, sir!" the lieutenant answered.

Twenty minutes later, after moving across the terrain at a trot, the soldiers, breathing hard, hacking, spitting and snuffing, moved into the trees. Several sank to the ground, the sudden exhaustion draining away their reserves of strength.

But First Sergeant Robertson was having none of that. "On your feet! Nobody told you to bunk out!" he yelled furiously. "Squad leaders! See to your men, goddamn it! Do I have to play corp'ral as well as do my own job?"

A defensive position was quickly arranged and the soldiers, knowing they would be on a fifty-percent alert, settled into the routine they were beginning to know so well. They removed their blanket rolls and haversacks, setting them up as rifle props while they arranged their individual positions among the trees.

While the men adjusted their places for the night, Captain Riker stood in the middle of the perimeter. "Go on with your work, men," he said. "But listen to me."

Most, curious as to what their commanding officer had to say, stopped all their activity to listen.

"We lost four men today," Riker said. "Three of them died fighting, and nothing they or we could have done would have altered their deaths. But the fourth man brought about his own tragedy."

Harold Devlin, upset, uncharacteristically spoke out. "His name was Larson, sir."

150

Riker's voice remained calm. "I know his name. And I know yours too, Private Devlin." He slowly walked around the circle of soldiers. "In fact, I know all of your names. Military protocol and custom does not permit officers to mingle socially with the enlisted men. But that does not mean you are not individuals to me and that I do not care to learn about you and know who you are."

Harold felt better knowing that the officer who had such legal authority over him also knew him as a living, breathing person.

"I am sincerely sorry when one of you is lost or hurt," Riker went on. "Larson's death was brought on by blind panic. If he had stayed in formation and obeyed his orders like a good soldier, he would be with us this very minute. His actions should be an excellent lesson to all of you. What do you think would happen if everyone suddenly broke loose and started running away in blind fear?"

Tommy raised his hand. "We'd all get killed, sir."

"That is absolutely correct, Private Saxon," Riker said. "So you all now know the consequences of not doing as you are told when you are told to do it."

Mike Mulligan, emboldened by this uncharacteristic and informal talk, asked, "Are we gonna run out-a bullets, Cap'n?"

Mack Baker laughed. "If we do, you can run over to the Indians and steal some for us, Mulligan."

"Shut up!" Robertson roared. "Goddamn your eyes, the captain is talking to you!"

"That's all right, Sergeant," Riker said. "Yes, men, we are getting short of ammunition." Then he lied. "But if you fire only when ordered to, we'll have plenty. But remember! We cannot afford to waste any, so there'll be no plinking or individual shooting. That is

151

most important." He took another look at his troops. "Now, you corporals take charge of your squads and continue settling in while Lieutenant Worthington and I have a meeting with the sergeants."

The senior ranking men squatted down in the center of the formation, whispering to each other so they wouldn't be overheard by the men.

"I'm going on a scout," Riker said. "We can't just blunder around out here blind. With some luck, I might be able to locate one or two of the Indian camps and plan a route to avoid them for as long as possible. If we could have a day or two without fighting, we can last that much longer."

"I'll go with you, sir," Worthington volunteered.

"No, Mr. Worthington," Riker said. "You stay here in command. Sergeant Robertson will assist you. I'm going to take three experienced privates with me." He looked at Robertson. "Do you have any suggestions for the job, Sergeant?"

"Yes, sir," Robertson said. "Private Callan from the first squad, Private Baker from the second, and Tomlinson from the fourth."

"Get 'em for me, Sergeant," Riker said. "I want them ready to go as soon as it's good and dark."

"One thing, sir," Robertson reminded him. "When you return here, remember to answer loud and clear when any of the sentries challenges you."

"I shall, Sergeant," Riker said with a wry grin. "I know how trigger-happy these youngsters can be. You make sure they know we're going out and are coming back in."

"Yes, sir," Robertson said. "Don't worry. I'll stay awake 'til you're back inside the position." He motioned to Sergeants Donahue and McCarey. "Go round up Callan, Baker, and Tomlinson."

152

The three men, informed by the sergeants of their mission, reported to the company commander with grim expressions on their faces. This was no new game for the veterans. They were already prepared for the dangerous work ahead. Carrying only their rifles, they had shucked all nonessential gear, including their hats. The only accouterments they sported were the canvas cartridge belts with their personal knives and bayonets attached. Baker had tied his bandanna around his head Apache-fashion.

Riker, attired like the rest of his patrol, gathered them around to give them a quick, urgent account of the purpose of their mission.

"The main reason we're going out there in the dark is to find and note the locations of any Indian encampments," Riker said. "From the way the Sioux have been coming at us, I am of the opinion that there are several small groups scattered about rather than one large one."

"And thank God fer that, sir," Callan said. An ex-sergeant, he'd recently been broken down for insubordination to Lieutenant Worthington. His reduction in rank had brought about the promotions of Marteau to corporal and McCarey to sergeant.

"It is of vital importance that we succeed," Riker said. "By noting the physical placements of the hostiles, we can chart the safest route possible through them. It may take us all night, and we'll probably be close to exhaustion in the morning, but we're all old soldiers and know what must be done."

"And we can do it, too, sir," Mack Baker added.

"Yes, sir!" Tomlinson said.

"Exactly!" Riker said, with a grim smile of appreciation for their fighting spirit. "Now, let's get on with this job."

The four infantrymen moved out of the trees and across the open country in the dark. They walked slowly and deliberately to avoid making unnecessary noise. All had fought Indians before and knew that the warriors, with their closeness to nature and animals, had spiritual instincts that gave them uncanny senses of perception. A soldier did not stumble upon those people unless they wanted him to.

The slowly moving patrol traveled for an hour across the gentle rolling swells of the flatlands. Finally they noted a dancing light on the horizon. They immediately squatted down.

"Looks like we've found the first one," Baker remarked.

"Right," Riker said. "Let's close in a bit and see what size it is."

Nerves raw with apprehension, the seasoned patrol renewed their calculated trek forward. Drawing closer, they could hear the faint sounds of chanting and the irregular staccato of an Indian drum.

Tomlinson, in the rear of the quartet, stifled a chuckle. "Sounds like that Injun on the tom-tom is drunk."

Riker, continuing on, listened carefully. After a few moments, it was very easy to tell that everyone in the camp was intoxicated. Shouts—some joyful and some angry—burst out now and then to interrupt the singing.

"I bet they ain't got guards out," Baker suggested.

"Hell, no!" Callan said. "They're getting drunker'n English lords after a foxhunt."

"We'll close in on them as much as possible," Riker said. "But stay on the alert just in case there's a teetotaler somewhere."

Baker grinned. "You figger there's a Good Templar Chapter in the tribe, sir?" he asked referring to the sol-

154

diers' temperance societies.

Riker smiled back. "Could be. And they're the ones that will catch us."

But when they were finally able to close in on the encampment, the patrol noted it had been located within a grove of trees. When they sneaked inside the dense vegetation, they halted.

"Hold up," Riker said. He went forward to make a final check on the situation. In five minutes he returned to the three soldiers. "No guards," he reported without surprise. The Indians were notorious for their lack of vigilance and discipline at certain times. "Let's get up closer."

When they reached a vantage point, the infantrymen could see that the entire group of warriors was roaring drunk.

"I can't catch no sight of women or kids," Baker whispered. "And better yet—no damned dogs."

"It's a war camp," Tomlinson said. "They ain't even got theirselves to home yet."

"Right," Callan said. "Them darlin' lads has just stopped to take a wee nip o' the white man's firewater."

Riker agreed. "It's loot from the main column." He looked at Baker. "Taken from your quartermaster teamster friend, no doubt."

Baker grimaced. "The dirty bastards!"

"Look, sir!" Callan said. "Over to the side."

Riker glanced in the direction indicated. There was a stack of familiar-looking government crates. The sight of the wooden boxes immediately raised the spirits of all four soldiers. The patrol knew they contained .45-caliber cartridges for Springfield rifles.

Riker felt a surge of want for the ammunition. He knew he couldn't pass up the opportunity. "Those Sioux are going to be passed out before dawn. The four of us

155

should be able to lug at least two of those crates back to the column."

Baker did some fast calculating. "You're talking two thousand rounds of ammunition, sir!"

"That ought to be enough," Riker said.

Callan wasn't that happy. "We're still outnumbered a couple o' hunnerd to one. All the bluddy bullets in the world ain't gonna save us if them heathen bastards catch the comp'ny."

Tomlinson shifted the chaw in his mouth. "At least, by God, we can kill more of 'em afore they does us in."

"Let's settle down and wait," Riker said.

The hours of darkness went by slowly. The celebration in the camp grew louder and wilder as a couple of altercations broke out among the thoroughly drunk Indians.

"God!" Callan said. "If the whites can't whip 'em with guns, they'll do it with whiskey."

"That or smallpox," Baker added.

Tomlinson laughed. "Or syphilis."

The final effects of the liquor were hours in coming, but when the passing out started, it went fast. The warriors, a proud race of fighters and hunters, could not resist the effects of civilization's liquor. They turned into staggering, vomiting wretches toward dawn. Those who were moving did so slowly, with no perception of what went on around them.

"Let's go!" Riker said.

It took less than thirty seconds for the four men to step inside the camp, grab the roped handles on each end of two crates, and haul them back into the woods. After adjusting their loads, they began the return trip to their own camp just as dawn was pinking the eastern sky.

156

Now damning caution, they moved as rapidly as possible, pausing only to change hands when the heavy burdens caused cramping and discomfort. Traveling almost twice as fast as they'd done the previous night, they finally sighted the trees where the company was camped, after forty minutes of the backbreaking hike.

"Oh, shit!" Mack Baker exclaimed.

A war party of ten Sioux appeared on the horizon a hundred yards away. Evidently heading for the war camp, they were cold sober and alert. There was no need to issue orders. The patrol dropped the crates and prepared for an attack.

It wasn't long in coming.

The Indians, surprised and happy at this unexpected sight of four white soldiers, rode forward to start the fight. Yelling and firing, they rapidly closed in.

The patrol couldn't wait for them to get closer. They had to put out a swarm of bullets as quickly as possible. The accurate shooting of the veterans brought down two of the Sioux right away. The others veered off sharply, but kept in close enough to maintain pressure on the infantrymen.

Baker, excited, laughed aloud. "By God, we got enough ammo here, ain't we, boys?"

The heavy recoil of the Springfields slammed time and again into their shoulders as they maintained the steady rate of fire for which the infantry was famous. The Indians, taking a couple more casualties, knew they could not lose this one, so they became bolder. They also increased their fire as they moved in closer to bring the battle to an end.

Tomlinson caught a slug in the jaw. It blew away the bottom portion of his face, spinning him around and dumping him on his back. With none of the others able to give him aid, he choked to death on his own

157

blood as the fighting continued.

The Sioux did not know about the infantry camp in the woods a half mile away. When Lieutenant Worthington and the second squad appeared, the Indians did not even notice them until the extra firepower slammed into the backs of four more of their number.

Riker, glad to see the pressure taken off, reacted quickly. "Grab the crates!"

He picked up one while Mack Baker and George Callan grabbed the other. The trio went as fast as they could toward Worthington and the other men. When the two groups finally joined up, Riker handed off his crate to Tommy Saxon and Harold Devlin.

"Get back to the camp!" he ordered. "Follow Baker and Callan!"

The Indians were thoroughly confused by then. They could not figure where the other soldiers had come from or if there would be more arriving. They thought they had killed all the troops in the battle back at the Powder River. Looking in confusion at one another, they milled about aimlessly for a few moments.

Riker formed up the squad and began a retrograde movement back to the safety of the trees. Worthington, filled with battle ardor, took his time. Firing deliberately spaced shots with his Colt revolver, he moved slowly backward.

Riker had started to yell at him to catch up, when the lieutenant suddenly doubled over and fell to the ground. He struggled back to his feet and turned around, staggering toward the squad. His face bore a surprised expression and he smiled an apology.

"Fred!" Riker instinctively hollered.

The second bullet struck Worthington in the back of the head, coming out the front and popping his eyeballs out of their sockets while blowing his nose off.

At that point, the Indians were not sure of the true situation, so they pulled back and rode away, heading for reinforcements at the war camp.

Riker led the second squad back to the woods to join the rest of the company.

Chapter Thirteen
Riker Goes Hunting

All the loops in the men's canvas cartridge belts were now stuffed with government-issue .45-caliber cartridges. The remaining ammunition was carefully packed away in the first crate while the second was broken down and passed among the troops to be used as firewood. The split boards were either stuffed into haversacks or tied on the outside. The column could not always be certain they would be near trees or be able to police up buffalo chips for cooking, so the remnants of the wooden box might come in handy during times when cookfires might be needed. Also, in the case of a rain that wet down natural fuel supplies, the remnants of the crates made excellent kindling.

Before the men began the day's march, Lieutenant Worthington and Private Tomlinson were quickly buried and given a brief ceremony. Although it was obvious the Sioux knew the column's location, Riker still would not permit the playing of Taps from Melech's bugle. The sound might serve to encourage any other straggling war parties to investigate the source.

When that silent, sad chore was finished, First Sergeant Robertson assembled the men to resume the hike that would, they hoped, reach the safety of Fort Keogh.

"We've got a crate of ammunition to tote, men," he reminded them. "So before we leave we'll take down one of these thick saplings and rig it up so two men can carry the load. Mulligan will be permanent porter. The rest o' you can take turns with the miserable thief."

Mulligan, knowing he was still regarded as an undesirable, didn't much care one way or the other. He'd gotten a pretty good break from the manual labor of digging holes, so he still considered himself better off than when the hike first began. In his world, any physical advantage was always to be worked to the limits.

After detailing a couple of men to arrange the load for carrying, Robertson reported to Captain Riker for a last minute conference. With the lieutenant gone, the first sergeant was now second-in-command.

"We've plenty of ammunition now," Riker said, watching the sapling being stripped of limbs. "But that's not the end of the problem."

"Yes, sir," Robertson said. "We're still outnumbered. All the bullets in the world ain't gonna help us if we don't have repeaters to load 'em into."

"I wonder when the powers-that-be in the ordnance department will come up with an acceptable repeating infantry long arm," Riker wondered aloud.

"It's too late to help us now, sir," Robertson said. "When all them scattered Sioux finally get together, they're gonna be able to roll over us just using the weight of numbers."

"And that's exactly what they're going to do if we tarry here much longer," Riker said. "We're going to have to strike out cross-country. That means we won't have much natural defense until we reach the Tongue

River."

"We'll be like ants on a picnic tablecloth, sir," Robertson said. "Easy to spot if somebody wants to squash us."

Riker smiled wryly. "We're doing quite a job in pointing out our problems to each other, aren't we, Sergeant?"

"We got to be practical about it, sir," Robertson said. "It ain't gonna do us or the men no good to play like ever'thing is fine."

"You're right, of course," Riker said. "Our only hope is to run into another column of troops from Fort Keogh. But there isn't much chance of that. I'm not aware of any plans to send out any more units into the field."

"And they couldn't have found out what happened to the main column yet, either," Robertson said. "I suppose when they finally notice that General Leighton ain't sending dispatch riders back, the staff at Fort Keogh will figger something awful happened." The sergeant was a seasoned noncommisioned officer. He knew the conversation going on with Captain Riker was mainly an opportunity to give the commander a chance to think and plan as he talked. Robertson's responsibility was to help that process along with comments and a few suggestions.

"It's all up to us, Sergeant Robertson," the company commander said with a tone of finality in his voice. "Our chances of being found and rescued are nil, but there always exists that wild chance of a little luck."

"If we don't have any, sir," Robertson said, "we'll soon be paying the devil his due." He glance over at the column to see that they were now ready to move out. "Shall I take the point, sir?"

"Thank you, Sergeant," Riker said.

162

Robertson, having already confirmed his estimate of the war camp's location with Riker, Callan, and Baker, chose a more southerly direction to avoid it. From the description of the warriors' antics he knew that when the Sioux who had attacked the patrol arrived there, they would find no effective fighters—only sleeping, helpless, and sick drunks. If there was any whiskey left, they would undoubtedly consume it. That would cause even more delay and confusion on the Indians' part.

Because of the possibility of an attack from all directions, the column was formed into a diamond formation, each man charged with a certain area over which to maintain watch. The countryside was wide open, giving them plenty of visibility, so at least they didn't have to worry about being ambushed or suffering a surprise assault.

Riker took a position toward the rear where he could keep an eye on everyone. The exact middle of the configuration of men was occupied by Trumpeter Melech, Mulligan, and whoever was assigned to work with the thief in carrying the crate of ammunition.

Tommy Saxon was the first man detailed to help the New Yorker carry the vital load of Springfield bullets. Both young soldiers followed Charlie O'Malley's suggestion and also put their haversacks and blanket rolls on the pole cut from the sapling. With the burden evenly distributed and balanced, it really wasn't too uncomfortable.

Tommy didn't mind the situation too much, but he wished he was with Harold Devlin instead of Mike Mulligan. Like the other men, he'd never gotten to know the thief very well. Mulligan always stuck to himself most of the time, even when everyone wasn't angry with him.

163

"How're you doing up there, Mulligan?" Tommy asked. He thought it would be more pleasant to talk a bit.

Mulligan, lost in his own thoughts, turned his head as much as he could to look back. "What?"

"I asked how you was doing," Tommy said.

"Awright," Mulligan answered. Then he asked, "How's it wit' you, then?"

"Pretty good," Tommy replied. He tried to think of something to talk about. "The weather's nice, ain't it?"

"It's awright."

"It'd be nice back home right now," Tommy said. "Unless it was raining." He walked a bit more. "Would it be nice where you're from?"

"It'd be awright."

"You're from New York City, ain't you?" Tommy inquired.

"Yeah."

"You got family back there?"

Mulligan shrugged, making the pole bounce a bit. "Just my ma," he said. "And my big brudder. I t'ink they're still living together. You got family?"

"Back in Ohio? Sure," Tommy said. "There's my folks and aunts and uncles. We lived on a farm."

"Wit' pigs and shit?" Mulligan asked.

Tommy laughed. "Yeah."

"I lived on the toid floor of a doity ol' building," Mulligan said. "On the Bowery. There was a saloon on the foist floor. It was called McGinty's. When my old man was home he'd send me down there for buckets o' beer."

"Did your pa die?"

"I dunno. He went outta the house one evening and never come back," Mulligan said. He blurted out a sardonic laugh. "And Jeez! Was that ever a blessing? You

164

bet!"

"What's it like there in New York City?" Tommy asked. "I bet she's pretty big, ain't she?"

"It's great for a sharper like me, kid," Mulligan said. He didn't get much chance to talk with anyone. "I had a gang. They was a bunch o' tough bruisers, you bet."

"Yeah?" Tommy used to read about robber gangs in dime detective novels. "Were you the leader?"

"Don't you know it! We called ourselves the Doiby Hats on account o' it was the rules I made up, see? All them oafs wore one," Mulligan said. "And, say! Let me tell you, they done ever't'ing I told 'em to do. Din't they, though?"

"Really?" Tommy was impressed.

"Sure, kid. You know what we did? We'd go up to a store owner, see? And we'd say, 'Hey, you got a nice store here. You wanna keep it this way?' They shake in their shoes, see? And we'd say, 'Kick in five greenbacks a week and it'll stay that way, see?' Did they pay up or what?"

"Did you make a lot of money that way?" Tommy asked.

"Did I? Hey, kid, that's why the judge made me join the army, see? The bigwigs in the mayor's office was afraid o' the Doibies, see? They seen that the day was coming that New York was gonna be run by Mike Mulligan and his boys. Was they scared or what?"

Mournful Melech, striding nearby, listened to the exchange. He'd paid protection money on his handcart to gangs in several neighborhoods. He'd learned to hate the petty tyrants, but had been helpless to do anything about them. Melech knew that no sneak thief like Mulligan ever ran a gang or had the gumption to collect from merchants in a racket. The real gangs would have broken every bone in his body.

165

Mulligan, enjoying himself, went on. "You know what, Saxon? I been thinking about getting up a gang in the army, even. How'd you like to join, huh?"

Tommy shook his head. "I don't think that's my style, Mulligan."

Mulligan was thoughtful for a moment. "Yeah. You ain't the type, anyhow. And am I choosy? Say! You better believe it. Maybe we could go talk to the store owners in town, huh?"

Tommy wasn't certain that was a good idea. "I don't know, Mulligan. Don't all them fellers out here carry guns?"

Melech laughed. "You could shake down the sutler, maybe, Mulligan.

"Hey! Mind your own business, Jew-Boy," Mulligan snarled. "Maybe I'll bounce that bugle off your noggin. Would I do that or what?"

Tommy, unhappy that the conversation was taking an unpleasant turn, quieted down. He shifted the pole to his other shoulder and plodded on.

Riker finally decided to call a halt in mid-afternoon. He would have preferred to keep moving, but his experienced eye noted the awful fatigue setting in on the men. They'd been too long without proper rest. The soldiers walked listlessly, even in that dangerous situation, stumbling a lot. Several even fell fast asleep on their feet, waking up only when they tripped over something.

When the column reached a shallow, wide ravine that offered a bit of a defense, Riker gave the command. "Comp'ny, attenhut!" The men came out of route step and picked up the cadence, marching as if they were on a parade ground. "Comp'ny, halt! First Sergeant!"

Robertson left the front of the formation and trotted in to receive his instructions. After speaking with the

166

captain, he situated the men for an hour's break. Half would be allowed to sleep for the first thirty minutes, the second half could nap the final period. When he inspected each position, he also took a close look at the soldier manning it.

He didn't like what he found.

Robertson returned to Riker's place in the middle of the ravine. "We got problems, sir."

Riker looked at him and laughed. "I thought we had already determined that, Sergeant Robertson."

"I mean something else now," the first sergeant replied. "The men's shoes is getting bad now. Most of 'em are on their second pair."

"God!" Riker moaned. "Now, that's all we need is to try to get a company of barefoot men across this cursed wilderness."

The footgear issued to army troops was manufactured in the military prison at Fort Leavenworth, Kansas. The shoes, made of coarse leather with the soles attached to the uppers with brass screws, were uncomfortable under the best of conditions. Most were so badly made that it was virtually impossible to tell the rights from the lefts. That didn't make much difference, since they were as bad a fit on either foot. An old soldier's trick, adopted quickly by the Johnny Raws, was to rub soap on the feet to reduce friction and blisters while on the march.

"If some of the men's footgear wears out, we'll have to share, somehow," Robertson said. "But I'm afraid we're gonna finish this here march looking like a band o' goddamned tramps."

"I'll settle for that if we get back to Fort Keogh," Riker said. "Frankly, I don't think shoe leather is going to be the most important thing on our mind."

"It's my duty to report it, sir," Robertson said.

167

"That's correct, Sergeant," Riker said. "And I appreciate your attention to your duties."

"We're also running short on rations," Robertson said. "Most o' the men are down to their last hardtack biscuits. And there ain't any saltpork left in the comp'ny.

"I'm out, too," Riker admitted. He sank deep into thought for several long minutes. "Son of a bitch!" he finally said. "I'm going to have to split out some men to go ahead and hunt game."

"Yes, sir," Robertson said.

"We can't take the whole damned outfit," Riker pointed out. "Any game around would be alerted by the noise and the scent." He stood up and pointed. "See that hill way off there to the northwest?"

Robertson also stood up. "Yes, sir."

"I'm going to take a couple of men to go hunting," he said. "We'll meet you there."

"Yes, sir. Who are you taking?"

"Baker and Callan," Riker said. "They proved to be pretty good on that scout. They're experienced men and should be a lot of help on a hunt."

"Yes, sir," Robertson said. "I'll fetch 'em for you now."

The first sergeant went over to the first squad, where he found the ex-sergeant asleep. Shaking him, Robertson said, "You're going hunting with the old man. Report to him."

Callan instantly came awake. As a veteran soldier, he was not surprised by any orders or instructions. "Right, Sergeant." He stood up and grabbed his gear, hurrying over to the company commander.

Robertson hurried to the second squad where Baker and O'Malley shared a common position. "On your feet, Baker."

Mack Baker groaned. "Oh, shit."

"Move it," Robertson said.

Baker reluctantly stood up. He turned and faced the first sergeant. "Yes, Sergeant!" He swayed a bit, displaying a silly grin.

Robertson's face blanched with anger. "You son of a bitch! You're drunk!"

Baker continued his idiotic grinning. "Yes, Sergeant."

"Where in the hell did you get the goddamned liquor?" Robertson demanded to know.

"In the Indian camp," Baker said. "There was a bottle laying by the ammunition crates. A little ol' pint bottle some dumb Sioux dropped. I picked the little darling up and shoved her in my blouse."

"It looks like Mulligan is going to have some permanent company with that load of bullets," Robertson snarled. He kicked O'Malley. "On your feet!"

"Jesus," O'Malley said, rubbing his sore leg. "What's the idea? I ain't drunk, Sergeant."

"You damned well better not be," Robertson said. "Come with me. You're going hunting with the captain."

The two joined Riker and Callan. Riker wondered why O'Malley was with the first sergeant.

"Baker is drunk, sir," Robertson said. "He swiped a bottle when the patrol snuck into the Sioux camp."

Riker fought a desire to laugh. "I am beginning to think that Private Mack Baker and Mister John Barleycorn were made for each other."

"A match made in heaven, sir," O'Malley said, grinning.

"Shut up!" Robertson snapped.

"Yes, Sergeant!"

"We'll leave now," Riker said. "My reckoning is that the break will be over within a half hour, Sergeant.

We'll see you on that hill and you know what to do if we're not there."

"Yes, sir," Robertson said. "I'll proceed on to the Tongue River and follow it up to Fort Keogh."

Riker nodded to his two companions. "Let's go." He waved to Robertson.

"Good luck, sir," Robertson said. As soon as the hunting party walked out of the perimeter, he turned and hurried over where Mack Baker had already situated himself with Mike Mulligan. "Where's that bottle, goddamn you, Baker?"

Baker pulled the empty container from his haversack. "All gone."

Robertson hit him hard, knocking him to the ground. "You're gonna pay for this, you bastard! You don't get drunk on me in the field and get away with it."

"Shit, Sergeant," Baker said, wiping at the blood on his mouth. "We're gonna die out here. Can't an old soldier get drunk just one more time?"

Robertson kicked him once, then did it again. "Don't hang your gear on the pole, Baker. You wear it, hear?"

Baker got to his feet, warily watching out for more kicks. "Yes, Sergeant."

A half hour later, right on the dot, Robertson had the column moving once again. They traveled across a gentle swell in the land that eased upward toward the hill where they were supposed to meet Captain Riker and Privates Callan and O'Malley. The men weren't rested much, but they were still slightly better off than they had been before having the hour to take it easy.

It took them two hours to reach the hill, but a mile from it, they could see the three-man hunting party waiting for them. Although the vision was distant and blurry, it appeared they had a horse with them. When

170

the company finally arrived, they found a happy trio.

"What do you think of our luck, Sergeant?" Riker asked.

They stood with a cavalry mount that had an elk buck slung over its back. Robertson was amazed. "What happened, sir?"

"Our shot brought down the elk," Riker explained. "And it also attracted this horse to us." He patted the "US" branded on the animal's flank. "He's a good soldier and knows a Springfield when he hears one.

"I reckon the Indians stole him when they massacred the column, huh, sir?" Robertson asked.

"It would have to be so," Riker said. "It probably got away from those drunks and started wandering around. When it heard us, it figured a feed of oats wasn't too far away."

Robertson laughed, but not with humor. "Well, the son of a bitch isn't any better off than we are. He'll have to wait 'til we reach Fort Keogh before he gets any government chow." Then he added, "If we get there, that is."

Montana River in the patrol, they had fully well in water.
way down to where it met the Crazy Woman River. The
proximity of water made it no problem to keep their canteens filled. In the dead heat of early summer, the men

Chapter Fourteen
The Charge on the Tongue River

Tommy Saxon staggered sideways, colliding with Harold
Devlin. Both young men lost their balance and fell to the
ground. Tommy, the stronger, was on his feet first, though
he was slow and clumsy about it. He helped his friend to
stand.

"I'm sorry, Harold. I reckon I stumbled," Tommy said.

"That's all right," Harold replied. "We're all getting dog-
tired." He pointed to the column where the weary members
of Company L moved like the walking dead.

Both young men hurried forward a few steps to regain
their place in the formation. None of the other soldiers
who had seen the incident saw any humor in it. They gritted their teeth and pushed on, weariness soaking down to
their souls.

The elk was long gone. Due to the necessity of speed, the
animal had been inefficiently butchered. Hunks of the red
meat were passed out and the men given a few moments to
roast the food over a fire and eat it before the march resumed. The portions not consumed were put in haversacks, making the bottoms of the packs greasy.

That had been two days before, and now stomachs were
once again empty and fatigue was taking its toll.

Another problem, which they now faced for the first
time, was thirst. Before moving cross-country, the column
had followed the Powder River, staying within sight of its
banks on the northward movement from Wyoming into

Montana. Even on the patrol, they had followed the waterway down to where it met the Crazy Woman River. The proximity of water made it no problem to keep their canteens filled. In the growing heat of early summer, the men perspired heavily with the hard physical exertion. Functioning with parched throats made the job much more difficult.

Unfortunately, when Riker decided to cut cross-country to the Tongue, the company moved away from all water sources. The captain, not knowing the country, had hoped they would find some source of water in unknown creeks or even some unmarked lake or pond. But there had been none—not even a buffalo wallow filled with brackish, muddy water. Now the final drops were left in the canteens, and it took every ounce of bullying that Sergeant Robertson could muster to keep them from guzzling it down all at once. Some of the men were on the verge of dry canteens with the next swallow or two. The old soldiers, as usual, proved to have conserved more of the life-giving liquid. Their eternal pessimism kept them always prepared for the worst.

The only relief in the grueling routine had been the presence of the recovered cavalry horse. A travois of two saplings was constructed by a couple of the experienced campaigners and attached to the animal with bits of rawhide and rope donated by various individuals in the company. Now the animal pulled the load of ammunition, sparing Mack Baker and Mike Mulligan from the burden. Even blanket rolls had been piled on the device, but more than a month of hard, relentless marching—first with the main column and now on their own—was taking its toll.

The men were not reacting to exhaustion all at once, however. It hit individuals at different times. Most showed the effects by becoming morose or irritable. Some, almost giving up, sank to their knees in dejection and were en-

173

couraged to continue by sympathetic bunkies who helped them up. If that didn't work, the poor wretches were kicked back into action by one of the noncommisioned officers. Others, like Tommy and Harold, stumbled about clumsily from time to time.

On that second afternoon after the elk had been killed, the horse unexpectedly raised its head and whinnied. The old campaigners knew what that meant.

"Sure, and the darlin' Tongue River's nearby, boys!" Paddy Donegan cried out.

"That's right," Charlie O'Malley shouted. "He can smell that sweet, cool water."

The good news bolstered their sagging spirits. As if given a tonic, the men's step increased and there was even some friendly bantering between a couple of the good-natured Irishmen.

"Now, Cawpril O'Rourke," ex-sergeant George Callan called out to his squad leader, "if it's a trade yer wantin', I'll give ye all the whiskey I can buy on me next month's pay fer yer canteen full o' fresh cold water to have as me very own. How does that bargain sound to ye, then?"

"Ye're bluddy daft, ye Kilcullen bastard!" O'Rourke retorted. "Even a stout Irishman like meself can't make it to the next payday wit'out sweet water to soothe me t'roat while trompin' about in this devil's wilderness."

"Quiet in the ranks!" Robertson barked. "And keep the column moving!"

The men continued onward and finally topped a rise that had cut off their forward view. Spread out before them was the beautiful view of the Tongue River, its lush banks sporting thick stands of tall trees and brush.

"Water, boys! We got water!" somebody shouted.

Cries of happiness in several languages followed, as happy emotions caused several riflemen to fall back to their native tongues.

174

"Hurrah!"
"Evviva!"
"Hurra!"
"Hurry, fellers!"

"Shut your yaps!" Robertson bellowed. "And stay in formation!" He had glanced back from his position on the point and noted the men were losing their squad integrities.

Suddenly Nathaniel Jones of the first squad broke ranks and raced toward the river. His canteen had been bone-dry for three hours and his throat was parched and dry. He didn't give a damn what Robertson would do to him later; all he wanted was to slake his thirst and cool the hot torment in his mouth.

Zlato from the third squad quickly followed suit, as did his messmate John Holihan. The two ran after Jones as fast as they could, ignoring the enraged shouts of their noncommisioned officers. Bounding down the gentle slope in long strides, the three soldiers ran crazily toward the cool, wet comfort offered by the river.

Ragged shooting abruptly broke out from the trees ahead of them. Jones went down in an undignified, tumbling heap. Zlato looked as if he'd run into a wire when the head shot hit him solid. His upper torso went back while his legs kept running, and he slammed down flat on his back.

By then Holihan had caught sight of the Sioux in the trees. He came to a shuddering halt and turned to go back to the column. A shot hit him in the shoulder, twisting him sideways, but he kept his balance and continued forward. A second and third shot slammed into his back simultaneously, and he performed his next three running steps as a dead man before going down.

"Enemy to the rear!"

Riker, with his pistol in hand, whirled around and saw a

large group of mounted warriors coming at them from the opposite side. Angry regret swelled up like bitter bile as he instantly realized the Sioux had correctly guessed the company's destination. Having horses, the Indians had beaten them there. Consequently, Riker had marched his men into a position where they were caught between the Sioux horsemen and their comrades in the trees by the river. There was no choice in the matter.

"To the bayonets!" Riker shouted. "Charge!"

The men obeyed blindly, putting their faith in the captain's quick reaction as they headed for the trees. Trumpeter Melech, excited for a change, trotted along sounding the Charge on his bugle. The insistent staccato of the notes blared above the sound of Indian shooting.

Lars Snekker in the first squad went down with a bullet in the forehead. He was quickly followed by Harry Brown of the third squad.

"Fire at will!" Riker ordered, knowing it would have been impossible to set up a controlled volley under the wild circumstances in which the battle had erupted.

Every man had a round in his rifle, and all made quick hip shots as they bounded forward in their ragged assault. It was highly inaccurate, but concentrated. The close-packed swarm of bullets was enough to make the Sioux inside the trees duck for cover as two of their number were cut down by the heavy slugs from the army rifles.

Tommy Saxon was unaware of anything but a wild rage, as he raced toward the riverbank. As thirsty as he was, the young soldier was willing to kill anybody who seriously considered keeping him from water. He'd found the brutal kick of the Springfield satisfying when he'd let loose a round on the captain's order. Now he leaped across a stand of bushes and charged into the treeline. A young Sioux warrior faced him. The Indian, caught loading, thought fast and swung his carbine like a club.

Tommy, screaming insanely, instinctively ducked under the blows while rushing forward. Filled with battle lust, he jabbed with a forward thrust of his bayoneted rifle. The blade went into the Sioux's neck, instantly causing blood to gush from the warrior's ears, nose, and mouth. The dying Indian grabbed at the rifle as he fell, almost dragging it from Tommy's strong grip. The Ohio farmboy violently shook the weapon to free it, making his opponent's final moments of life a brief but agonizing hell.

Less than ten feet away, Harold Devlin had clubbed down another warrior as his intellect evaporated under the heat of battle ardor and rage.

More ragged shooting exploded, and within a matter of fifteen seconds the ten Indians who had lain in wait in the woods were all dead. Badly outnumbered, they had needed their horse-mounted brethren for support, but the unexpected infantry assault had caught them in a bad way.

"Turn about!" Riker ordered. "Load!"

The men, with a fresh round in each weapon, faced outward toward the mounted warriors charging in on them.

"Aim! Fire!"

This volley was regulated and simultaneous, hitting the Sioux hard as their first ragged rank was wiped out. The others pulled back, making a wide circle as they rode out of range of the deadly Springfields.

"They got Sergeant McCarey!" an excited rifleman shouted.

McCarey was being held by a couple of Sioux as he struggled to get free. Somehow he'd lagged too far behind the charge and had been caught. Other Indians rode up and dismounted. They gestured toward the soldiers to make sure they could see the prisoner. One of the Indians took an arrow and began jabbing the sergeant hard with the point. Bits of blood began showing on his blue blouse.

"They're gonna drag the poor bastard away," Mack

Baker said. "God! They'll take the rest o' the day and all night in killing him!"

Tommy was barely aware of anyone beside him until he noted Captain Riker speaking to him.

"Sir?"

"I said give me your rifle," Riker said.

"Yes, sir."

Riker took the Springfield and brought it to his shoulder. Aiming carefully, he gently squeezed the trigger. It belched the .45 slug that hit McCarey in the head.

Blood and brains splattered over the enraged Indians. Angry and disgusted, they could be seen trying to get a decent scalp, but the split skull made it impossible.

"The captain just did a great kindness to Sergeant McCarey," Robertson said loudly. "Them Indians would've drug him away to a long, cruel death. Remember that, boys, and always save a last bullet for yourselves. If they're gonna cut you up and roast you, let 'em do it to you after you've gone to your Maker.'

Tommy took his rifle back from Captain Riker. He remembered hearing that sort of talk in the barracks, as tales of Indian torture and torment to captives were told and retold by the veterans. He'd wondered if they did it to throw a scare into the rookies. Now he knew it was all true.

"Corporal Schreiner!" Robertson barked. "You're acting sergeant and section leader of the first section." The loss of a noncommisioned officer meant a quick reorganization if discipline and order were to be maintained. The first sergeant looked at the survivors of the second squad. He carefully but quickly noted each one, finally saying, "O'Malley, you're acting corpral. Take over the second squad."

"Yes, Sergeant," O'Malley said. "Let's go, Second squad." He realigned them in the trees as they waited for the next Indian attack.

After spending a bit more time violently chopping up

178

McCarey's body, the Sioux remounted and pulled farther back until they were completely out of sight. Robertson, meanwhile, took some leadership pressure off Riker by personally assigning the squads to protect certain areas of the new position. When he was satisfied with their placement, he hurried across the position to make an official report to the company commander.

"Sir, L Comp'ny has one officer, one first sergeant, one sergeant, one acting sergeant, three corp'rals, one acting corp'ral, one trumpeter, and twenty-five privates present 'n' accounted for." He added up the numbers in the impromptu strength report he'd written in his notebook. "That gives us a strength o' thirty-four. We've had a total o' twelve men killed."

"Thank you, Sergeant Robertson," Riker said. His hand trembled from what he'd just done to McCarey. But he fought down the horrible rush of emotions. To add to his distress, the captain was more than slightly irritated by this parade-ground mentality that Robertson could display at the most outrageous moments. "Now all I must do is figure out some way to get us thirty-four survivors through all those Indians and back to Fort Keogh."

"It's a big order, sir," Robertson stated, missing the sarcasm.

"Then, of course, I'm going to have to make a full report on the circumstances surrounding Sergeant McCarey's death," Riker said. "I've just shot and killed one of my own noncommisioned officers."

"The circumstances will stand in a hearing, sir," Robertson assured him. He didn't want the captain to start going to pieces on him. The best thing to do was turn his mind to the present circumstances. "Any plans for right now, sir?"

"I'm not going to plan any last stands unless the situation has become completely hopeless," Riker said. "By God, we'll fight hard 'til they've beaten us down so hard we can't get up again."

"I'm glad to hear that, sir," Robertson said, trying to put a show of spirit in his voice. "I think the men will—"

"Enemy front!"

The cry was given several times along the short perimeter line. Both Riker and Robertson went forward to take a look at the situation. A group of Sioux, yelling and gesturing, rode across the open country toward the trees. Riker noted they didn't seem as numerous as before. Then an alarming thought occurred to him.

"Guard the flanks!"

"Fourth squad to the left!" Robertson yelled. "Second to the right!"

"Let's go!" Charlie O'Malley yelled at his new command. "To the right and keep a sharp lookout in them woods there!"

Second squad quickly responded. They reached the new position in time to meet some Indians on foot coming through the trees.

"Aim! Fire!" O'Malley commanded.

The accurate fire was effective, cutting down a good portion of the Indians. The others, surprised at having their sneak attack broken up, returned the shots but did so hastily and without any accuracy. The Sioux were plains Indians who liked to move rapidly on horseback across wide, open country. Sneaking around in the woods was not their idea of proper warfare. They quickly abandoned their foray and pulled away.

The story was the same on the other flank, where Corporal O'Rourke's fourth squad met another flanking movement. A determined volley by the soldiers broke up the attack.

The mounted Indians who had hoped to create a diversion with their antics in front of the company's position also paid a price for the effort. The first and third squads each delivered three devastating fusillades that slapped into the mounted group with a violent impact. No less than a half dozen of the Sioux were dumped from their horses, and three of the animals also went down.

Riker watched the hostiles melt back out of sight. "I just had a rather strange realization dawn on me, Sergeant," he remarked to Robertson. "Those Indians are used to running battles with cavalry. I don't think they've quite figured out how to deal with regulated volley fire from infantry situated in a strong defensive position."

Robertson found no comfort in that. "It won't take 'em long to come up with something, sir."

"That also occurred to me," Riker agreed with a tired sigh.

The men waited for another attack, but nothing happened as the long afternoon wound down into twilight. Finally night's dark curtain began to set in and, as always, the company went on fifty-percent alert.

Tommy Saxon and Harold Devlin once again shared duties. They set up a position next to a ponderosa pine, arranging their gear as rifle rests. They wordlessly settled in and waited to see what would happen.

Harold caught a last glimpse of Tommy as the sun finally sank away, making it impossible to see.

"How're you doing, Tommy?" Harold asked. "You've got a real strange expression on your face."

"I was just thinking," Tommy said seriously. "When I get home and my uncles start yapping about their service in the war, I'm gonna tell 'em to shut up." He paused and spat. "I mean *if* I get home!"

Harold, making no reply, turned away and stared out over the dark expanse of the wide countryside.

Chapter Fifteen
A Gathering of Hostiles

Dawn was a rustling, nervous affair as those troops who
had been sleeping were awakened. None quit their slumber
gradually. The fierce fighting of the previous day had left
them unsettled and edgy. When shaken by their bunkies,
they abruptly sat up with eyes opened wide, their nerves
raw, expecting the worst.

And a glance outside the trees showed the worst might
certainly be in the offing for that day.

The pickets on duty, rifles locked and loaded, could see
numerous Indians out of rifle range but near enough to
keep the area under close observation. The Sioux had the
company trapped between themselves and the river. At
first light, Riker had sneaked down to the water and
peered across it to the other side. After a few minutes, the
seasoned Indian fighter caught the sight of several Sioux
concealed in the trees there. Even if the water were shallow enough to wade—and Riker was glad it was not—
there would be no escape in that direction. The deep,
swift water protected L Company as the moat of a medie-
val castle had sheltered the inhabitants centuries before.

The captain returned to his makeshift headquarters in
the middle of the position. He hadn't slept more than an

hour through the whole night. It hadn't been the tactical situation that bothered his rest, as much as it had been thoughts filled with images of Lurene and his children. He missed his family terribly and damned the situation that showed every indication of preventing him from ever seeing them again. And for the first time he began to regret choosing a lifestyle that kept his wife from the comforts and luxuries that many American women took for granted. A woman wed to an army man on the frontier lived in stark austerity no matter what rank the husband.

First Sergeant Robertson was waiting for him when he came back from the riverbank. "How's it look, sir?"

"They've got us hemmed in tight, Sergeant," Riker replied. "There'll be no crossing of the river."

"That's a sort of blessing, sir," Robertson pointed out. "If we can't get over *there* then them redskins can't get over *here*."

"They can get over here, but they'll have a hell of a time swimming across that current," Riker said. "But the fact remains, we're pinned down tight here and can't move." He looked over at the men on the defensive perimeter. They seemed forlorn and bedraggled. "It appears our troops are evolving into ragamuffins, Sergeant."

"Yes, sir," Robertson said. "I made a quick inspection while you was down to the riverbank. Their clothes is torn and a lot of 'em have used up the last of the thread in their sewing kits. And, like I told you before, most of their shoes is worn out. And I'm talking about their extry pairs, sir."

"Yes, you've told me," Riker said, a bit irritated with Robertson's persistent habit of repeating reports. "However, if things go to hell here, that won't make much goddamned difference, will it?"

"No, sir," Robertson replied calmly. "I reckon it won't. And I think it's a pretty good assumption that things is

183

surely going to hell."

"At least we've got plenty of ammunition," Riker said.

"That might not do us no good either, sir," Robertson said. "It's starting to look like them scattered bands o' Sioux are getting together."

"Yes. I suppose the news of our existence has now been sent among the whole tribe," Riker said. "It's logical to assume that every warrior wants to be in on our demise."

"An Indian is a professional soldier, sir," Robertson remarked.

"Why, Sergeant Robertson," Riker said, "that's a compliment."

"Just 'cause I fight 'em don't mean I don't respect 'em," Robertson said. "I reckon I respected the Johnny Rebs in the war." Then he added, "But I still hated the raggedy son of a bitches."

Riker had to grin. "And now *we're* the raggedy sons of bitches."

"I'd say that's right," Robertson said. He gestured at the company. "Any orders, sir?"

"Tell the men they can brew up some coffee," Riker said. "The Sioux know exactly where we are. A little smoke isn't going to worsen the situation."

"Yes, sir," Robertson said. "They'll appreciate that."

Over in the second squad, the men welcomed the chance for coffee. O'Malley, however, got them together for a short meeting because of the ration problem. "Boys," he announced. "We're running short on coffee, so I'm gonna put something to you. Instead o' one or two of us settling down to boil some up, let's make a squad mess outta it. Ever'body chip in what they've got, no matter how much or how little, and we'll ration it out. Maybe that way we can always have at least a cup in the morning before we get back to Fort Keogh. It might be weak, but it'll be better'n nothing."

"Sounds an excellent suggestion to me," Harold Devlin said.

"Sure," Tommy said. "I'll go for that idea."

Mack Baker also agreed. "That's the way us old soldiers always does it."

Tim O'Brien had a further suggestion. "What about Mournful Melech? He ain't got any messmates."

"Sure," Tommy said. "He's a nice feller. Let's ask him to be in our mess."

"It's all right with me if it's all right with you," O'Malley said. He stood up and hollered at the trumpeter. "Hey, Mournful. You want to join our mess and throw your coffee in with ours? It don't matter how much you got. You're welcome to join and share."

Melech came over and pulled a cloth bag of beans out of his haversack. He looked very old standing there in his ragged uniform with his thick locks of graying hair sticking out from under his field hat. "Thank you very much."

Tommy also had another proposal. "What about Mike Mulligan?"

"Piss on him!" Mack Baker hissed.

"He could mean a few more cups of coffee," O'Malley counseled them.

"Shit!" Baker said. "If you fellers want, go ahead."

A brief discussion took place as the constituency of the second squad took another vote. The result was O'Malley calling over to Mulligan. "Hey! Come here a minute."

Mulligan, as usual by himself, wearily got to his feet and walked to the squad. "Whatayez want?"

"We're pooling our coffee; want to throw in?" O'Malley asked.

"Why should I?"

"This is the army, you son of a bitch," O'Malley said calmly. "Soldiers look after each other. When bunkies is short on stuff they share so's ever'body can have

185

something."

"I ain't got any coffee," Mulligan said. "Can I join in anyhow?" Then he laughed. "Let's see how you look after me, huh?"

"We asked you," Harold Devlin said. "It didn't matter whether you could contribute to the communal larder or not. So you may become part of the group."

"You're a generous bastard, ain't you?" O'Malley snapped.

"Yeah! Just a minute, Devlin," Baker protested.

"It's the only decent thing to do," Devlin insisted. "The rules were that anybody could join in no matter what their coffee supply."

"He'll get coffee when he ain't chipping in!" Tim O'Brien pointed out.

"Devlin is right," O'Malley said, finally relenting. His position as squad leader made him look at things differently than if he'd been a rifleman. "We asked him, so he has a right to join."

Mulligan grinned. "T'anks. I'm in."

But O'Malley was a seasoned soldier with a seasoned soldier's jaundiced view of people with highly individualistic styles. He stood up and walked over to Mulligan. "Gimme your haversack."

"What for?"

"Gimme it!" O'Malley insisted.

"You go to hell," Mulligan said. "Yez can take yer coffee and shove it up yer asses!" He turned around and started to walk away.

But O'Malley went after him, pulling the haversack off his shoulder. He opened it and turned it upside down. Among the extra socks, the shirt, and the worn-out pair of shoes that fell to the ground was a quarter of a bag of coffee.

"Looky there!" Tommy Saxon said, shocked. "He lied

to us!"

Harold Devlin frowned. "That's a despicable thing you've just done, Mulligan."

O'Malley, like the others, was infuriated. He grabbed Mulligan and dragged him across the crude bivouac to Schreiner. He gave the acting section leader a quick report on what had happened about the coffee agreement.

Schreiner wasted no time in taking them to the first sergeant. He explained the situation to the senior noncommisioned officer in his butchered English.

Robertson's expression was calm, but his voice was icy cold with rage. "You are a stingy, lousy son of a bitch, Mulligan. For the first time in your useless, miserable existence you're with a group of men you could form a true, life-long friendship with, but you're too stupid and evil to realize it."

Mulligan, stood stony-faced, saying nothing.

"O'Malley, keep his coffee, but he don't get to share, understand?" Robertson said. "If I catch him drinking coffee, I'll take it out on you."

"Yes, Sergeant."

"As for you," Robertson said, jabbing at Mulligan with his finger, "go collect the canteens and fill 'em down by the river. And I hope them Indians on the other side put a goddamned bullet into your thieving, lying skull!"

Mulligan went to his task. Everyone waited for the sound of shots, but the Sioux contented themselves with a few shouts at the timorous soldier who filled the canteens at the river's edge.

The morning drifted by. By noon, Mulligan had filled and refilled all the canteens in the company several times, but still had not been shot at by the Indians on the other side of the river. When he'd finished the final time, he went back to his place in the bivouac and sat down by himself.

Early in the afternoon the Indians edged closer to the company's position.

The Sioux made no overt motions, simply milling about at a distance. At first there seemed to be between seventy-five and a hundred of them. But from the way they moved about, disappearing off the horizon and reappearing, it was impossible to make an accurate estimate.

An hour later, things looked a bit worse. Sergeant Robertson, using the field glasses that had once belonged to Lieutenant Worthington, spent a careful quarter of an hour observing the hostiles. "I'd say two hunnerd of 'em now, sir," he reported to Captain Riker.

"You know what they're doing, don't you, Sergeant?" Riker asked in a whisper.

"They're waiting for some o' their pals to join 'em, sir," Robertson said. "I reckon ever' damn warrior in the Sioux nation wants to get in on this kill."

"Under these circumstances, I don't have too many decisions left to make, do I?" Riker remarked.

"You sure don't, sir."

"Get the men up on line," Riker said. "Make sure that each of them has one round locked and loaded."

"Yes, sir!"

The men, tense, irritable, and apprehensive, stood at the tree line, watching the growing throng of Indians in front of them. With nerves strained, there was no talking among them as they waited for the inevitable.

It began with the sudden thunder of hooves that could be felt in the ground.

"On your feet!" Riker commanded in a loud voice. "Line sergeants and trumpeter man the rear to watch the river. Everybody else to the tree lines. Any position — squat, kneel, lay down, stand up. But load!"

Robertson found a good firing place beside a pine that was near the company commander. "We're gonna have to

188

hit 'em at least three times before they close in on us."

Riker only nodded. "Aim! Fire!"

A scattering of the attacking Sioux, still at a distance, either went down with their horses or tumbled off their mounts to the ground.

"Goddamn your eyes, you bastards!" Robertson shouted in fury. "Fight like infantry! Kill 'em, goddamn it! Aim at their horses' chests!"

"Load! Aim! Fire!"

This time the volley struck hard, hitting so many of the attackers that several of the Indians farther back rode into their falling comrades, the horses going down and throwing the riders.

"Load! Aim! Fire!"

Again the Sioux suffered heavy losses from the deliberate, disciplined fire of the army riflemen. The momentum of their attack was broken.

"Fire at will!"

Now, as individuals, the men of L Company aimed and fired as fast as the single-shot rifles permitted. With improved proficiency, the bullets slapped in an uneven but rapid staccato, killing more of the hostiles until they turned away and galloped out of range.

"In the river, there are Indians!" shouted Acting Sergeant Schreiner.

Riker slapped Robertson on the shoulder. "Check that out!"

"Yes, sir!" The first sergeant went to the bank where Schreiner stood with Donahue and Mournful Melech. He laughed at the sight of the Sioux swimming across toward them. "Them dumb bastards don't know their pals out front have been beat back."

Donahue also chuckled. "Must be part o' their battle plan, huh?"

"Well, shit!" Robertson said. "Don't just stand there.

189

Shoot the son of a bitches." He took careful aim at one of the Indians bobbing toward them. He fired, the round making the man's head explode in a crimson spray.

Then Schreiner got one and Melech another. Robertson claimed one more when the other Sioux, realizing something had gone wrong, turned and tried to get back to the opposite side. All ended up floating away with the current, their skulls blasted by the .45-caliber slugs.

When Robertson returned to the front line, he was grinning. "There ain't no more Sioux on the other side, sir," he reported to Riker. "They was trying to sneak up on us. We got 'em all."

"The ones out front here have pulled back," Riker said. "I don't think we'll see them again today."

"No, sir," Robertson the veteran Indian fighter said. "But they'll spend the rest of the day and all night mulling over what happened."

"Correct," Riker remarked. "And that means they'll try to get us again tomorrow."

Robertson slowly shook his head. "Sir, there ain't no way we're gonna be able to keep this up again. When they attack again, we're gonna end up dead meat."

Chapter Sixteen
The Night Walkers

Captain Charles Riker and First Sergeant Gordon Robertson stood together at the edge of the tree line watching the Indians gathering up their dead.

"How many do you reckon we got, sir?" Robertson asked. "I been trying to figger it out, but it's kinda hard to tell. Some of 'em may have been able to ride away and fall outta sight when they died."

"I estimate the hostiles' casualties at no less than a dozen." Riker said, after some reflection. "And not more than twenty." He took a deep breath, exhaling slowly to help ease away the tensions left over from the previous battle. "We've stung them bad. They're not whipped, but they'll certainly be more careful tomorrow.

"The Sioux are madder'n hell, sir. They're really gonna work themselves up tonight," Robertson said. "By morning they're gonna be ready to come all the way into here. And it don't matter if we shoot a hunnerd of 'em off their horses."

"That's their nature," Riker said.

"Some old war chief is gonna stand up and make a real fiery speech," Robertson said. "He's gonna tell them young warriors they're nothing but a bunch o' women for

191

not pushing the attack all the way today."

"And one of those fighters will talk about our volley fire," Riker said. "They've never experienced attacking massed infantry before. All their fights in the past have been skirmishes with fast-moving cavalry. Concentrated firepower is new to them. But the Sioux are a determined people — unfortunately for us — ferocious enough that they may be willing to sustain high casualties to wipe us out."

"There's a real certainty that we'll cost 'em plenty, sir. No doubt about that. The British infantry squares at Waterloo whipped Napoleon's cavalry," Robertson said. "His horsemen couldn't penetrate 'em."

"I'm afraid we haven't enough men to form the necessary depth for such an effective formation, Sergeant," Riker said. He frowned in puzzlement. "Where did you hear about the Battle of Waterloo?"

"From Lieutenant Worthington," Robertson answered. "He used to talk about Napoleon a lot."

"I suppose he did," Riker said. He recalled the lieutenant's almost insane love of battle. Riker also remembered the shots that had blown the man's eyes out of their sockets. The captain shuddered a bit.

"Anyhow, some old man is gonna whip up the warriors at the council fires tonight," Robertson said, returning to the original subject of the conversation.

"Yeah," Riker said with a nod. "He'll shame them into making a big effort to wipe us out."

"Which they can do," Robertson stated flatly. "Even if the old man don't, there's all them women that lost men today — all twelve or twenty of 'em. They'll be weeping and wailing and cutting themselves. They'll be wanting the others to go out for revenge." He took a deep breath. "It means pure shit for us, sir."

"Yeah."

Robertson took a closer look at his commanding officer

in the dimming light. He noted the pensive gaze in Riker's eyes. "You got something in mind, sir?"

"I don't want to die in these trees," Riker said. "And I certainly don't want to get all sliced up tomorrow and have my scalp hanging in some warrior's lodge."

Robertson snorted. "Hell! Who does?"

Now it was Riker's turn to study his companion. The sergeant had been through some of the Civil War's bloodiest battles. He'd also fought in hundreds of skirmishes in the war against the Plains Indians. Crude, bullying, and uneducated—but incredibly brave in a rather stupid way at times—he was the perfect image of the professional soldier-leader who worked at the small-unit level. He was facing certain death when the sun next rose, yet he discussed the possibility of the event in a matter-of-fact tone. Not only did he ignore the frightfulness of his death, he also gave no thought to the uselessness of it. Or the more appalling fact that the people he was dying for—the entrepreneurs and sharpers—couldn't care less about him. In fact, the very people for whom he was fighting to get land looked down on professional soldiers, particularly the enlisted men. It didn't matter if the citizens were rich railroad barons or simple homesteaders. All sneered openly at the soldiery.

"We're walking out of here," Riker finally said.

"Sir?"

"As soon as it gets dark, we're going to resume the march," Riker said. "We'll go out far enough into the open country to avoid stumbling across the underbrush by the river, but we'll keep it in sight to guide us."

"I don't know about that, sir," Robertson said in a hesitant tone. "You said before it wasn't a good idea fer the men to march at night. It'd be too hard to control 'em."

"Do you have any alternate suggestions, Sergeant?" Riker asked.

193

"No, sir. But if they catch us out in the open like that—in the dark o' night with the whole comp'ny stumbling around—not able to see good—"

"Then they'll massacre us," Riker said. "Which is exactly what they're going to do tomorrow if we stay here."

Another, more logical aspect of the idea slowly dawned in Robertson's mind. "Yes, sir! And if them goddamned Indians is pissing and moaning about today's battle, they won't be out tonight anyhow, will they?"

"Let's hope they won't," Riker said. "But if some of them are, so what?"

"Yes, sir! So what?"

"We won't be able to follow the regular march routine, of course," Riker pointed out. "This scheme is going to call for a change in our habits. Special circumstances call for special actions, right, Sergeant?"

"Yes, sir," Robertson said. "What do you want me to do, Captain?"

"Issue out enough ammunition to fill the empty loops in the cartridge belts, Sergeant," Riker said. "Then pass the word to the noncoms. We will move in a single file. Noise discipline is a must."

"What about the horse, sir?"

"We'll use blankets over his hooves," Riker said. "That will help."

"Yes, sir. I'll see that the thief Mulligan and the drunk Baker make generous donations," Robertson said.

"Let's get this organized before it is completely dark," Riker said.

The company prepared for the night walk with only the slimmest of guards staying on the alert. Working fast, they drew enough ammunition to fill out all empty loops in their cartridge belts. Mack Baker and Mike Mulligan had to do more than just give up their blankets. Robertson made them fold up the covers and wrap them securely

194

around the horse's hooves. The animal, used to having things strapped on him, stood dumbly and endured the treatment with the same acceptance he would have displayed if a Gatling gun had been put across his back.

Finally, taking advantage of the time between the sun's disappearance and the moon's emergence, Robertson hurriedly but quietly made the men fall in. They'd already been told of the importance of keeping as quiet as possible, and they formed up without speaking.

The desperate nature of the escape also was not lost on them.

Tommy Saxon stood in the second squad between Mack Baker and Harold Devlin. Harold, as usual, didn't have blind faith in Captain Riker's decision. "I hope he knows what he's doing," he whispered.

Mack Baker looked over Tommy's shoulder and remarked, "There ain't a hell of a lot of choice, Devlin. If we stay here, them Sioux is gonna butcher us like the main column."

"Shush!" Acting Corporal Charlie O'Malley walked up to them. "Keep your mouths shut! Save your energy for walking, cause that's what we're gonna be doing until we got to stop and fight."

The squad settled down, each soldier feeling lonely in the darkness in spite of the closeness of the other men around him. A bare five minutes passed before the word was given for them to move out. The column began that phase of the march slowly, snaking out of the treeline and turning due north to follow the river up toward the far distant sanctuary of Fort Keogh.

Tommy was barely able to see Harold in front of him. He was terribly tired. His legs felt sluggish and his feet seemed terribly heavy. As the fatigue settled in more heavily, so did his homesickness. Each step seemed an individual, painful effort. He thought about home, picturing the house that sat in the middle of the farmyard not far from the barn. For a moment he felt like crying. It would be easy to do in the dark; nobody would know about it if he kept his sobbing silent. Sadness and regret pulled down on his spirits as the awful tiredness did on his body.

He suddenly remembered the Indian he'd killed with his bayonet. The fellow was about his own age, and Tommy remembered the wide-open eyes and the gurgling croak when the blade sliced into the young Sioux's throat. The last time he had seen the corpse was when some of the fellows from the fourth squad had thrown it on the pile of other dead Indians left in the trees.

Harold Devlin's physical and spiritual well-being were in as bad a shape as his young friend's. He was third in line in the second squad. O'Malley was first and Tim O'Brien second. He could barely see O'Brien's bleached field hat ahead of him. It bobbed a bit with every step the soldier took.

Harold realized his rash act of leaving Drury Falls had indeed been a headstrong, foolish act. He should simply have swallowed his pride and stayed there at the bank while making job applications in other towns if he wanted to leave. There were plenty of opportunities he'd not even considered because of his hurt feelings. But at that point, in a lost column of infantrymen stranded in hostile country, it was too late to do anything about past imprudence.

"Stupid! Stupid!" Harold mouthed in a silent castigation of himself.

An image of pretty Nancy Reardon swam into his mind. He felt a stab of hurt. She had such a lovely smile and a charming way about her. She had been so graceful and lovely in her party dress. Knowing that she felt him beneath her cut deep into Harold's most sensitive feelings. He fully knew that he hadn't been in love with her, but he'd quickly developed an overwhelming crush that had kept her constantly on his mind. He'd even wondered if they might get married someday, and the idea had seemed wonderful. His imagination created a picture of a good and happy life as he continued to grow in the business world.

Now he felt angry.

He was damned well going to do something about that whole situation, Harold decided. When his hitch in the army was up, he would strive toward nothing less than becoming extremely wealthy. It could be done out west, in this new country. There had to be literally hundreds of ways for a man to amass wealth if he was smart enough to recognize the opportunities and take advantage of them. The new idea and resolution made him feel a bit better. He unconsciously stepped out a bit faster as the surge of determination overrode his fatigue.

"Oof!"

"Excuse me, Tim," Harold whispered. "I didn't mean to bump into you."

"That's all right," Tim O'Brien said, grinning in the dark. "You must have really been deep in thought."

"Yeah," Harold said.

"I heard you whispering to yourself," O'Brien said. "What was you talking about? That Indian you beat to shit? I seen you, Harold. You was really a wild man. You whacked that son of a bitch like a lumberjack taking down a tree."

Harold grimaced as he suddenly recalled the incident when he had turned into a primitive, enraged animal. He pressed on silently, damning the army in general and Captain Riker and Sergeant Robertson in particular. He turned and looked out into the darkness where the Sioux were. He mouthed a silent curse: "And goddamn you, too!"

The hours of walking through the dark night melted

into each other until time meant nothing. Life for the riflemen of L Company had been reduced to simply trudging after the dim figure of the man ahead, forcing the aching fatigue from the conscious mind as the small column snaked its way up the Tongue River.

After a long period of the strength-draining routine, Tommy Saxon noted that it had grown a bit lighter. He could clearly see his feet, the worn-out army shoes he wore in plain sight. Even the dew sticking to them was visible. Now Harold Devlin in front was easy to view. Tommy turned his head and glanced back at Mack Baker. He was shocked at the appearance of Baker's face: it was drawn and sallow, with dark circles under the eyes. The strain was telling plainly on the hard-drinking old soldier.

Tommy wasn't doing very well himself. He wanted to lie down and go to sleep. He didn't give a damn if the grass was sopping wet and cold. The young man simply wanted to get some blessed, refreshing sleep. And then something to eat.

"Enemy right!"

A half-dozen Sioux horsemen appeared in the heavy morning mist. Now knowing they'd been spotted, they gestured and yelled defiant threats at the soldiers.

"Comp'ny, halt!" Captain Riker's voice was loud and strong. "Right, face! Load!"

The Indians responded by bolting forward, approaching the formation at an oblique angle. They brandished bows and arrows rather than rifles. Riker, afraid they might be a feint for a larger group that would come head-on at his command, did not order a volley to be fired. He wanted to take no chance of having to go through a loading and aiming procedure while a large number of hostiles closed in on the company. The Indians were smart enough to have figured out that that was the best way to break through the limited volleys of the company.

The Sioux shot several arrows and immediately turned away, galloping into the mist and disappearing from view.

"Oh, man! Shit!"

Tim O'Brien, with one of the shafts deep in his shoulder, dropped his rifle and staggered in a circle. He finally knelt down, moaning softly.

First Sergeant Gordon Robertson immediately leaped into action. "Get that gear off the travois!" he barked to Tommy and Harold. While they obeyed, he went to O'Brien and helped him to his feet. He led him over to the travois and allowed him to lie down on it.

Riker came over to see what had happened. He quickly summed up the situation. "You men grab your haversacks and blanket rolls off the travois to make room for O'Brien. Quickly! We can't stay here."

The riflemen complied, sorting through the gear for their own stuff, donning it speedily.

Robertson made O'Brien as comfortable as possible. "We'll get that arrow outta you the first chance," he said. "Just hang on 'til we get to a better place." He glanced up at Riker. "Ready to go, sir."

"Right, Sergeant." The company commander took another look out into the mist to see if any more Indians were approaching. There was nothing but vapory silence. "Company, fall in! Sling arms! For'd, march! Route step, march!"

With O'Brien lying on the travois and clasping at the arrow sticking from his shoulder, the column renewed their march across the Wyoming wilderness.

Chapter Seventeen
The First Sergeant Plays Doctor

Newly appointed squad leader Charlie O'Malley hurried forward through the first section to Acting Sergeant Karl Schreiner. "Hey, Corp'ral," he called out.

Schreiner, his head bent with the effort of walking, turned around. "Sergeant Schreiner," he said. "To be called *Sergeant* Schreiner I am. Is the same being acting as for real."

"Oh, yeah?" O'Malley said, almost sneering. He read the Prussian's insistence on proper protocol through the mangled syntax of his sentences. "You ain't getting paid for it."

"I am still sergeant!" Schreiner insisted.

"Well, I ain't taking this acting corporalcy too serious 'til they gimme orders to slap a coupla stripes on my arms," O'Malley asked. "And I want to see that extry two dollars a month when I make pay call, too."

Schreiner, not wanting to get into a deep discussion involving American logic, sighed. "What is it about which you wish to speak, Corporal O'Malley?"

"I think O'Brien has got to get that arrow pulled out," O'Malley said. "He's hurting something awful."

"Is bleeding badly O'Brien?"

"I can't tell," O'Malley said. "He was already soaked in blood when Sergeant Robertson laid him down on the travois. But it's starting to look like a fever is building in him. That's a bad sign."

Schreiner nodded. *"Ja.* To the first sergeant I go." He picked up the pace, making his way to the head of the column where Robertson led L Company's march across the wilderness. "Sergeant Robertson, O'Brien has hurting very bad. Out must come the arrow."

Riker, nearby, overheard. "We'll stop long enough to remove it. Who's good for the job?"

"I can do it, sir," Robertson said. He raised the flap of his haversack and fished around inside, finally withdrawing a piece of hooped wire. "This here is perfect for jerking out arrows. I seen a surgeon with one, so I had this made in case I ever caught one o' them damn things in my own carcass."

"Company, halt!" Riker called out. "Go to it, Sergeant."

Robertson hurried down the column, grabbing ex-sergeant George Callan by the arm. "You got a chaw working?"

"Yes, Sergeant," Callan said. "Are you goin' to pull out that great bluddy arrow?"

"Yeah. C'mon."

The two went to the travois and found Private Tim O'Brien in a great deal of pain. He was speaking with Tommy Saxon and Harold Devlin.

"I'm real sorry to be the cause o' you fellers having to pack them blanket rolls and haversacks," he said between groans.

"Don't worry about it, Tim," Harold said. "You just relax and rest up."

"Sure, old feller," Tommy said kindly. "We don't mind a bit."

201

Robertson wasted no time. "Get that ammo crate off the travois."

Tommy and Harold got the wooden box that O'Brien had been lying beside on the carrier. They set it down and waited to see what was going to happen.

The first sergeant was primed and ready to operate. "I hear you're having a rough time of it."

"I seen better days," O'Brien remarked.

"We'll take care o' that now," Robertson said. "Devlin, get his feet. Callan, hold that right arm, and you, Saxon, kneel down here with me and keep a good grip on the left." He looked at O'Brien. "You look like death warmed over, O'Brien."

O'Brien grimaced, his face an ashen color. "I suppose I do. To tell you the truth, Sergeant, I feel sorta poorly."

"Then we got to get that arrow outta there, soldier," Robertson said. He pulled back the bandage that had been made from the wounded man's extra shirt. "If we don't, the damned thing is gonna move around and cut you worse. Then some real bad festering is gonna set in."

"Yeah," O'Brien said. "I think—ow! I think it'd be better if 'n it got pulled out."

Robertson adjusted the size of the wire hoop. "Indians used to make them arrowheads outta flint, they tell me. But that was a long time ago. Now they make 'em outta sheet iron they get from trading with no-good, whiskey-peddling bastards."

Callan worked the chaw in his mouth. "Yeah. Them traders would sell their own sisters to a Mexican whorehouse if they had a chance."

"That's for sure," Robertson said. "They carry sheet iron just 'cause they know the Indians want it."

Callan said, "Yeah. And them kind o' arrowheads

202

can bend real easy when they hits you. That's what makes 'em hard to come out."

"That's what this wire is for. I'm gonna put this hoop in beside the arrow, and work her over the point," Robertson said. Then he added, "It's gonna hurt."

"I figgered that," O'Brien said.

"It's gonna hurt like hell," Callan added.

"Then let's do it and get it over with," O'Brien said, bracing himself.

Robertson stuck the loop of the wire in his mouth to wet it, then leaned down toward the wound. Opening up the slash caused by the arrow's entry, he slipped the device into the interior, probing a bit as he felt it slide along the arrowhead.

O'Brien grimaced, gritting his teeth so hard that they squeaked. Tommy and Harold held on tightly, both looking away from the awful sight. Callan, on the other hand, slowly chewed on his tobacco, watching the procedure with a sort of detached interest.

"I hit the bottom," Robertson announced. "Now I gotta slip her over the point." He looked at O'Brien. "You ready, young soldier?"

O'Brien nodded.

Robertson worked rapidly and violently as he maneuvered the loop into position. Finally O'Brien emitted a loud, piercing shriek that lasted for three full seconds. The first sergeant ignored it as he felt the wire slip over the arrowhead. He nodded to Callan. "Is that chaw all worked up?"

"You bet, Sargint," Callan answered.

Robertson pulled a bit to make sure all was ready. "Here we go!" He jerked violently upward. The arrow came free with a spurt of blood as O'Brien yelled again. Callan leaned forward and spat deep into the gaping wound that Robertson held open. O'Brien

203

fainted as the bandage was slipped back into place.

Robertson stood up and dropped the arrow on the travois beside the unconscious wounded man.

"O'Brien'll want to keep that. He can tell his grandkids about the time he got a arrow shot into him by the Sioux." The first sergeant signaled to Riker. "Ready to move out, sir!"

The column shuffled forward as the first sergeant trotted ahead to take the point.

Tommy and Harold walked beside the travois, keeping an eye on their friend. Tommy, noting that the outside seam of one his trouser legs was coming loose, asked, "How's your thread, Harold?"

"I have a bit, but I'm running short," he said. "I see you're about to get some unwanted ventilation there. I can let you have enough to mend that."

"These dang clothes just keep coming apart," Tommy complained. "I ain't got a speck o' thread left to fix nothing."

"We're giving them a lot of wear and tear," Harold said. "Of course, they're not made too well in the first place."

"Why is that, Harold?" Tommy asked. "You'd think the army would want us soldiers to have good clothes to wear when they send us out in the field."

"I'm sure they do," Harold said. "But the companies that manufacture for the government cut corners where they can."

"I reckon these uniforms is good enough if you're back east at some fancy-pants fort," Tommy said. He remembered drawing the clothing at Columbus Barracks and having the post tailor make alterations. "They oughta have a special field uniform or something for out here on the frontier."

Harold grinned. "Why don't you make a suggestion

to them?"

"Sure," Tommy said, smiling back. "And I'll also tell 'em about my idea of doubling our pay." He started to say something else, but he noticed Tim O'Brien on the travois. "Tim is awake!"

Harold looked down at him. "Hello, Tim. How're you feeling?"

O'Brien answered by leaning over the side of the travois and vomiting. He hacked and spit as he lay back down. "God! That hurt!" He moaned. "It still does."

Tommy got the soldier's canteen, lying beside him. He pulled the stopper. "Want some water?"

"Yeah," O'Brien said. He took a couple of sips and handed it back. "Thanks."

Harold pulled his extra bandanna from his haversack and poured some water on it. He folded it and laid it across O'Brien's forehead. "How does that feel?"

"God! That's real good, Harold. Thank you," O'Brien said weakly. He closed his eyes and drifted back into unconsciousness.

Mulligan, close by, chuckled. "Say! Don't youse two look like a coupla old hens clucking around him or what?"

Harold looked at him. "What's the matter, Mulligan? Haven't you ever seen a human being show compassion or care for another one,"

"Hell, no, I ain't," Mulligan said sneering.

Tommy felt a flash of anger. "Well, keep watching us. You'll see a hell of a lot more of it."

"It's the best part of human nature, that's what it is," Harold said.

Mulligan chuckled disdainfully. "What a load o' bunkum!"

Tommy and Harold ignored the next few gibes and comments by Mulligan. Realizing they weren't paying attention to him, the New Yorker went back to his silent, solitary walk among the other soldiers.

The day's heat increased, adding to O'Brien's discomfort. Even with his hat laid across his face and wet bandannas applied to his forehead, the young man tossed and turned as he slipped in and out of consciousness.

Tommy was alarmed. "I think he's getting worser, Harold," he said. "Look at his face. It's red one minute, then real pale the next."

"You're right," Harold said. "I'll talk to O'Malley."

When the acting corporal was summoned, he made a cursory examination of the patient. "Things look normal to me," he said.

"How can you say that?" Harold demanded to know. "He's getting worse by the minute."

"We done ever'thing we could do," O'Malley said. "You can't expect a feller that got hit by a arrow to look fit as a fiddle. Anyhow, Callan even spit tobaccy juice in the hurt, didn't he?"

"I don't think that was a very good idea at all," Harold said.

O'Malley became angry. "You listen here, Devlin. You maybe have a lot of book learning, but you don't know ever'thing. Spitting tobacco in wounds is an old soldier's trick that goes way, way back."

"That doesn't mean it does the job," Harold protested. "You better tell Sergeant Robertson that O'Brien is sinking."

"What for?" O'Malley remarked. "There ain't nothing more the first sergeant can do. He ain't got any medicine or nothing with him. Not even extry bandages. O'Brien has to wait 'til we're back to Fort Keogh. The regimental surgeon can help him then."

"He might die," Tommy said.

"Yeah," O'Malley agreed. "In the meantime all you can do is keep him comfortable." He went back to his position in the column.

While Tommy and Harold worried about Tim O'Brien, Riker decided it was time to put out flankers. He chose two veteran soldiers — George Callan and Christopher Harrigan — giving them orders to get out far enough to be able to warn against any attacks or appearances by the Sioux, yet be close enough to the column for a quick return.

Taking no breaks and eating the last of the elk meat — much of which smelled bad and seemed rancid — L Company continued unmolested on their way north. By late afternoon O'Brien had begun mumbling incoherently to himself. A couple of times he flung the hat off his face, but Tommy or Harold retrieved it for him.

Tommy took the bandanna from O'Brien's forehead and dampened it with water from his canteen. Walking along, he replaced it as gently as he could.

"What time is Mass, Ma?" O'Brien asked.

"What?" Tommy asked. He looked down at the wounded soldier's face. It was red and flushed. "Hey, Harold! Tim is burning up with fever."

Harold put his hand on O'Brien's face. "God! Yes he is."

"Are we gonna go see Uncle Paddy after Mass, Ma?" O'Brien asked.

"What's he talking about?" Tommy wanted to know.

"Sweet Jesus," Harold said softly. "He's getting delirious."

"What's that mean?" Tommy asked.

"It means his condition is growing more serious," Harold answered.

"Maybe we should stop, then," Tommy suggested.

"It's like O'Malley said," Harold remarked sadly.

"There's nothing we can do."

"Indians!"

The call came in from the flanks as Callan and Harrigan ran back to the column. They quickly found Captain Riker. "Sir," Callan said, "there's a big group of bluddy Sioux. But they ain't headin' this way."

"Right, sir," Harrigan said. "They're headed off to the northeast."

"Let's have a look," Riker said. He gestured to Robertson. "Take over the company."

Forcing themselves to trot, the captain and the two riflemen hurried out from the formation and headed straight for the horizon. They'd gone but fifty yards when they halted.

"For the love of God!" Riker exclaimed.

It seemed the whole of the Sioux Nation was on the move. Warriors, women, and children traveled together. Dogs scampered around the horses that pulled travois stacked with tepees, buffalo robes, and other belongings.

"They must not like it around here," Callan commented. "I'd say them Injuns is moving to new campgrounds."

"They most certainly are," Riker said. He smiled. "After the attack on General Leighton's column and the set-tos with us, they must be expecting a big show of troops. They want to get their families to a safer area."

"That could be a blessin' fer us, sir," Harrigan said.

"It'll give us some more time," Riker said. "But not much. When the warriors are satisfied their women and children are secure, they'll be back after us with a vengeance. At any rate, I intend to take advantage of every minute available. You men stay on the flanks. I'm going back and kick up the speed a bit."

"That could kill the men, sir," Callan the ex-sergeant

208

warned him. "They're runnin' ragged as hell now. It's a good bet that some of 'em'll drop from the exhaustion of it all."

"They'll pick up the speed come hell or high water," Riker said coldly. "Or, by God, they'll die by the Sioux anyhow."

Chapter Eighteen
Private Mike Mulligan

Timothy O'Brien died the night following his wounding by the Sioux arrow.

His blanket roll was broken open and spread on the ground. Privates Tommy Saxon and Harold Devlin, who had grown close to him during his last hours, tenderly lifted the corpse from the travois and laid it on the coverings. His personal effects were removed from the body and turned over to Sergeant Robertson for safekeeping. The NCO had taken the haversack of the first man killed—George Hammer—to carry the dead soldier's property. Now the canvas container was beginning to be packed with wallets, photographs, letters, and other property of the dozen men who had died since the company had left General Leighton's bivouac only a short time ago.

After a final look at O'Brien's now peaceful face, Tommy and Harold folded the canvas over their dead friend.

Under Robertson's stern supervision, Mike Mulligan dug the grave. Mack Baker walked over to the corpse and squatted down where the dead soldier's feet stuck out. He began unlacing O'Brien's shoes.

"What're you doing?" Tommy Saxon asked.

"Getting his shoes," Mack said. "I'm on my last pair and they've just about give out." He showed one in which the sole had a large hole.

"Hey!" Tommy protested. "I don't think you ought to do that, Mack."

"And why not?" Mack said, taking off the first one. "Me and Tim has the same size feet. We borried footgear between us lots o' times. He sure as hell won't use 'em no more."

Harold Devlin frowned in disapproval. "That isn't exactly a socially approved custom, Mack."

"What the hell do you mean by that?" Mack angrily asked. "Sometimes I don't care for your way o' speaking, Harold."

"I don't mean to imply you're doing something terribly wrong," Harold said. "But in normal society, taking something from a corpse isn't considered acceptable behavior."

"Listen, smart boy," Mack said. "Society's opinions don't get you shit in the army. Particular when we're out here in this god-awful empty country. We're away from all the fancy rules and laws most folks live by. Hell, I suppose that holds true in the barracks, too." He took the other shoe from the dead soldier and began to discard his own. "This ain't grave robbing, y'know. And it ain't against army regulations, neither. These shoes is U.S. government property, boy. Don't you forget that for a minute, neither. Tim's gone and I need them shoes to keep going." He slipped into the better footgear, tying them and standing up. "And I'll tell you boys what. If I croak, you're welcome to anything I own. I'll report to Colonel Devil naked as a jaybird. If he ain't got a quartermaster sergeant in hell, then I'll spend eternity on short rations and a shorter clothing issue. I don't care. All I ask is that you put something over my face to keep the dirt off it when you bury me."

Harold Devlin was thoughtful for a few moments. All normal values and moral judgments faded away in the primitive world of campaigning in the wild West. "You're right, of course, Mack." It was just another ideal he was forced to ignore while serving in the army out on the frontier. Like beating another human being to death with his rifle butt.

Mack Baker nodded. "I meant what I said. All I own goes to my bunkies."

Riker and Robertson joined the group. The first sergeant was impatient. "Let's get this over with, boys. The Sioux ain't gonna tarry none."

Private Tim O'Brien was put into his final resting place, quickly covered, and given a brief good-bye by the men of L Company. Haversacks and blanket rolls were deposited back on the travois that he had occupied.

"Fall in!" Riker commanded. "Sling arms! For'd, march! Route step, march! The point, if you please, Sergeant Robertson."

"Yes, sir!"

The column trudged on, some of the men close to reeling with fatigue in spite of the rest while tending to O'Brien's burial. Stronger bunkies, grabbing their arms and saying encouraging words, continued to hold off any desires to sink down and give it all up.

Mike Mulligan, as usual, walked by himself in the group of men. Even if others were within spitting distance of him, Mulligan was still alone. The only difference now was that he was beginning to feel lonely for the first time in his life.

Mulligan had always been a solitary sort of fellow. Even as a youngster in the Bowery, he'd had a tendency to distance himself from other people. A lot of the times, he had to admit, it was because others didn't care for his company. But he was the sort who was more comfortable

212

thinking as an individual.

The best thing about keeping to yourself, Mulligan always thought, was that people couldn't really get to you. They couldn't hurt your feelings, in particular, if they didn't know enough about you to really know how to wound you. That attitude was the result of the way in which Mulligan had been raised in various slum dwellings along the crowded, noisy, and dangerous streets of shanty-Irish neighborhoods.

His father was a brute named James Mulligan. A drunken lout who had married a dimwitted immigrant girl from Connaught, he was loud and bullying. A monumental failure, even as a minor criminal, he always entered the family's humble abodes by kicking the door open and roaring out, "What the hell's goin' on here, then?"

That was the prelude to drunken rages in which Mike Mulligan, his mother, and his older brother could either stick around and take some painful punches and kicks, or get the hell out of the place until the intoxicated sire passed out. In the summer it wasn't so bad to flee out to the streets. But huddling on the stoop on a cold winter's evening, with a frigid wind blowing, was unpleasant. The neighbors, knowing the likelihood of James Mulligan breaking in on them if his family sought refuge in their own apartments, offered no hospitality.

This repeated violence continued until, after the father's long absence, the family concluded that he would not be coming back. He'd either gone away or somebody had slit his throat in one of the many altercations James Mulligan was forever involved in.

But that wasn't the end of Mike Mulligan's problems.

With the father gone, his older brother Joseph took over as bully. Although Joe never raised his hand to the mother, he beat the hell out of Mike on more than one occasion. Mrs. Mulligan, glad that any threat to her own physical well-being had been eliminated by her husband's disappearance, didn't care one way or the other how her younger son fared.

That was when Mike Mulligan decided to look after himself and damn the rest of humanity.

Like all boys of the Bowery, his life centered on the street and the activities there. Among the handcarts, coal wagons, and milling, cursing, pushing people, Mike sought a place for himself in the hectic scheme of things. When he was thirteen years old, he fell in with another couple of fellows his own age. One, David McCarthy, was, like him, a drifting hunk of flotsam in the Bowery sea. The other, Brian O'Keefe, although from the same background, was a clever organizer with plenty of ideas for improving his lot in life—none of them legal, legitimate, or moral.

It was Brian who figured out the scheme of breaking into the neighborhood pawn shop that was as much a fencing outfit for burglars as it was a loan establishment. The plan was to avoid the obviously expensive watches and jewelry brought in by the local thieves. They would be hard to fence and would surely attract attention if three youngsters tried to pass them off. But the boys could turn some quick cash by grabbing clothing from the racks in the rear of the place. Brian even had picked a good hiding spot in the alley just behind the shop, where the stuff could be stashed until the theft had cooled down for a couple of weeks. Then the loot could be gathered up and quietly carted away to a different fence in a different neighborhood.

It was a good plan and would have worked if it hadn't been for Mike Mulligan. He went back early, by himself, and grabbed the clothing. Mulligan sold the stuff for his own benefit and kept the money. It didn't take long for Brian O'Keefe and David McCarthy to figure out what had happened. They beat Mulligan senseless for his disloyalty and treachery. Mulligan took his lumps without a care: he still had the money.

After a couple more dirty tricks played on other fellows, Mulligan was branded an outcast in his own neighborhood. Forced into a solitary criminal career, he paid a price for his lack of friendship and support, with several arrests. After more beatings from the police and many trips to jail, he learned to work another angle while in custody of the authorities. By being an informer, he could get extra food and a better cell. As time went by, he continued the habit on the outside, working with detectives by passing on tips from the underworld where he lived.

Finally, however, after the tenth trip before the same judge, things turned bad. The magistrate was tired of seeing him. He would have given him a good long stretch of five to ten years in Sing-Sing, but Mulligan's career as a snitch paid off. Instead of jail, he was given the option of enlisting in the army and getting the hell out of New York City. When he agreed to the deal, the bailiff marched him straight down to the nearest recruiting station and watched as the happy sergeant signed up the petty crook for a five-year hitch.

Mulligan carried on his thieving ways in the barracks. At David's Island, while waiting for orders assigning him to a regiment, he not only stole from his own barracks mates, but managed to sneak into other companies to go through locker boxes. He was pretty lucky at the game until Mack Baker finally caught him in the bivouac by the Powder River. The beating he received from Baker and Schreiner was nothing, as far as Mulligan was concerned. He'd already gotten away with plenty. That was only a minor setback.

But, during the previous three days, Mike Mulligan's attitude had begun to change a bit.

Spasms of loneliness overtook him for brief periods of time. He began to wish that some of the fellows liked him a little or cared at least something about his well-being. The company was in one hell of a dangerous situation. The Sioux they faced had no jails or deals to make. They offered only two sorts of punishment—a slow death or a quick one.

Mulligan wondered what would happen if he got killed. The men in the column probably wouldn't even bother to bury him. They'd strip him for whatever he had that they wanted, and leave his body to be hacked up by the Indians.

Or maybe, if he was hurt bad and couldn't help himself, they'd just walk away and leave him to be tortured by the hostiles.

At that moment, walking dog-tired in the column of infantry, Mike Mulligan made an enormous and deeply meaningful vow. He wouldn't steal anymore—at least not from anybody in L Company.

"Halt!"

Robertson held up his hand and signaled to Captain Riker to come forward. When the company commander joined him, Robertson pointed ahead. "Sioux, sir. See 'em?"

By then Callan and Harrigan had trotted in. "The heathen devils are off by the trees there," Callan said.

"Right," Harrigan said. "That's how you seen 'em afore we did from the flank."

"There're only two of them," Riker said, studying the Sioux through his field glasses. "They're just sitting there on their horses."

"There wasn't no more out on the flank," Callan said. "What do ye suppose they're up to, then?"

"We don't face much of a threat here," Riker admitted. "But I want to be careful." He nodded to Robertson. "Ser-

216

geant, take two men and move forward on scout. I'll have Callan and Harrigan go back on the flank and keep watch there."

"Yes, sir!" Robertson waved at O'Malley. "Send me two men, quick!"

Tommy Saxon and Harold Devlin trotted forward. Ragged and worn to the nubs, they didn't make much of a fierce martial picture.

"We're gonna walk toward a coupla Indians out there. They're sitting nice and cozy on horseback, and we can't figger out what they're up to," Robertson said. "I want one o' you on each side o' me. Don't try nothing unless they fire on us."

The trio moved forward as Callan and Harrigan went back on the flank. All three soldiers held their Springfields ready, their eyes darting about as they scanned the woods ahead and the open country to the right.

"Walk slow!" Robertson cautioned the two young soldiers.

"There ain't but two of 'em," Tommy said.

"Might be more," Robertson said. "We'll see."

They moved closer and the pair of Sioux simply watched in a bored fashion, gazing over the heads of their mounts. When the three got within effective rifle range, the Indians pulled on the reins of their horses and slowly rode away. After a last look at the army men, they disappeared.

"Let's get back to the comp'ny," Robertson said.

When they returned, Riker was anxious for a report. "What seem to be their intentions, Sergeant Robertson?"

"I don't know for sure, sir," the first sergeant answered. "They rode away when we got close enough to take shots at 'em. I reckon they're just out keeping track of us."

Riker stuck his field glasses back in the carrying case.

217

"The tribe is moving. None of the warriors wants to leave his women and children while they're vulnerable. These two were probably sent out on a scout just to see what we were up to."

"You're right, sir," Robertson said. "But once they're settled into their new campgrounds, them braves is gonna be back here to settle the score."

"Let's keep it moving, Sergeant," Riker said.

The commands were again shouted, and the soldiers of L Company stepped out again in their slow, agonizing trek.

Chapter Nineteen
Horsemeat and More Sweat

Mike Mulligan glanced ahead in the column where Tommy Saxon and Harold Devlin walked together. He had an overwhelming desire to join their company. The only thing that held him back was a sincere fear of rejection. That was something he'd never given a damn about before. If he said a word or two to somebody and they either ignored or snubbed him, he hadn't much cared. In fact, he was used to such treatment from others and he generally shrugged it off. But this time, he really wanted to chat with someone. He felt an overwhelming need for human companionship and some sort of rapport with another person.

Finally he picked up his step a bit, increasing his stride until he was directly behind Tommy Saxon and Harold Devlin. "How many Indians was back there?" he asked, to make conversation. He waited for their reaction.

Tommy, surprised at this unusual behavior, answered, "We figure there wasn't more'n two. We watched them and they watched us for a while and they rode away.

"Yeah? What do you figger made 'em do that, huh?" Mulligan asked, as he pressed for more conversation.

Harold, as astonished as Tommy at Mulligan's sudden socializing, slowed down to allow the New Yorker to catch up with them. "We don't know. They seemed to be simply observing us."

"Yeah," Tommy said. "Sergeant Robertson and Cap'n Riker seem to think the Indians are staying away from us long enough to move their families someplace."

"I imagine that's correct," Harold said. "Our valiant leaders are of the opinion that these were young warriors sent out by the others."

"I reckon they're bachelors," Tommy added.

"Yeah," Mulligan said. A few moments passed while he tried to think of something to say. "I suppose the captain and the first sergeant should know more about Indians than anybody else in the comp'ny, huh?"

"Charlie O'Malley has a lot of knowledge," Harold said. "And so does Mack Baker."

"I reckon Cap'n Riker knows more'n all of 'em put together, though," Tommy said. "Remember when he grabbed my rifle and shot Sergeant McCarey? He knew what would happen to him if he got took away alive."

Everyone in L Company had gone through unconscious pains to avoid speaking of the awful situation. Mulligan's artless conversation making had brought up a painful subject.

The New Yorker realized what he'd done. He wanted to keep up the friendly rapport with Tommy and Harold. His mind raced rapidly for a subject of conversation. "Hey, did youse know that Callan was a sergeant before youse come to the comp'ny?"

"I heard he was reduced in rank after telling off Lieutenant Worthington," Harold said.

"I heard that, too," Tommy added.

"Yeah. That's the truth of it," Mulligan said. "I seen it all wit' me own peepers. Callan din't like Worthington wort' a shit."

"What brought about the argument between them?" Harold asked.

"I t'ink it was over some inspections in the evening," Mulligan said. "The lieutenant was allatime coming in the barracks and t'rowin' surprise checks on our equipment. And he'd look to see if the floor of the billets was clean, and even if there was dust up on the rafters. Callan was gettin' tired of that shit and wanted Worthington to stop doin' it.

"Lieutenant Worthington seemed to have the soul of a tyrant," Harold remarked.

"He was driving us crazy," Mulligan said. "He'd come in and tip over the bunks and yell. No matter how careful we was, he'd find something the matter."

"It rather sounds like Callan stood up for his men," Harold said.

"Sure he did," Mulligan said. "But a lot o' good it did him."

They nodded and continued to trudge. "I'm hungry," Tommy finally said.

"When is the last time we ate?" Harold wondered.

"Day before yestiday," Mulligan said. "Maybe the cap'n will go hunting again, huh?"

"Yeah," Tommy said. "At least I hope so.

The three young soldiers fell back into silence. Mulligan's thoughts turned inward. He remembered the tenderness and care shown O'Brien in his last hours. The New Yorker had rarely seen such concern or affection among human beings. Mulligan's own mother had never as much as reached out and touched him, except to take a swat at his face when he'd done something to anger her.

Mulligan pondered the possibility of getting wounded. Everyone knew the chances of getting back to Fort Keogh were growing slimmer and slimmer. In actuality, Company L was on foot trying to outrun Indian horsemen. Even if they managed to pull off such a miracle, it would still mean that a few more of the soldiers were going to go down by way of Indian bullets or arrows.

The thief from the Bowery wondered what would happen if he was hurt. Would the fellows give him drinks from their canteens and wipe his face with wet bandannas to comfort him? Probably not. They'd take all his stuff, more than likely, and leave him somewhere to die alone. The best he could hope for would be to bounce around on the travois, ignored until he finally expired from bleeding to death. Nobody—not one single other soldier in the company—liked him a bit. A couple, like Mack Baker, actually hated him.

Such thoughts confused and disturbed Mulligan. He wasn't used to pondering the consequences and effects of his actions. The possibility of quick and easy reward was always enough to justify his conduct. After another hour of walking and thinking, the reason behind this mental turmoil finally dawned on him.

He needed those other fellows.

And if they felt they didn't need him, they wouldn't mind abandoning him in the slightest. If he was a necessary or valuable part of the team, the company would never leave him behind as long as there was even the shallowest of breath in his body.

Mulligan made a momentous decision. He was going to make damned sure he became a significant and worthy member of Company L.

The next time they were attacked by Indians, he'd aim and shoot as carefully as possible in order to kill the maximum amount of Sioux. And he also vowed to keep an eye out for game. Perhaps if he sighted elk enough times, and the soldiers were able to fill their bellies, they would start to like him. Mulligan even daydreamed about them coming up to him and saying they were sorry that Schreiner and Baker had beat the shit out of him back at the bivouac on the Powder River.

"Company, halt."

Riker's loud shout broke into Mulligan's reverie of forgiveness and friendship. The soldiers, instantly nervous, glanced around to see if something was the matter. When all seemed normal, they turned their attention to their company commander.

Riker waited until Callan and Harrigan came in from the flank. He waved at them. "Stay out a bit as pickets," he ordered. "I want to have a talk with the men."

"Do you want a formation, sir?" Robertson asked.

222

"No," Riker said, shaking his head. "Everybody gather round and get comfortable. Sit down if you like, but I want you all to listen to me."

The riflemen, curious about this unaccustomed happening, obeyed in the same manner in which they'd been walking—lethargically.

"I've noticed how tired you are," Riker began his address. "The pace is falling off at an alarming rate. I know you're tired, but I don't want you to lose heart. We have a damned good chance of making it."

There was more than one expression of skepticism on the faces of the soldiers.

"And I have a damned good reason for thinking we'll march through that front gate at Fort Keogh," Riker continued. "The Sioux are moving their villages. I don't know why, and I don't care. Perhaps another expedition has been sent out from the post. At any rate, the individual warriors have decided to stay with their families before going back on the warpath. That gives us a good breathing spell and a chance to move that much closer to Fort Keogh."

Robertson roughly nudged a couple of the men who were dozing off.

"But the main reason we re going to make it is the same reason the whites are going to win the West from the Sioux and their brothers. That rationale is based on the Indians' lack of discipline. Nobody—no one chief—is in overall command. Now and then some individual takes charge of a particular warmaking effort on their part, but most of the time they do pretty much as they want to as individuals. Even guard duty around their camps is voluntary. They do no serious planning that they stick to. The Sioux squabble among themselves about those plans they do make. When they do decide to fight, they place too much emphasis on individual battle honors and not enough on accomplishing the overall mission."

Harold Devlin, realizing he was listening to a man seasoned in both fighting and living among Indians, was attentive and interested. He stood up and went to the back of the group so he could see a bit better.

"Without that discipline — which we have — the Sioux, the Cheyenne, and other tribes that include even the Apaches, are sure to lose out in the fighting," Riker said. "And, as I stated, that is the primary reason why the white man can take their land away from them." He paused as he noted the men absorbing his words. "So we are going to buckle down and move rapidly and purposefully toward Fort Keogh. We shall do so in a calm but vigorous manner, strengthened by both our resolve and our discipline. After our return, we will rest, re-equip ourselves, and come back out here to beat hell out of those Indians."

The men seemed to feel a bit better.

"I know you're hungry," Riker said. "But we can't go hunting. It will slow us down too much." He pointed to the horse. "That brave old soldier has one more duty to perform for the army. He'll feed us."

Robertson, knowing what to do, grabbed the horse and led him away a few yards. Without hesitating, he chambered a bullet and aimed at the animal. The shot exploded over the silence of the scene and the cavalry mount went to its knees, then struggled to get up. A second shot finished the job. "Baker!" Robertson yelled. "Donegan! Do the honors."

Pulling their large knives, the two veterans did a quick butchering. While that was being tended to, other men were sent to get dried limbs from the deadfall beneath the trees by the river. Hunks of meat were passed out and the men allowed to quickly roast them over a bonfire lit away from the woods.

Mike Mulligan, gnawing at a piece of meat on the end of a stick, walked over to the second squad. Mack Baker saw him and growled, "Get the hell outta here, you son of a bitch!"

"Let him stay," Harold Devlin said in a serious tone.

"Sure," Tommy said. "Why not?"

224

"Let bygones be bygones," Harold added.

Baker, in no mood for an argument, shrugged. "Suit yourselves. I don't give a shit no more."

Mulligan was inwardly happy. He made a silent vow to do something nice for Tommy and Harold. They might just turn out to be his very first friends.

The rather slipshod and untidy mess call went on for less than a half hour. When the column moved out to renew their march, greasy horsemeat was stuffed both in their bellies and in haversacks.

The march continued for another two hours before dusk began to darken the sky. Riker would have liked to press on, but he knew the men had to stop. Their hunger was satisfied, but they needed rest badly. He picked a good defensive position in the nearby trees and moved L Company into it. Section and squad leaders quickly arranged their men and appointed the first guard relief. Those scheduled to stand watch first sighed wearily and braced themselves for the dreary hours ahead. The ones who could sleep immediately lay down and sank into the deep, dreamless slumber only hard physical exhaustion could bring on.

The exception was Mulligan. He seemed strangely agitated. Although slated for the second relief, he volunteered to stand the first for Mack Baker, in addition to his own turn on guard.

The old soldier was suspicious. "I ain't paying you nothing for this, Mulligan."

"I know," Mulligan replied. "But I ain't sleepy, see? So why should we both stay awake?"

Baker looked over at O'Malley. "Whattaya say, acting cor'ral?"

"It's all right with me," O'Malley said.

Baker, afraid a good thing might come to an end, quickly flopped down, using his haversack for a pillow. "Wish me sweet dreams, you son of a bitches!" he said happily.

Mike Mulligan stood with Charlie O'Malley as the moon

came out. The pallid light dimly lit the landscape around them. "Y'know," Mulligan said. "I was t'inking I might stay in the army."

O'Malley gave him a hard look. "Maybe you're learning something about comradeship, Mulligan." He hadn't failed to notice that the New Yorker had been friendly with Tommy Saxon and Harold Devlin.

"Yeah," Mulligan said. "Ever't'ing out here looks different, y'know? I mean it's like I've loined me somet'in'."

"You better stop stealing stuff," O'Malley said coldly.

"Yeah. You're right."

O'Malley vaguely wondered if there had been a real change in the soldier. The possibility that he would quickly revert to his old self if they made it back to Fort Keogh was pretty certain. But nobody could really tell — only Mulligan.

The first two hours of guard duty ended with the rustle of men getting up and the usual yawning and sleepy muttering. Mack Baker, his Springfield rifle in hand, joined O'Malley and Mulligan.

"I'm off to beddy-bye," O'Malley said. "You got your regular relief to stand now, Mulligan."

"Sure. I'm fine," Mulligan answered.

Baker settled in beside the thief. For a long time, they said nothing, only looking out into the open country in front of them. Finally, Mulligan spoke.

"Hey, you, Baker," he said.

"Yeah?"

"I'm sorry I lifted your watch."

Baker's mouth dropped open. But he said nothing.

The long hours of guard duty drifted on.

Chapter Twenty
A Soldier's Deed

The smoke of the cookfires drifted slowly across the
primitive bivouac through the heavy air of early morning.
The men occupying the campsite were ragged and sleepy,
going about their routine in lethargic, numb acceptance of
the situation they were in. Several looked at rips and tears
in shirts or trousers, trying to mend them with the small
bits of thread left in their haversacks.

Mack Baker poured himself a cup of weak coffee from
the communal pot shared by the members of the second
squad. He paused, thoughtfully, then glanced over where
Mike Mulligan was tying up his blanket roll. Several times
he started to holler over to the New Yorker. But each time
he changed his mind. finally, after one more hesitation,
Baker called out:

"Mulligan!"

Mulligan, the brim of his worn and salt-encrusted campaign hat drooping over his rugged young face, looked
over. "Yeah?"

"Why don't you have some coffee?" Mack asked.

Tommy Saxon grinned. "Sure, Mulligan. C'mon and
have a cup. It's nice and hot."

The gesture was not lost on the New Yorker. He felt a

surge of emotion that choked off his words. He pulled his cup out of his haversack and walked over to the fire, saying nothing, but his hand holding the utensil trembled slightly.

Baker took his cup and filled it, handing it back. "There you go."

Mulligan had never expressed gratitude to another human being in his life. The young soldier simply did not know how. He took a sip from the cup. "That's good, fellahs." One more gulp and he felt awkward at not being able to say what he meant. The best he could do was, "Well, I gotta get back and tie up that blanket roll." He went over to his gear and squatted down, finishing off the cup with small swallows, savoring both the taste and the friendly gesture shown him. After sticking it in his haversack, he donned his equipment and joined the second squad.

O'Malley got the men on their feet and checked them out. After taking a look at his small, shabby command, he grinned. "Well, you ragamuffins, ain't you a sight? Now, what would the post commander think if you ever showed up for a Sunday parade looking like this?"

Mulligan answered. "He'd make us stand downwind from the mules so's they wouldn't be offended."

The squad exploded into laughter.

Baker slapped Mulligan on the shoulder. "Ain't you a caution, though?"

Mulligan was surprised and pleased. No one had ever found anything he said amusing before. He liked the feeling.

Any further joking was interrupted by Sergeant Robertson's command to form up the company. The other men obeyed dully, showing little life as they assembled in squad and section formations. Only Mike Mulligan seemed to show any enthusiasm. The second squad, their spirits lifted by the sudden laughter, stepped a bit livelier than the others. Mike Mulligan was the most active of the

228

group. He took his spot in the squad, snapping to attention and bringing his rifle to a soldierly position of order arms.

Riker noticed the second squad in particular when he gave the command to resume the march. He watched them as Company L shuffled through the thick prairie grass, moving northward, renewing their desperate bid to escape the persistent Sioux.

The second squad, under Acting Corporal Charlie O'Malley's supervision, maintained a close formation. Some of the high spirits had simmered down and O'Malley wanted to keep them in a lighter mood. He gave his men a quick visual check. "How's it feel to be toting those blanket rolls and haversacks again, boys?" he asked. Since the butchering of the horse, the travois had had to be abandoned.

"It ain't a bad bargain to get something in your belly," Mack Baker said. "Even if it is horsemeat."

"I woulda volunteered to pull that travois myself," Mulligan said. "But I was afraid youse fellahs would do me like that horse and butcher and eat me when you got hungry again."

The squad burst into laughter at Mulligan's joke.

"You wouldn't be near so tasty, Mulligan!" Baker said. "And besides, you stand guard a hell of a lot better'n a damn ol' horse, anyhow."

"Yeah," Mulligan said. "But you gotta admit I'd make a genuine Irish stew, wouldn't I?"

The men laughed again.

Captain Riker, moving along in the column not far away, heard the conversation. He smiled to himself. It was good that the men had something to laugh about — or could muster enough feeling to see the humor in a few inane remarks.

Riker had seen loners come around before in the army, and that included West Point. Even the most antisocial individuals learned they had to rely on others in dangerous

229

situations. The lessons might be harsh, but at least they eventually appreciated and respected their fellow soldiers.

Robertson joined the company commander. He had also noticed the difference in the relationship between Mulligan and the other men of second squad. "I'd say that Bowery boy thief is coming around, sir."

"Yeah," Riker said. "Mulligan will probably be a better soldier from now on."

"Hell, sir," Robertson said. "I seen it before. There's a hell of a good chance that he might even stay in the army. Private Mulligan could just be a thirty-year man. I know a sergeant over in the Fifth Infantry that was a reg'lar hooligan when he first come into the service."

"Perhaps Mulligan will follow that example," Riker mused. "But even if he doesn't, the world at least has a better human being."

"Yes, sir," Robertson said. He changed the subject. "The reason I come over, sir, was to talk to you about Callan and Harrigan."

Riker looked out on the flank where the pair of veteran soldiers plodded along with their Springfield rifles ready for trouble. "What's on your mind where they're concerned, Sergeant?"

"Them two is getting wore out, sir," Robertson said. "I wouldn't say nothing under normal circumstances, but even old soldiers get careless when they're overused. And them two sure as hell ain't spring chickens. We got younger feet that could be walking out there."

"You're right, of course, Sergeant," Riker said. "Thank you for pointing that out to me."

"It's my job as first sergeant, sir."

"Put two more men out there," Riker said. "And you're right. They don't necessarily have to be the older men. I think every soldier in this column is a veteran now."

"That they are, sir," Robertson said in agreement. He shouted to O'Malley. "Gimme two flankers!"

"Yes, Sergeant," O'Malley said. "Saxon! Devlin! Report

230

to the first sergeant!"

The two friends wasted no time in obeying. They trotted over to the senior noncommisioned officer and waited to see what he wanted.

"Go out on the flank and relieve Callan and Harrigan," Robertson said. "And stay alert. Somewhere in that open country the whole damn Sioux nation is gonna show up. Don't let 'em surprise us." Then he added ominously, "Because if they sneak up on the company, you two'll be the first to die."

"Yes, Sergeant!"

"Yes, Sergeant!"

They hurried out to where the two older soldiers stumbled along. Callan and Harrigan were extremely happy to be relieved from the arduous duty. The two went back to the column where they could at least walk along with their heads bowed without having to continuously glance along the horizon.

Tommy and Harold settled into their new duties. Although they had to be vigilant, they could at least talk with a bit more freedom than when Captain Riker or one of the NCOs was in their proximity.

They walked in silence for fifteen minutes before Tommy said something. "I wish the army paid more money. If they gave us soldiers decent wages, I'd be able to save enough to buy a farm when I get back to Ohio."

Harold chuckled. "I thought you were going to stay in until you could retire as a sergeant major."

Tommy grinned. "I got to tell you, Harold. I just about had my fill o' being a soldier in the reg'lar army."

"I was disenchanted by the end of my first day at David's Island," Harold said.

"There's things about the army I like," Tommy said. "I feel grand at the Sunday parades when we're all dressed up in our full dress with them helmets on and all."

"We're not such a grand sight now," Harold said. He snorted as he looked at the uniforms they now wore. Almost rags, the clothing lacked any martial sparkle whatsoever.

Tommy raised his shoe and showed the loose sole that flapped when he shook his foot. "I reckon the way we look now is something the recruiting sergeants don't like young fellers to know about, huh?"

"I am certain they would not find us fine advertisements for army life, Tommy," Harold said without humor.

"But I still like to drill and wear a uniform," Tommy said. "And I like to shoot my Springfield, now that I learned to hold her in tight to keep the butt from bucking straight back into my shoulder."

"That was a most painful experience for all of us," Harold said.

"You know what I was thinking I'd do after my hitch is up?" Tommy asked.

"Sure. You said you wanted to purchase a farm," Harold said.

"No. I mean besides that," Tommy said. "I think I'll join the militia."

"The militia!" Harold exclaimed.

"Sure. We got a comp'ny in the town near the farm," Tommy said. "My two uncles is sergeants in it."

"There was a militia company in Drury Falls too," Harold said. "Some rich men from Riverside—that's the wealthy part of Drury Falls where I came from—get together once a month to put on fancy uniforms and march around on the green. Some of the fellows that work in the mill are in it, too. But they just joined up to get in good with the bigwigs."

"A rich old feller runs our militia comp'ny too," Tommy said. "He owns a bunch o' farms and stores and stuff. He paid for the uniforms and ever'thing. That's how come he's the captain."

"I hope the uniforms are better than these rags," Harold said.

"Yeah. Anyhow, if anybody served in the reg'lar army,

they get to be a corp'ral or a sergeant," Tommy said. "That's what I'd like to do."

Harold sighed. "Well, Private Tommy Saxon, if it means that much to you, fine! As for me, once I've finished my enlistment, I'm not going near a uniform again for as long as I live."

"I could even be an officer in the militia," Tommy went on. "A man in Salem is a captain on a brigade staff. He goes by train over to Columbus whenever the brigadier general has a meeting."

Harold shook his head. "Ridiculous!"

"No, it ain't," Tommy argued. "If there's ever a big war like the one with the South, the militiamen go on federal duty. Anyhow, if I was in the militia, I could do all the soldier things I like and there wouldn't be nothing going on I didn't like."

"Such as a first sergeant that will beat and kick you if you make a mistake or get into trouble?" Harold asked.

"Yeah! And they don't buck-and-gag nobody, neither," Tommy said. He laughed. "I reckon they'd better not. Ever'body gets drunk right after the drill."

A shrill shouting sounded to the east.

Tommy and Harold quickly glanced that way. Numerous Indian horsemen were bounding across the prairie country, heading for them.

"Oh, God! Harold!"

Harold looked frantically around. "Sweet Jesus, Tommy! Where is the column?"

The two had been so engrossed in conversation that they'd wandered off the route followed by the column. There wasn't a single soldier in sight.

"That way!" Tommy said.

They began running in a blind panic. After a couple of minutes, Harold realized they were going the wrong way. He grabbed Tommy's arm and steered him as he changed course. Looking back over their shoulders they could see the Sioux gaining on them.

"Oh, Lord!" Tommy said. "Oh, Lord help us! Please!" His shoe flapped as he ran.

They topped a rise and could see the column. Never had the line of blue-coated soldiers looked so good to them.

"Indians!" Tommy yelled.

"Behind us!" Harold shouted.

The company quickly formed up to meet the attack as their wayward flankers streaked toward them. Tommy and Harold got within twenty-five yards when Tommy suddenly tripped over his bad shoe. He went down in a tumbling heap.

Harold stopped and grabbed him. He pulled so hard, as Tommy struggled to his feet, that they both slipped.

Cries from the column told them to hurry up. The pounding of the Indian horses' hooves could be plainly heard and felt in the rumbling ground.

Tommy and Harold ran once more, but the bottom of Tommy's shoe came off and he went down again. As before, Harold refused to leave him. He helped him back to his feet.

"God, Tommy! Please hurry!"

A lone figure came running out toward them. It was Mike Mulligan. When he arrived, he fired a shot at the Indians and immediately reloaded.

"Hey, youse two! Get a move on, huh?"

Tommy, his foot hurt now, limped as fast as he could toward the company. Harold still held onto his arm and tried to hurry him along.

Mulligan, moving slowly backward, covered them. He fired again, quickly reloading. Now the air popped with incoming bullets from the Indians. The next time Mulligan raised his Springfield to fire, he staggered backward and fell down. Getting to his feet unsteadily, he tried to aim once more. But again he was hit, the blow of the bullet slamming him straight onto his back. He twisted a bit, then was still.

Mulligan stayed down.

234

Riker ordered rapid volley fire. The swarms of heavy slugs smashed into the attacking Indians like steel hornets. After three of the fusillades, the Sioux pulled back.

The entire second squad damned whatever First Sergeant Robertson's reaction might be. Concerned and angry, they ran out to Mulligan. When they got there, they found he had died instantly from the strike of the second bullet. His eyes were open and there was a grimace on his face that almost seemed like a smile.

Mack Baker knelt down and gently laid a hand on Mulligan's chest. "Brave soldier lad," he said.

The first sergeant's voice bellowed loudly in the rear. "Get your goddamned asses back here—*now!*"

Second squad quickly obeyed.

Chapter Twenty-one
The Last Salute

Captain Charles Riker formed up L Company in two ranks of fifteen men each. Sergeant Aloysius Donahue, Acting Sergeant Karl Schreiner, and Trumpeter Uziel Melech had been detailed as riflemen and sent to join the firing line.

Only the company commander and First Sergeant Gordon Robertson stood to the rear in order to command and control the action.

Robertson's face was ashen, but that was the only emotion he showed. He snuffed a bit and wiped a hand across his moustache. "This is it, sir."

Riker nodded. The awful thing he had been trying to avoid was undeniably upon them. The run for safety was over and the final scene was about to be played out.

L Company, because of the combination of trees and river, was protected from attack on the flanks and in the rear. But that desperate last stand made such advantages seem pointless in light of the terrible consequences the riflemen now faced. The captain glanced to the north in a wild hope that a relief column would suddenly and conveniently appear. Then he damned the childish action, reminding himself that he was in command of men about to do battle.

For fifteen minutes the countryside in front of L Company was empty. Then the Sioux began to appear. The first group was a weak, strung-out line that rode into sight without any particular coordination. Wide gaps showed clearly between the Indian horsemen. It was almost as if what they were doing was all coincidental, but their war regalia showed exactly what their intent was. Gradually, those empty spaces were filled as other warriors slowly came forward over the horizon and joined their brethren. These reinforcements continued to build up for another quarter of an hour.

The battle—if that was what to call it—would be more than a thousand Sioux fighting men against thirty-two soldiers. That overwhelming number indicated to the veterans in L Company that many clans and warrior societies had joined in the deadly activity.

"Front rank, kneel!"

Riker's voice was commanding and loud but it displayed a tone of coolness, too. The last thing he wanted to do was to appear nervous to his men. The company commander's own personal conduct would lead them either to fight confidently and deliberately or to behave in wild fear. He wanted them as sure of themselves as possible. Riker felt he owed the soldiers at least that much. He would do his best to see that the company's last moments on earth were not ones of panic and terror.

The men in the forward line obeyed the captain. They dropped to kneeling positions, their eyes gazing at the multitude of aboriginal warriorhood they faced.

"Load!"

The company was so well practiced in the firing drill by then that the opening and closing of thirty rifle chambers was almost simultaneous. The clank and click of metal against metal was sharp and distinct.

"Remember to wait for the commands," Riker cautioned them. "Do not anticipate what must be done."

Across the open space, an old Indian appeared in front of the assembled warriors. Even at that distance it was easy to tell that he was an ancient fighter. He wore a buf-

237

falo headcovering complete with horns and carried a long lance bedecked with feathers.

"That'll be the medicine man, sir," Robertson remarked. "And I'll bet my next month's pay that he's the wicked old son of a bitch that's been getting them Indians up for this." Then he added in an undertone, "But I don't think I'll be making pay call no more."

The old man rode toward the soldiers and chanted loudly for several long moments. He gestured wildly with the lance, shaking it toward L Company as if casting a spell or a curse on them. After a few moments he rode back to the young warriors. He pointed the weapon at a group off to one side and shouted at them.

Battle cries sprang from the group and they burst into action, charging at the company from an oblique angle. Eager to gain war glory, they exhibited no hesitation in doing what the medicine man had commanded them to do. After bounding forward for about fifty yards, they opened fire. The ragged volley slapped the air around the soldiers. Suddenly George Raleigh and Hiram Gold of the first squad went down.

"Aim!"

The Indians, now bellowing loudly, closed in.

"Fire!"

The volley sent three-quarters of them tumbling to the ground. Men and horses alike were hit, leaving only a dozen survivors to pull off to the side and speed back to the huge Sioux force still waiting.

The soldiers hollered and jeered at the withdrawing Indians. Some waved their sweat-stained field hats as if they were cheering a baseball game back at Fort Keogh.

"Quiet!" Robertson roared. "Listen for the commands!"

"Load!" Riker shouted.

The old medicine man waved his lance again. This time he shook it at the opposite side of the Indian group. The warriors there quickly responded, galloping toward L Company. They shrilled loudly, their horses pounding across the flat grassland in the savage assault. Gunshots began to explode from their mass and, once again, bullets zinged around the soldiers.

This time a man in the fourth squad was hit. Old soldier Christopher Harrigan was spun completely around when the bullet struck. He staggered forward, then tried to get back into ranks. "I'll dress right and cover down," he said in a strangely calm tone. But he collapsed to his knees. After a quivering effort to rise once more, he fell over on his face.

"Aim!"

The Sioux crowded together as each warrior tried to reach the flank of the army formation.

"Fire!" Riker yelled. Then he quickly followed with, "Load! Aim! Fire!"

All twenty Indians in the attacking group were down by the time the roar of the second of the rapid volleys died down. Several horses galloped wildly away, but their riders lay sprawled over the ground.

Once more the ancient medicine man came forward a few yards. He repeated his little ceremony, shaking the lance and shouting words the soldiers couldn't understand. Then he turned around and went back to the warriors.

"This is gonna be the big one, sir," Robertson. He spat on the ground. "That mean old bastard just used his strongest medicine on us. He'll have them young Sioux thinking our bullets can't harm 'em now."

More gesturing and shouting by the old man resulted in the entire Sioux band bounding forward.

"Load! Aim!" Riker waited a couple of beats. "Fire! Load! Aim! Fire!"

The men could feel the earth shaking with the pounding from the hooves of more than a thousand Indian horses. The soldiers loaded, aimed, and fired in a sort of dreamy calmness as the Sioux came on in an exploding, bellowing mob of enraged warriorhood. Sergeant Aloysius Donahue went down, as did Privates Silver, Czarny, MacReynolds, and Carpenter.

But the Indians paid a horrible price before their assault broke up. The close-packed horde made an easy target for L Company. The men didn't even have to aim as they simply pointed their rifles in the right direction and blasted away with each of Captain Riker's commands to fire. The disciplined fusillades were enough to break up the warriors' attack.

The Sioux warriors returned to their original position to join the medicine man who waited for them. A strange, eerie silence settled over the scene. The dead Indians were strewn across the open space. Downed horses were scattered among the corpses. The moaning of a few wounded could be heard. Several of the injured struggled weakly in an effort to crawl back to their brothers.

Tommy Saxon and Harold Devlin stood shoulder-to-shoulder. Their unfortunate friends, cut down by Sioux bullets, lay at their feet and elsewhere along the line. The eight dead soldiers sprawled in the undignified positions in which they'd fallen, ignored by the living, whose total concentration was on the battle they waged in sweating desperation.

Tommy was panting as if he'd just run a mile. Unable to speak, he breathed hard, swallowing constantly with nervousness as he licked the salty sweat on his lips.

"God above!" Harold exclaimed. "How many more of them must we kill before they stop?"

Mack Baker looked at him. "They ain't gonna stop, Devlin! Are you stupid or crazy or both? Them son of a bitches is gonna keep coming until we're all dead. Ain't you figgered that out yet?"

"Shut up, Mack!" O'Malley snapped.

"Shut up yourself, Acting Corporal," Baker said bitterly. "It's about time the babies around here figgered things out. We're here to die." Mack pointed to the army dead. "Look at them poor soldier boys. It's our turn next!" He started to sob, but with anger, not fear. "And I'm gonna kill me a whole bunch o' them redskin bastards before they cut me up!"

Once more the ground rumbled.

"Load!" Riker shouted. "Aim!" He waited. "Fire! Load! Aim! Fire!"

Corporals Bakker and Mateaux, along with Holihan and Braun, collapsed in the hail of incoming bullets. This time the men got off four volleys before blasting the Sioux into another withdrawal.

Riker wiped at the sweat streaking down his face as he counted his men. Including the first sergeant, he now commanded a total of eighteen riflemen. So far he'd lost a dozen in less than an hour. The captain figured that he and the others had another sixty minutes to go—if they were lucky.

Across the stretch of open country, the medicine man was giving a big talk to his warriors. He shook the lance wildly, his shrill voice barely audible across the distance. Suddenly he whirled his horse around to face the soldiers, pointing his weapon straight ahead.

A group of Sioux galloped out to the attack.

"They're coming in waves, sir," Robertson said.

The first group came in hard and fast, losing heavily but still retaining numerous warriors for more fighting, as they turned to the side and galloped out of range of the Springfield rifles. Their rapid shooting took out Corporal O'Rourke and Privates Nero and Schwartz.

The second bunch was a repeat of the first, but their shooting was much more deadly. A total of five soldiers— MacTavish, Black, Franklin, Patterson, and Albertson— died in the fusillade fired by the warriors.

The third and final band came in on the heels of the others. Although smaller than the previous groups, they suffered no casualties. But before they galloped off to the flank to return to their medicine man, their combined fire had killed Donegan, Asztalos and Raleigh.

The last nine men of L Company now stood alone.

Once more the bizarre stillness settled over the scene. The Indians, still in overwhelming numbers, were once again assembled across that awful field. This time the old medicine man did not address the warriors. Instead, he rode slowly forward toward the soldiers. He held his lance over his head in both hands. He did not stop in the usual place. The ancient warrior continued to draw close to L Company.

Mack Baker started to raise his rifle to his shoulder.

"Stand steady!" Robertson bellowed at him.

"Hold your fire!" Riker ordered.

The venerable Sioux religious leader still did not stop. Holding the lance, he glared at the soldiers as he approached. He finally stopped when he was within hailing distance. For a long minute he sat there, the lance held aloft. Then abruptly he hurled it down, making it stick in the ground.

"White soldiers!" he shouted. "Hear me!" His elderly voice cracked with the effort of hollering. "Your medicine is strong. You are brave! Today you no die! But when we see you again, we kill you!"

Pulling on the reins of his horse, the old man rode slowly and with dignity back to the warriors.

"Goddamn my eyes!" Robertson exclaimed under his breath. "We just been saluted!"

Riker stood dazed. Sweat ran from the brim of his field hat and coursed down his face in heavy rivulets. For a moment he was speechless.

Robertson uncharacteristically nudged him. "They're leaving us go, sir. Goddamn my eyes! Those son of a bitches is gonna leave us go!"

Riker suddenly remembered a similar thing happening to him by the bridge that ran over Cub Run during the Battle of Manassas. Only it had been a Confederate officer saluting with a saber rather than an Indian with a lance.

"I'll never understand Indians as long as I live," Robertson said. "They got us nailed to the wall here, but there's something in that damned spirit belief of theirs that's telling 'em to leave this fight."

"I suppose the old man had a vision or something," Riker surmised.

The men stood in silence for a while, looking at the Indians, who made no more moves. Robertson glanced at Riker. "We'll have to leave our dead, sir. We can't hang around here long or some o' them warriors is gonna tell that old medicine man to stuff it and come in here to finish us off."

Riker nodded. "Yes, Sergeant. We shall have to leave our dead." He took a deep breath and shouted, "Company, fall in!"

The men numbly formed up, dressed to the right and waited.

"Left face! Sling arms! For'd, march! Route step, march!"

243

Chapter Twenty-two
Fort Keogh

The sentry, with binoculars hanging around his neck, was entering his second hour on post. He was stationed in the observation tower constructed on the top of Fort Keogh's post headquarters. He leaned against the railing, enjoying the warmth of the morning sun. The dawn had been a cold, drizzly affair, but the clouds had gone away and the day promised to be bright and balmy.

Yawning, the soldier almost drifted off into a brief nap, but snapped awake in the knowledge that he was in full view of the entire garrison. If some officer or NCO caught sight of him asleep, he'd spend the next month in the guardhouse. Shaking his head to rid himself of drowsiness, he cursed the slow movement of time in such a boring routine. The soldier raised his eyes and glanced outward over the open country. A slight movement on the horizon caught his attention. The guard grabbed the binoculars for a better look. After several moments of intense gazing, he leaned over the railing of the tower.

"Corp'ral of the Guard! Post Number Two!" he yelled in an anxious voice. "Corp'ral of the Guard! Post Number Two!"

Within moments the noncommissioned officer the sentry had summoned made an appearance. Looking up, the corporal angrily shouted. "What's got ye worked up then, McGillicuddy? It sounds like ye kin see Crazy Horse and the whole bluddy Sioux nation chargin' at us."

"There's some soldiers approachin' the fort," McGillicuddy answered. "They're maybe a mile away. I been watchin' 'em for near a quarter hour."

The corporal, as aware of missing men as any other member of the garrison, quickly ascended the ladder to join the sentry. He grabbed the field glasses. After a moment of viewing, he slowly shook his head. "Sure now, and may the good saints preserve us! It's Captain Riker and a few of his men."

"Now how do you suppose they got away from them heathen Indians?" McGillicuddy asked.

"That's not fer us to worry about, lad," the corporal said. "But tidin's like this can't be left waitin'!" He dropped the binoculars and slid over the rail to go down the ladder two and three rungs at a time.

Out in the countryside, Captain Riker now could see that he and his men were within sight of Fort Keogh. The garrison's flag was barely visible in the blurry distance, shimmering just over the horizon.

"Hold it up. Form up in two ranks," he commanded. "Sergeant Robertson, take the position of right guide, if you please."

"Yes, sir."

The seven other men fell in behind the first sergeant. The right file was made up of Acting Sergeant Schreiner, Trumpeter Melech, and Private Callan. Acting Corporal O'Malley and Privates Saxon, Devlin, and Baker were on the left.

"Company, atten-hut!" Riker said. "We may be starving and ragged, but by God we're still L Company. Sharpen up and let's show them what real infantrymen look like. Right shoulder arms! For'd march! Hut! Two! Three!

Four! Left! Right! Keep in step, men. Hut! Two! Three! Four!"

Minding the cadence, L Company marched across the open country toward the post. A quarter of an hour later, Captain Charles Riker brought the remnants of his shattered command into the garrison. They passed through the quickly formed post guard that stood at the fort's entrance. The sergeant of the guard brought his men to present arms.

Riker returned the salute as he and his riflemen continued on their way across the cantonment area. Exhausted, starving, ragged, and as threadbare as tramps in their worn, ripped uniforms, they marched with backs straight and heads erect, keeping in step as if they were passing in review. Riker finally brought them to a halt in front of their regimental headquarters, where the colonel in command stood ready to greet them. The old officer looked at the survivors of the column. "God in heaven, Captain Riker! I thought you and your men were dead."

"Sir, I beg to report L Company has returned from detached service with General Leighton's command," Riker said with a sharp salute. "One officer and eight enlisted men present and accounted for."

The colonel's voice was a whisper, and he was so shocked he momentarily forgot protocol. "I can't believe I'm standing here looking at you." He returned the salute as if in a daze. He recovered slowly before he could properly respond. "Captain, dismiss your company."

"Yes, sir!" Riker performed a faultless about-face. "First Sergeant!"

Robertson left his post as right guide and marched up to a point in front of the company commander, saluting with a flourish. "Sir, the first sergeant reporting as ordered."

"Dismiss the company."

"Yes, sir." Another salute and Robertson turned to face

the men. "On my command, fall out and return to the barracks." He took a deep breath. "Comp'ny! Fall out!"

The men broke up the formation and turned away to walk slowly back to their billets. The campaign officially ended for them at that moment.

They returned to the barracks they'd left weeks previously. The company quartermaster sergeant, who had stayed behind, stood in the doorway. His mouth was open and there were tears in his eyes. "Is this all o' yez, then?"

"That's it, Flanagan," Robertson said. "We'll be drawing our bedding after the men dump off their gear."

Robertson led the men into the billets. He went directly to his own room at the end of the squad bay. The men tramped in after him. The extent of their losses became poignantly apparent as each went to his bunk. The unoccupied beds, empty and forlorn, had once been resting places of men who now lay scattered along the bloody route that Riker's column had followed.

Tommy Saxon pulled off his haversack and blanket roll, dumping them on the floor. Then he sat on his locker box and stared numbly at the floor. He closed his eyes and clasped his hands together as he suddenly began to pray.

George Callan and Charles O'Malley also discarded their field gear, but instead of throwing it down, the two old soldiers began to unroll it and pack it away in its proper place on the shelf above their bunks. Acting Sergeant Karl Schreiner went one step further. He opened his locker box and pulled out a fresh uniform to change into when he got a chance to clean up.

Trumpeter Mournful Melech and Mack Baker took off their equipment and laid it down on the floor by their bunks. Then they sat down. Harold Devlin followed their example, but when he sat down he began to tremble.

"Amen," Tommy said, ending his prayer of thanksgiving. He glanced at Harold, noticing his friend's anguish. "Is something the matter, Harold?"

Harold tried to answer, but he suddenly began to cry. Uncontrolled weeping wracked his body as he sobbed loudly in the barracks room.

Robertson, who had changed into another uniform, came out of his room. He had heard Harold weeping. The first sergeant walked over to the young soldier. He sat down beside him, saying nothing for a long time.

"It's over, Devlin," Robertson said in a soft voice. "Now let's pull ourselves together. We've got to go down to the supply room." He stood up and pointed to Mack Baker. "You're barracks guard. Watch the weapons while we're down there drawing our bedding."

"Yes, Sergeant," Mack responded.

Robertson walked to the door and turned around. "All right!" he said in a loud voice. "Company formation outside. Let's go!"

The men obeyed, going out to the company street to form up and be marched to their supply room. After drawing bedding, they returned and made up their bunks in the proper military manner. A trip to the bathhouse followed that. After they were cleaned up and wearing fresh uniforms, they went to the mess hall.

The other troops from the post were already in line when L Company marched up. Suddenly and spontaneously, they stepped aside to let the survivors of Riker's column proceed them in to eat. Someone applauded and the clapping was picked up by the others.

After messing, the men spent a quiet evening in the barracks. They talked little, preferring to nap a bit and settle in with their own thoughts. Finally, an hour after dark, Mournful Melech suddenly stood up. Wordlessly, he began to change into his full dress uniform.

"What're you doing, Melech?" Mack Baker asked.

Melech didn't answer. He put the plumed helmet on his head, picked up his bugle, and walked out of the barracks. He strode purposefully across the garrison to the

248

headquarters building, where he ascended the ladder to the lookout tower.

The sentry on duty there frowned in puzzlement. "What the hell are you doing up here, Melech?"

Still Melech said nothing. Instead he turned and faced the south where L Company's dead were scattered down the Tongue River and across the wilderness to the Powder. He put his bugle to his lips and played Taps for them.

The notes were long and sad, drawn out by the grief of the trumpeter who made this last gesture to dead comrades. When he'd finished, he left the tower and walked back to the barracks.

L Company, including First Sergeant Robertson, were outside by the door when he returned. They said nothing as he walked through them and went into the billets. After a few moments, they turned and joined him inside.

During the weeks that followed, L Company became minor celebrities on the post. After throwing away their worn uniforms, they were issued fresh sets from the post quartermaster's stores to augment the ruined clothing. Although it was a time of relaxation for them—the colonel saw to it that they performed only light duty, and excused them from guard, fatigues, and drill—their company commander was soon ensnared in an insidious paperwork trap.

The first battle he did was with the quartermaster. All lost and destroyed items of government property had to be listed and accounted for. Not only were the Springfield rifles abandoned with the dead noted, but even personal items of equipment as minor as field hats, trousers, and shirts had to be accounted for and listed in the proper documents. The locker boxes of the dead men were opened and the contents listed either for return to army stores or, if personal effects, to be sent to next of kin.

When the quartermaster's administrative needs were met, then the adjutant took over.

His were the simplest demands. A listing of all the dead men was made from the company roster. Their pay and allowances due would be passed on to the listed next-of-kin or, as in the case of those without families, returned to the finance department.

Both Riker and Robertson pooled their memories to list the details of each death. The one problem that occurred was the demise of Sergeant Thomas McCarey, whom Riker had killed while the NCO was in the hands of the Indians.

A preliminary hearing was held. After the facts were brought out, they were watered down with a version that indicated the sergeant's death was the result of misadventure due to his proximity to the enemy during a battle in which Captain Charles Riker was firing in his direction.

That was the colonel's idea.

By the time the paperwork on the incident wound its way through the army's various bureaus and reached Department Headquarters, more statements were added in the appendices of the original document, until it appeared that the entire company was firing at the time the sergeant was killed.

Since McCarey had no family, the entire incident simply died away in the dusty vaults of the military archives.

Company L soon got back to as normal a schedule as possible for a terribly understrength company. They messed and drilled with K Company while waiting for reinforcements to join them from the recruit depots at Columbus Barracks and David's Island.

The final report and summation of the incident of Riker's column was summed up with a statement that read:

It is the studied opinion of the official Board of Inquiry that the Indian enemy was unable to break

250

through heavy infantry volley fire without suffering enormous casualties. The hostiles, due to the growing activity of army units in the field, more than likely abandoned the battle against Company L because suffering such heavy losses against a small unit did not make the effort worth the terrible cost to them.

Finally, officially and literally, the campaign had come to a close.

Chapter Twenty-three
The Traditions Continue

Corporal Thomas Saxon, his new stripes fixed solidly on his arm, stood at the dock watching as the steamer eased closer across the waters of the Tongue River.

Tommy wore the brand new uniform recently issued to him to replace the one ruined during the long march. He'd used some of the pay raise in his promotion from private to noncommissioned officer—an increase of $13 to $15 per month—to have the post tailor cut it down to fit well. Now, natty in shiny shoes and belt, with a new, freshly creased campaign hat sitting jauntily on his head, the junior NCO waited for the riverboat to go through its docking procedures.

In five short minutes after the gangplank was thrown out, the newly arrived recruits and replacements, fresh from the infantry depots back east, marched off the boat and onto the wharf. Tommy strode forward to meet them.

"Fall in!" he barked. "Quickly! Quickly! Didn't they teach you nothing at Columbus Barracks and David's Island?" He waited impatiently as the men shuffled into a formation. He could spot the old soldiers by the way they easily arranged themselves in the proper fashion. Tommy gave them all a long glare, walking back and forth in front

252

of them. Finally he commanded, "Stand at ease!"

The men relaxed, looking at him in anticipation for whatever was going to happen.

"My name is Corp'ral Saxon. I am here to welcome you to Fort Keogh and to our regiment in particular. You have been assigned to L Comp'ny," Tommy announced. "We've just got back from a campaign in which we lost thirty-seven men out of forty-six." He paused, enjoying the disturbed look on some of the new arrivals. "If you think that means we were poor fighters, you're damned mistaken. We faced over a thousand Sioux warriors down and fought so hard that at the end they saluted us and rode away." He walked about some more letting that bit of news sink in. "But we still want to avenge them thirty-seven fellers that got kilt." Now he shouted. "And that's what you're here for! And, by God, your only purpose in life from this point on is to march with the comp'ny back out there and get the rest o' them Sioux! That's all us old soldiers has been thinking about and that's all you recruits is gonna think about too!"

The story of Riker's column had already spread through several western garrisons and the batch of recruits had heard embellished and exaggerated accounts of the incident. They were impressed.

"Now. I'm gonna take you —" Tommy stopped speaking when he noticed an older soldier in the second rank. "You! What's your name?"

"Duncan, Corp'ral," the man answered.

"Wasn't you a sergeant at Columbus Barracks?" Tommy asked.

Somebody laughed. "Yeah, Corp'ral, 'til they caught him and the sutler cheating the recruits."

Tommy grinned. "Got yourself busted down, did you, Duncan?"

"Yes, Corp'ral," Duncan answered sullenly. "And I'm shipped out to a line regiment too."

"I remember you, Duncan," Tommy said in a coldly gleeful manner. "I went through recruit drill under you. So I'm gonna give you special attention."

"I been a private before," Duncan said. "Soldiering is something I've done plenty of."

"But not under *this* corp'ral by God!" Tommy shouted. He enjoyed the ex-sergeant's look of discomfiture. "Now! Let's get you men up to the barracks and settled in." He took a deep breath. "Detail, atten-hut! Shoulder your gear! Right face! For'd, march!"

The detachment of new men marched to Tommy's shouted cadence, the new men doing their best to keep in step while they paraded through the garrison. As they passed the guardhouse, Mack Baker stared through the barred windows of his cell at them. His bloodshot eyes burned and the monstrous pain of his hangover pounded through his head. But he grinned to himself.

"I wonder if any of them new fellers would loan me the price of a bottle o' whiskey when I get outta here," he said to himself.

The recruits went out of sight on their way to their new martial abode. There would be only a short time to run them through dry-firing exercises before they went into the field for active campaigning.

Post Script

CAPTAIN CHARLES RIKER retired from the army with the rank of major in 1890. He and his wife moved to Saint Paul, Minnesota, where the major went into business with his eldest son, operating a variety theater in Minneapolis. He died in Saint Paul in 1924 at the age of 86.

FIRST SERGEANT GORDON ROBERTSON was murdered by another sergeant at Fort Robinson, Nebraska in 1883. The crime was the result of an altercation over the attentions that Robertson was showing the other NCO's wife.

SERGEANT KARL SCHREINER left the army in 1887. He moved to a German-American community in North Dakota, married and raised a large family while prospering as a farmer. He passed away in 1948, aged 96 years.

CORPORAL CHARLES O'MALLEY remained in the army. He retired with the rank of regimental sergeant major in 1895. He died in 1931 in Lawton, Oklahoma, at the age of 76.

CORPORAL THOMAS SAXON took his honorable discharge from the army in 1885. He returned to Ohio where he became active in the state militia while going into business as a merchant. He married and fathered a large family. Saxon saw active service again in 1898 in the Spanish-American War as a lieutenant colonel and second-in-command of a volunteer infantry regiment. He served once more in World War I as a brigadier general in the Ohio National Guard. The general passed away in 1955 at the age of 93.

TRUMPETER UZIEL MELECH eventually took his discharge from the army. In 1889 he settled in Wichita, Kansas, where he became a music teacher. Melech never remarried, but lived a long and full life forming several musical organizations and concerts in that city over the years. He died in 1937 at the age of 92. A street and an elementary school in Wichita were named in his honor.

PRIVATE MACK BAKER, because of bad health, petitioned for admittance to the Old Soldiers Home in Washington, D.C., in 1891 after twenty years of service. He expired from acute alcoholism in 1893 when 41 years old.

PRIVATE GEORGE CALLAN quickly worked his way back up to the rank of sergeant. He was killed in action during the year following L Company's return to Fort Keogh.

PRIVATE HAROLD DEVLIN finished out his army career on detached service as post librarian at Fort Keogh. After an honorable discharge he went to California and eventually settled into the banking business in San Francisco, where he married into a prominent local family. He and his wife raised a family of two daughters and a son. When he was killed in the Great Earthquake of 1906, he was 51 years old and the vice president of the Commerce and Merchant's Bank of that city.